# The Bloodline Watchers

## The Awakening

Orion R. Veil

Cosmic Quill LLC

Published by Cosmic Quill Publishing

www.CosmicQuill.pub


This is a work of fiction. Names, characters, events, and dialogue are products of the author's imagination. Some real-world places, organizations, and historical references appear for narrative depth but are used fictitiously. Any resemblance to actual persons, living or dead, or real events is coincidental.

# Author's Note

This story is written in Neo-Scriptural Prose, a narrative style shaped by breath, rhythm, and memory. It reads the way oral stories once moved, carried in cadence rather than fixed form.

Lines break where pulse breaks. Meaning sits in the spaces as much as the sentences.

The structure is intentional. It mirrors the way truth arrives: layered, quiet, and felt before it is understood.

The Bloodline Watchers began as a reflection on family, trauma, and the hidden patterns inside ordinary lives. It became a myth about lineage, awakening, and what rises when the blood remembers itself.

Read it at the pace your breath gives you. Let the quiet parts speak.

— Orion R. Veil

# Dedication

For the families who kept memory alive when the world tried to erase.
For the bloodlines that carried silence as inheritance.
For the minds that wrestled the dark and refused to let it win.
For the women who held the line when no one else would.
For the broken, who learned that cracks are where the light gets in.
For the daughters who bore divinity in secret, keeping balance when the world forgot she was equal.
May memory awaken, and the flame remember its source.

# Contents

Chapter 1

# The Frequency

Four streetlights on Dauphine lined the block. Three died when Sam passed beneath them.

Sam stepped through the chipped glass door of Good Friends, water streaming off his Mavericks hoodie. His boots squelched on worn wood. Oak steeped in decades of whiskey. Citrus cleaner battling the lingering grime. Above it all, a buzzing neon sign washed the liquor bottles in restless glow.

Pressure rose beneath the warmth, gnawing his molars. Metallic pressure, high and needle sharp. A wire drew tight behind his eyes. Always when the city tilted. Sideways. Wrong.

The jukebox spun low and blue in the corner. Billie Holiday's voice curled through the room like smoke carrying memory. It had been skipping all week. Jules had cursed it, unplugged it, cursed it again. The moment Sam crossed the threshold, the skip vanished and the room aligned. The jukebox smoothed. The lights steadied.

The door thunked shut.

Jules straightened from rinsing glasses, towel over her shoulder. She didn't ask questions tonight. Poured three fingers of Maker's Mark over a single cube and slid the glass across wood worn smooth by ritual.

"You look like hell," she said.

Sam caught the glass. Bourbon hit his tongue. Wayne's smell. Old Spice and cold warning. The man who raised him more than anyone else ever had.

"Strange night," Jules said. "Power's been acting up. Three customers swear their phones showed messages they never sent. Even the jukebox's playing songs I never loaded." She nodded toward Billie. "Old songs."

Around them, Good Friends held its rhythm. Ice clinked. Voices murmured. Underneath, threading through it all like electricity through water, a current.

"You feel it too," she said.

Sam nodded. Heat flared beneath his shirt. For a moment the bar thinned: walls translucent, voices split by old frequencies. Depth folded in on itself. Space breathing in ways it should not move. Then it passed.

"How long?"

"Couple weeks. Getting stronger. Small at first. Like being watched. Then sounds."

Jules poured again. "You're not the first. Regulars talking about shared dreams. Symbols showing up."

The words hit harder than they should. His chest tightened, the kind of pressure that pushed him toward another drink before thought could catch up.

"What symbols?"

She pulled a napkin from beneath the bar. Geometric spirals. Ancient marks shifting when he didn't look directly. In the center, a glyph that made his blood sing.

"Two nights ago," Jules said. "Filled six napkins before she realized."

Close. Not exact. Close enough.

"Anyone else?"

"Three. All different. Whatever this is, it isn't just you."

The room tilted. Subtle. Wrong. Conversations quieter. Lighting warmer. People turned without knowing why. Billie faded into older rhythms. A pull ran under the floorboards, through the walls, stitching this place to others across the city.

Thunder cracked. Bottles rattled. Sam flinched. Not from the sound. From the line that always followed it into childhood rooms. Where's your mother. What'd you do.

Heat rose under his palm.

"I need to go."

Jules waved off his money. "On the house."

"If anyone else comes in drawing symbols…"

"Get some sleep, Sam."

The door closed behind him. Rain had stopped. The street gleamed under lights beating too regular to be random.

His phone buzzed. Renee.

Renee. Critical build failure. S3 sync collapsed. Need you first thing tomorrow.

He ignored it.

Heat drummed beneath his shirt. Shadows bent wrong. Streetlights synced to what burned under his ribs.

A girl in a Saints jersey drew blue chalk spirals on wet concrete. Eyes too old for her face. He kept moving.

A streetcar rattled by. Windows dark. No driver. Tracks glowing with an unnatural sheen. Heat answered.

He turned down a narrow street.

A preacher stood in a shadowed doorway.

He hadn't been there a moment ago.

Black coat slick with rain that hadn't fallen. Half lit. Half swallowed. His head tracked Sam with mechanical precision.

"The hour is late," he said. Too many harmonics beneath. "Signs are everywhere. You must choose. Light or shadow."

Heat erupted beneath Sam's ribs, visible through fabric for half a second. Gold-green light.

The preacher's eyes went black. His mouth opened. Ink poured out thick and cold, a darkness that swallowed light.

"Ubi Lumen est?"

Where is the light.

Sam struck him. The survival punch learned before understanding language. Wayne's warning. Knuckles knew before the mind.

The preacher staggered. Ink sprayed brick. His face twisted. Skin pulled taut in ways a face was never meant to hold.

Sam backed away. Walked fast. Hoodie up. Head down. Gone.

The scream cut off in an instant, sharp as a snapped line. No footsteps followed. No breath. Only wet silence behind him. Sam kept moving.

He reached his apartment without looking back. Locked the door behind him.

The Quarter glowed wrong outside his window. Streetlights beating old languages.

He collapsed on the couch. Knuckles aching from hitting something not human.

Not external. Internal. Beneath his sternum. Heat erupted, brand-deep. He tore off his shirt.

Gold-green light carved across his chest. Spirals rising out of bone. A pattern older than anything he knew.

Air vanished from his lungs. The pattern spread, cutting through skin into bone, binding him to a network older than the city.

His spine lit like a fuse. Vision split across layers he had no language for.

An old presence stirred. Recognition. Opening.

The burning stopped.

The glyph settled. Glowing. Warm. Alive.

Every streetlight on Dauphine pulsed once as one.

Sleep refused him. The weight in his chest hummed, pulling him toward what waited. He stared at the pattern pulsing beneath his skin, at the Quarter answering him, and wondered if he had ever walked alone.

Or if he had always been answering.

Seventeen missed calls. Numbers he had never seen in any system.

A voicemail: his own voice.

His gut tightened hard. Hearing his own voice say words he did not remember speaking made the room tilt again. Made him question whether his mind was breaking.

Find the others before the fourth light dies.

Outside, three streetlights pulsed in slow unison.

The fourth stayed dead. And in that gap of darkness, Sam felt the city holding its breath, waiting to see how he responded.

## Chapter 2

# The Call

Just past dawn. The glyph pulsed beneath Sam's shirt, pulling him from dreams of ink pouring from mouths that spoke in frequencies older than language. He had been on the couch six hours, still in yesterday's clothes, hoodie stiff with dried rain. His knuckles ached where they had met the preacher's jaw.

The phone buzzed on the coffee table. He ignored it twice.

Renee's name lit the screen again. Three missed calls. Six texts climbing from professional to desperate.

"Build failed AGAIN. Client breathing down my neck. Sam please."

The real world called its due. Sam sat up, vertebrae popping, and typed with thumbs that felt disconnected from his hands.

"On it. Give me an hour."

He needed normal. Needed code that obeyed rules he understood. The mark thrummed, insistent, but he pushed toward the bathroom. Hot water first. Then he would fix what was broken in a world where problems had solutions instead of ink bleeding from possessed preachers.

By noon the fix was live. Green checkmarks rolled across his screen. Then Krishtan's text arrived.

"Sam-eee. Hex tonight. 8 PM sharp. Marisol been seein' you burnin' in da flame since da moon turned. Fire callin' fire, cher. Don't keep da old ones waitin'."

Seven hours. He stared at the wall. Time stretched thin, refusing to move. The waiting ate through him. The glyph pulsed steady as a second heartbeat, pulling him toward eight o'clock like gravity.

Fresh jeans, same hoodie. Smelled of rain and fear. Felt right.

Go. Before he talked himself out of it.

The pulse climbed his ribs.

Not thought. Not memory. Older than both.

He grabbed keys and phone. Stepped into the hall.

The atmosphere bent. Even two floors above Dauphine Street, the Quarter's symphony faded. Jazz and laughter dissolved to static. In their place, a low thrumming rose from the city's bones.

The Quarter transformed. Not shape. Truth. His breath shortened. What he was seeing now wasn't exhaustion. It wasn't drink. Something fundamental had shifted. The charm of the Quarter thinned at the edges, like paint peeling from truth.

Shadows flowed through narrow gaps between buildings that leaned inward, guarding secrets older than the French who built them.

Twice he caught movement on rooftops, shadows flowing too smooth for pigeons, eyes older than the stones under Jackson Square. The glyph grew warmer, compass-precise, pointing him toward what had waited all his life.

The Hex sat on Decatur, narrow storefront, old brick, blue-gray doors. A sign swung overhead, paint faded by salt and sun. Beside it, an iron gate closed a courtyard of folded umbrellas. Tourists passed without seeing.

But the block had changed. Streetlights hummed green. Air pressed close, heavy with unshed rain. Candlelight moved behind glass, steady but alive, as if the shop breathed.

Sam touched the threshold. The door opened on its own.

Krishtan Dauvee stood framed in candlelight, pressed suit sharp as ritual. Dreads bound with copper wire, rings flashing. His eyes stopped Sam's breath. Ancient. Knowing.

"Sam-eee! Look what da wind done blow to my door, cher. Come, come." He stepped aside, one hand on his gris-gris bag. "Ma cousine been pacin' since before da moon set. Girl got da sight strong as her gran-mère."

Sam crossed inside. Warmth rose from the floorboards, sweetgrass and dragon's blood. The glyph on his chest answered.

Shelves climbed the walls, glass bottles, herbs, photographs whose eyes seemed to follow. Candles burned everywhere, flames steady in still air, shadows moving on their own.

A woman parted a curtain of beads. Tall, composed. Eyes bright with lineage.

She studied him, seeing more than what skin allowed.

"I have dreamt of you for weeks," she said, English crisp, each word measured. "Every time I light a candle, the flame bends towards what it cannot name. Toward you. The pattern kept returning. Energy without a name. I thought it was symbolic until now."

Krishtan's laugh rolled low. "Marisol, ma belle, you still talkin' like you in a classroom. Let da spirit speak, cher, not da scholar. Dis girl been burnin' candles for dis man since she was knee-high to a grasshopper."

Her breath shook once, a tremor she tried to hide, something older rising behind her eyes.

Her posture shifted. Calm cracked. The rhythm in her voice changed, dropping into a rhythm older than grammar.

"I been seein' you in da flame...

Walkin' through fire dat don't burn. Carryin' light dat don't belong to dis world. Fire call to fire. Blood call to blood. You don't know me, but yo' blood do. Dey been whisperin' your name since before you took your first breath."

Sam's stomach dropped. Hearing his name in that cadence felt like someone calling him from behind the veil.

Krishtan moved deeper into the shop, steps silent on floorboards that should have creaked. "Come on, Sam-eee. What I got to show you ain't for da front room." He touched a candle. It bent toward him. Shadows leaned close, listening.

"Some talk need older ears," he said. "Deeper shade. Truth don't breathe right in all dis light."

Behind the curtain, the air cooled, damp with dirt and stormwater. In the floor, a square of dark wood framed in brass waited. Krishtan knelt, tracing faint glyphs.

"Been here since my people laid da first brick on dis street. Veil run thin under Decatur. My gran-mère said da earth remember every prayer."

He pulled the iron ring. The trapdoor rose slow, dust drifting through candlelight. Cold air rolled out thick with stone and smoke.

"Careful on dem steps, cher. Dey get slick when da spirits start movin'."

They descended single file. The stairs glowed with candles of green fire. Earth walls hummed like living skin.

"Dis part of da shop don't exist on city records," Krishtan said. "Been in da Dauvee family since before records was records. My gran-gran-gran-mère carved dese steps herself when da old ways was all we had."

His tone deepened. "What we about to show you ain't no tourist magic. Dis real. Older than da city. Older than what you think possible."

The walls below shifted with the light. Symbols breathed. Some matched the glyph on Sam's chest. Others spoke in shapes that never had alphabets. The mark answered, heat rising with each step.

At the base, Krishtan unlocked a door of beaten bronze. Thunder rolled. Warm air swept out smelling of ozone, wildflowers, rain on stone, copper, mineral heat.

"Welcome to da heart of da Hex," he whispered. "Da place my ancestors kept da old fire burnin'. Where da veil so thin you can touch eternity."

The chamber was round, walls carved from basalt dark as river night, green veins pulsing beneath the surface.

At the chamber's center rested a basalt tomb, dark and veined green.

On it burned a single green candle. No heat. No smoke. A slow pulse matching Sam's heartbeat.

"Da eternal flame," Marisol said softly. "Lit by my ancestor Ama in da 1700s when she smuggled da old knowledge in her songs and her scars. Protection and invitation both. Keep out what should stay out. Call home what belong."

Sam stepped closer. The fire pierced him, a thread of light diving through fabric and skin. A metallic chime rang through the chamber. The mark erupted. Not pain. Recognition.

Reality bent inward, folding along lines his mind wasn't built to follow.

Marisol bent and ancient for a heartbeat, leaning on a carved cane. The chamber drowned in rising water, the eternal flame burning blue beneath the flood. His mother alive in another version of the world, reaching for him through a curtain of light.

White marble corridors. Golden fire held in niches. Bodies at rest, one bearing his own face. Every vision overlapped, layered, time folding until he existed in all of them at once.

Krishtan went still. Truly still. Breath caught halfway. Eyes wide, not in fear but recognition of something he had been taught could never happen. "Bon Dieu," he whispered, voice scraped thin. "Da flame just crossed bloodlines, Sam-eee."

Sam was pulled through like thread through needles, unraveled and rewoven, his molecules remembering forgotten shapes.

Through the roar came a single voice inside his chest. His mother.

"Choose the frequency that lets you save them all."

The flames collapsed inward with a sound like every bell in creation. Blue-green light exploded. Alignment snapped into place.

Air slammed back into his lungs, thick with mineral heat and dust.

He braced on the stone, unsure if the world had moved or if he had. Neither answer felt safe.

His knees struck real stone.

The tomb had turned east-west.

Light shifted from nowhere.

Krishtan's copper wire shone silver.

Even their shadows had moved, falling in directions that did not belong to this room.

Glyphs rearranged themselves, more complex, alive.

"Your mother warned us this might happen," Marisol said, and his blood froze. His mother had never spoken of these people. Hearing her name here felt like a trap sprung in his chest. "Said the bloodline might pull us through if the synchronization went deep enough."

Words hit hard. Sinking through adrenaline. Body knew fear should come. Didn't. Only weight. Comfort.

Krishtan touched the silver wire, frowning as his fingers traced what had not been there before. "We ain't where we started, are we, Sam-eee? Feel like my bones remember things that ain't happened yet."

The eternal flame burned steady now, blue-green and patient, its frequency found. The candle older, wax pooled different, as if it had burned three hundred and five years instead of three hundred.

Silence settled. Air thinned, vibrating at a pitch that made his molars ache. The echo of the fire lived in his chest, warmth with its own gravity, its own pull toward what waited beyond sight. The light inside him held steady, but the world around him felt displaced.

Whichever timeline the flame had chosen, they were bound to it now.

Krishtan straightened, scanning shadows. Silver wire glinted in his hair.

"Da old ones just opened dey eyes in more worlds than one, cher. We best find which world we landed in before dey come lookin'."

Behind them, the passage dimmed, the world stitching itself closed where they had walked.

Stone breathed slow. Walls hummed, glyphs flickering like dying stars. Marisol rose, hand on the tomb for balance.

"We need to go." Her voice raw, scraped. "What woke here sent ripples through more than da Quarter. Every sensitive felt it. Dey comin' to see what woke up."

Above them, through layers of stone and wood, footsteps crossed the Hex floor. Deliberate. Heavy. Not customers.

Krishtan listened. "Three of 'em. Maybe four." His fingers traced quick patterns, pulling threads only he could see. "Dey got weight to 'em. Spiritual weight. Da kind dat come from carryin' things most folks can't even see."

Sam's legs trembled as he pushed from the tomb. The chamber resisted. Each step toward the stairs made the glyph itch, invisible threads pulling tight in his chest. Whatever bond the ritual had forged between him and this place would stretch but never break.

"Can you walk, Sam-eee?" Krishtan asked, already climbing. "We movin' now, not stoppin' till we see what world da flame chose for us."

Sam nodded.

They climbed in formation, Krishtan leading, Marisol behind. The walls pressed close, symbols shifting, marks carved in tongues that had not existed where they came from.

At the top, Krishtan paused, hand on the door.

"Brace yourself, cher. Quarter gon' feel different now."

The glyph tightened. The stairs felt narrower. What waited above the door pressed against the veil, close enough to breathe.

# Chapter 3

# Veil Lightning

Krishtan opened the door first. Quarter heat slapped.

His arm swept back, catching Sam's elbow, guiding him into the open.

Marisol stepped up fast on the other side, beads clicking a heartbeat rhythm, closing the formation around him.

Sam stood between them. Shielded without asking.

"Dat where you stand, Sam-eee," Krishtan said. Breath steady, eyes sharp.

"Time done slipped sideways. Rules walk crooked when da veil get thin."

Next door. Courtyard gone. Butcher shop pressed against Hex's brick. Pig carcasses in window. Oil through water.

Marisol's breath caught. "Dat wasn't there."

Across street. Tourist gallery gone. Empty storefront. Newspapers yellowing behind broken glass. Dated November 11, 2027.

Lightning split sky. Not white. Purple-blue. Cosmic electricity. No thunder. Crawled across clouds that hadn't existed minute before. Branching veins. Bruised tissue.

Mark under ribs pulsed blue-green. Wrong frequency. Wrong world. Bones hummed. Teeth aching. Vision blurring at edges.

"Look at dat sky," Krishtan said, voice tight. Fear held on a leash. "Dat's veil lightning, cher. Flame dragged us through more than one layer when it marked you."

Marisol's fingers dug into his arm. Knees softening.

"Chamber ain't done wit' us," she whispered. "Feel dat pull? River want back what's hers."

The pull rose from below. Through stone, through earth, through him. The eternal flame finishing what it started. Chest hollowed clean, glyph beating in the space where a heart should be.

Krishtan angled his body forward, shoulders tense, reading the street like a battlefield. "We gotta split, Sam-eee. Corner close enough to taste. Need to see what path we steppin' on."

Moved as unit down Decatur. Krishtan keeping Sam between them. Precious cargo. Rootworker's hand near elbow. Ready to catch. Marisol's fingers moving in patterns. Reinforcing protection. Shimmered faint. Heat distortion.

Tourists flowed past. Sleepwalkers. Never looking. Woman in a Saints jersey passed so close her shoulder brushed air where his should have been. Eyes skated over him. Frequency mismatch.

Thirty feet from door. Air changed. Thickened. Lungs worked harder. Pulling against pressure. Weight. Intention.

Stray cat crossed path. Paused mid-stride. Stared at Sam. Eyes reflecting silver in daylight. Opened mouth. Sam's name came out. Whispered. Voice belonging to something older than animal wearing its shape. Melted into alley that hadn't existed heartbeat before.

Krishtan's voice dropped low. "Dey huntin' your frequency, Sam-eee. Flame loud as church bells."

Crowd thickened. Bodies pressed. Tourists moving with wrong synchronization. Steps matching rhythm Sam couldn't hear. Felt in bones. Too many people. Too close. Moving with purpose.

"Krishtan," Marisol said. Warning sharp. "I see it. Turn back. Now."

Crowd surrounded. Human vise closing. Krishtan ahead. Cutting through. Marisol behind. Gripping shoulder. Trapped in middle. Feet barely touching pavement.

Man bumped into him. Middle-aged. Sun-faded polo. Khaki pockets sagging with weight. Phone pressed to his ear. Collision felt natural. Accidental.

Pain flared.

"Sorry, buddy," man said. Fingers catching Sam's wrist. "These streets all look the same."

Touch burned.

Mark detonated. White-hot fire. Drove every thought from head except pain. Terrible expanding awareness. Things moving in spaces between heartbeats.

Vision fractured. Twelve timelines. Versions of this moment stacked like transparent film.

The glyph spiked, tearing the veil thin around the man.

Tourist's form flickered. Polo shirt dissolved. Underneath, fabric remembering drowning. Suit clinging wrong to frame. Spent years underwater. Skin color of drowned flesh. Grey-green. Bloodless. Eyes sunken deep. Burning with light not life. Lips pulled back. Teeth too numerous. Gums black as old iron.

Quarter dimmed. Tourists faded. Translucent ghosts. Thing came into sharp focus. Only solid object in world gone transparent.

"Sam-eee!" Krishtan spun. Hand reaching. Thing moved with speed violating physics.

Grip on wrist tightened. Fingers too long. Joints bending angles bone shouldn't allow. Nails black. Cracked. Clawed through coffin wood.

Smell hit. Floodwater. Grave mud. Copper. Rot. Stench of bodies pulled from houses weeks after water receded.

Preacher's true form pulsed through decaying suit. Shadow. Drowned bone. Eye holes punched through reality. Mouth forming words. Language predating human speech.

Behind him, alley stretched into impossible distances. Lined with doors opening onto star-filled voids. Chambers where things never born waited. Patience measured in geological time.

"The spiral remembers," thing whispered. Breath cemetery soil against ear. "The watchers stir. The convergence comes whether you will it or not, child of flame."

Power poured through contact point. Mark expanded. Spreading fractals across chest. Burned through cotton. Skin.

The glyph cracked open, pulling bloodline resonance through him with no filter.

Vision hit.

His teeth rang.  His knees buckled.

Luke. San Juan Mountains. Rental cabin. Three in the morning. Lurched upright. Sheets tangled. Hiking gear scattered. Maps. Compass. Backpack lifted. Contents swirling in vortex. No source. Air moved wrong. Pressure dropped. Copper flooded mouth. Heat flared between shoulder blades. Two half-circles searing into skin. Wind howled through sealed cabin. Cyclone building from nothing. Scream was sound of atmosphere remembering how to rage.

Glyph ate deeper.

Audrey. Oklahoma kitchen. Dawn light. Sink. Washing dishes. Water ran cold. Ice formed across knuckles. Dropped mug. Shattered. Water erupted from faucet. Defying gravity. Spiraling upward. Ropes twisting like serpents. Right ankle burned. Blue-green light pulsed through jeans. Water answered. Hands moved through it. Conducting symphonies from rivers.

Fire pulled harder.

Celine. Hyde Park. Tornado cellar. Damp earth. Cold concrete. Mason jars. Peaches. Pears. Summer preserved. Heat built beneath skin. Not fever. Furnace. Inner left wrist throbbed. Fire carved name. Reached to steady jar. Glass blackened under touch. Syrup boiled instantly. Jar detonated. Molten sugar spraying walls. Smoke rose. Sweat evaporated before forming. Two hundred degrees. Shadows danced. Thermal distortion bending reality.

Sam collapsed.

Preacher's grip released. Krishtan's hand closed on empty air. The thing smiled. Lips peeling back. Black cavity of throat. Stepped backward into shadows. Swallowed like hungry water.

Tourist crowd solidified.

Sound returned in a rush, too loud. Flowing past. Faces blank. Sleepwalkers.

Wrist burned. Skin raised. Patterns. Symbols. Tracking mark carved in flesh. Pulsed with sick heartbeat.

Body rejected it.

His glyph hunted foreign frequencies on instinct.

Glyph flared. Foreign mark ignited. Not preacher's frequency. Older. Hotter. Wrong for pattern trying to take root.

Screamed. Symbols blistered. Smoking. Flesh cooking. Own fire turned against tracker. Ate it alive.

Marisol's hands flew to wrist. Couldn't touch. Heat too much. Watched mark burn itself out. Skin charred black. Symbols cracked. Fragmenting. Ash.

Finished. Raw meat remained. Wound size of silver dollar. Edges cauterized. Smoking.

Tracker gone. Scar remained.

Pause. A single beat of silence in the chaos.

Legs gave out. Marisol's arms kept him upright.

He shook. Teeth chattering.

"Inside," Krishtan snapped. "Now."

Ran. Thirty feet felt like miles. Legs wouldn't coordinate. World tilting sideways. Visions hollowed him out. Rejection cost more. Each cousin's awakening bled strength. Own body turned fire inward.

Half-carried. Weight distributed across shoulders. Hex's door stood open. Mouth waiting.

Fell through into gloom. Ten degrees cooler. Sweetgrass. Dragon's blood.

Krishtan slammed door. Threw locks. Pressed palm flat against wood. Symbols flared green. Wards activated. Sound like struck crystal. Door hummed. Reinforcing.

"What was dat?" Marisol's voice shook. "It touched him. Left somethin' behind."

Hands hovered. Wound too hot. Edges black. Weeping. Face pale. "He burned it off. Da mark tried to root. Fire rejected it. Ate it clean out."

"Can dey still track him?" Krishtan asked.

"Non. Not through dat." Pulled strip of linen. Wrapped wrist. Hands shook. Fabric stuck to cooked flesh. Hissed through teeth. "But da cost real, cher. Dis gonna scar deep. Might not never heal right."

Vision blurred. Pain white-hot. Constant. Radiating up arm. Every heartbeat sent fresh agony. Nerve endings trying to understand what body had done.

Throat raw. Scorched from inside. Glyph pulsed erratic. Blue-green light flickering. Candle dying in wind. Flame inside eating outward. Consuming.

Above. Glass shattered. Shop's front window exploding inward. Shards raining.

"Down," Krishtan said. "Sanctuary da only ground dat still know your name. Earth holds what wood cannot."

Velvet curtain. Pulled aside. Trapdoor. Pulled open. Cold air rushed out. Earth. Stone. Something burnt.

More glass broke. Footsteps crossing shop floor. Multiple sets. Deliberate. Heavy.

"Go."

Descended in formation. Moving fast. Stairs carved from earth remembering older secrets. Candles in iron cups burned. Patient green flame. Light felt thinner. Stretched. Working too hard to push back dark.

Legs gave out halfway. Caught himself on stone wall. Palms scraping. Wall exhaled. Cold breath. Copper. Ash. Residue of flame.

Marisol grabbed elbow. Hauled him upright. "Almost there, homme. Hold on."

Reached bottom. Basalt door. Surface absorbing light. Krishtan's hands shook. Worked ornate key into lock.

Behind. Above. Footsteps descended. Getting closer.

Lock clicked. Door swung inward. No sound.

Fell through. Circular chamber. Smell hit. Physical. Mineral charge. Coated throat. Burnt copper. Charred sweetgrass. Stench of organic matter consumed by heat not existing in physical world. Underneath, something older. Cedar smoke. Mineral earth. Scents belonging to chamber's bones.

Tomb sat in center. Basalt surface reflecting nothing. Iron plate empty. Eternal flame's candle gone. Consumed completely. Wax and wick and three hundred years of patient burning erased.

Heat and cold warred across the chamber, the air forgetting which season it belonged to. Stone walls hummed. Frequency rising. Falling. Trying to find stable rhythm. Failing.

Made three steps. Knees hit stone.

Impact drove breath. Couldn't pull more in. Chest too full. Packed with something not air. Not blood. Pure uncontained energy. Reshaping from inside out.

Glyph expanded. Fractals raced across chest. Mapping circulatory system in blue-green fire.

Felt flame inside. Distinct. Separate intelligence fused with cells. Rewriting DNA. Base pair by base pair.

Breaking him down faster than flesh could adapt. Vessel fracturing under pressure.

Krishtan and Marisol dropped beside him. Rootworker's hands moved. Patterns pulling heat away. Redistributing through protective geometry. But geometry broken. Fractured by flame's absence. Trying to hold form no longer possessed.

Marisol pressed palms against temples. Grounding. Bloodline resonated. Creating harmony. Hands burned where touched skin. Gasped. Pulled back. Stared at blisters forming.

"Il brûle, Krishtan. Flame eatin' him hollow. Dem visions, and what dey woke, took too much."

Vision fractured. Saw room from twelve angles. Perspective shattering. Tomb pulsed with residual heat. Walls breathed. Stone expanding. Contracting. Alive in ways violating geology.

Each heartbeat sent shockwaves. Dust suspended. Candles froze mid-flicker. Flames solid shapes. Light and shadow.

Footsteps reached bottom of stairs. Shadows stretched under door. Multiple figures waiting.

Krishtan pulled him closer to tomb. Center of chamber. Geometry strongest. "Chamber gotta choose, cher. Hold you or let da dark in."

Stone walls pulsed once. Hard. Heart remembering how to beat. Temperature stabilized. Locked. Geometry snapped into new configuration. Spiral patterns glowing faint on basalt surfaces.

Chamber had chosen.

A violent tremor seized him, every muscle locking at once, body rigid against stone.

Spine pulling tight. Flame peaked inside. Rewriting vessel into shape that could survive it. Light erupted. Bright enough to shield eyes.

Door trembled. Hunters pressing. Testing. Threshold held.

Marisol grabbed hand. Despite heat. "You hold on, homme. Chamber got you. Old ground. Sacred ground. It know who belong."

Lay gasping on stone. Absorbed three centuries of ritual. Flame winning. Reshaping him into what it demanded. Pulse slowing. Matching his own.

In mind, three cousins burned across map. Luke, air bending. Audrey, water rising. Celine, fire igniting.

Outside the door, the hunters went silent, waiting for his next heartbeat.

# Chapter 4

# **The Destination**

Silence breathed. Alive. Patient. Cold settling in bone despite the chamber's heat.

Lungs worked against air thick with copper. Sweetgrass memory, but twisted. Burned wrong. Flame wasn't gone. Lived in him now.

Ozone and copper from the alley clung to his tongue. Limestone's damp breath claimed it. Puddles that mirrored starlight upstairs turned here to slick black stone. Swallowing light whole. Stone watched back. Seams breathing slow. Hand-cut walls exhaled whispers. Syllables in languages belonging to buried civilizations.

Bone-deep cold knifed his spine. Not temperature. Recognition. The chamber measuring him. Deciding what parts of him still belonged to the living.

Air crawled along his arms, testing new edges.

Temperature shifted. Waves across exposed skin. Where flame touched, phantom heat bloomed. Patterns matching glyph's geometry. Cedar smoke clung to hair. Mixed with ozone.

Heartbeat pushed current. Arteries hummed. Struck wire. Basalt tomb radiated warmth under palm. Heat came from him. Breathed. Geometric afterimages burned against eyelids. Brands.

In glyph's violet light, memory crystallized. Flame's depths held surface reflecting souls. Not faces.

Own face. Older. Scarred by knowledge that bent spine. Eyes holding weight of watching worlds burn.

Details flooded back. Deep lines etched around eyes that had seen too much. Scar cutting across left temple. Disappearing into hairline gone silver at edges. Eyes holding galaxies of regret. Weight of choices no one should make.

Stomach lurched. Inevitability settled in bone. Not prophecy. Recognition.

Krishtan's gaze sharpened. No surprise in the look. No pity. Just the heavy, quiet nod of a man watching a car crash he knew was coming.

"Sam-eee." Voice slid low through breathing dark. River pulling silt. "You still walkin' wit' da livin', cher? Dat flame ain't no gentle kiss. She climbed down deep. Built herself a chair right in yo' marrow. I smell her now. Cedar an' stormwater. Dat's a mark da loa don't ignore. You lightin' beacons. Whether you ready or not."

Tried to speak. Mouth tasted of metal. Distant storms. Glyph erupted. Violent radiance. Filling chamber with light. Casting shadows against ancient stone.

"Saw myself," he managed. Voice rough. Sandpaper. "In the flame. Different. Like I'd been through war."

Marisol stepped closer. Academic composure fracturing. "There's a name for what you saw."

Paused. Voice dropped three octaves. Rhythms belonging to grand-mères whispering secrets older than written history.

"Ama warned 'bout da mirror flame. Said it show what you carry, not what you want."

Air shifted above. Weight moved across Hex's main floor.

Glass shattered above. A heavy shelf toppled. A snarl bled through old floorboards, wrong in pitch, wet at the edges. Claws or bones or both scraped across the ceiling, dragging slow as if savoring the scent it followed.

Vibration in stone. Newly sensitive bones reading density. Morse code spelling danger. Mark responded. Heat pulsed through chest. Tasting presence overhead.

Weight pressed down. Layers of wood and plaster. Low groan through beams. Scents that didn't belong. Ozone mixed with wet earth. Graves disturbed too recently.

Temperature dropped two degrees. Seconds. Breath misted despite warmth bleeding from tomb's basalt surface. Altered senses mapped presence above. Sonar. Reading density. Intent. Vibrations normal perception couldn't process.

Sound echoed. Footsteps on Hex's main floor. Too deliberate to be customers. Step leaked intention, seeping through cracks in ceiling, pooling in sacred air.

Oil on water.

"Here dey comin', now... keep still." Musical cadence sharpened. Blade steel. "And dey ain't here for palm readings. Dey huntin' somethin' dat smells like old flame. Whoever dey are, dey got weight to them. Not just body weight. Spiritual mass. Da kind dat comes from carryin' things most folks can't even see."

Glyph responded to tension. Flaring bright enough to cast shadows against walls. In sudden light, caught movement in alcove. Presence pressing forward. Testing boundaries. Light faded. Watching remained. Closer now. Drawn by scent of power no longer quite belonging to human flesh.

Turned. Darkness swallowed it. Shadows remained. Weighted with patient intentions. Presence pulled closer. Waves felt against altered skin. Cold moving with purpose. Mapping geometry through senses operating beyond sight.

New awareness catalogued shape. Not shadow. Static. A tall, angular glitch in the room's rendering. Carrying emptiness like a corrupted signal.

Glyph flickered weaker. Staggered. Caught himself on tomb. Energy drained. Water through sand. Chest showed mark had changed. Simple lines held spirals within spirals. Creating depth that shouldn't exist.

"It's different," he said. "Feel it moving."

"Da flame marked you proper," Marisol said. Voice staying in ancestral cadence. "Made you a conduit. But what flows through can change da shape o' what it touches."

"Time to go," she added. Tremors in voice. Speaking of more than unwanted visitors.

Footsteps stopped directly overhead. Absolute stillness. Heartbeat echoed off stone. Sound magnified. Thunder trapped in chest. Glyph pulsed once. Twice. Third beat, answer came from above.

Low vibration thrummed through ceiling. Subsonic. Felt in teeth before ears. Frequency made teeth ache. Vision blur. Dust rained from joints. Vibration built.

Silence returned. Deeper.

"Dey testin' da walls," Krishtan said. "Searchin' da seams where power seep like river through cypress roots. Da old ones taught 'em. Stone got memory. Memory got cracks where light try to bleed out."

Above, a presence whispered his name through wood thick as bone. Not in voice. In vibration. Every syllable carried the weight of graves that had never known rest.

Truth settled in bones. Hunters above knew exactly what they were looking for.

Mark flared one more time. Casting shadows across ancient stone. In radiance, older Sam watched from flame's memory. Still there. Still waiting.

And the older version looked right through him. Eyes focused on a war only one of them survived. To him, Sam wasn't flesh. Just a memory.

Light faded. New heat stirred in chest. Distant warmth. Echo calling from vast space. For a moment, felt pulse of another awakening bloodline member. Mark responding across distance. Connection lasted only a heartbeat. Carried recognition. Hope.

Sensation passed. Leaving him hollow.

Above, weight shifted. Moved away. Message clear. Found. Marked.

The mark inside him answered, not in heat but in recognition. As if some distant intelligence had opened an eye and fixed it on his spine.

Footsteps moved away across shop floor. Knew they'd be back. Hunters wouldn't stop until they found what flame had made him.

Chamber exhaled. Releasing pressure held too long. Silence remained. Carried weight. Heaviness after irreversible change.

Krishtan's eyes flicked to stair. "We movin' now, cher." Voice dropped heavy with oath. "To my ward, cher, 'fore dey circle back. Dat ground been watchin' us since da first Dauvee woman stepped in dis land. Sacred earth wit' teeth. She know who true an' who false. She know where da city breathe itself into da swamp."

# Chapter 5

# The Ward

Krishtan shoved him.

"Time done gone, Sam-eee. We movin' now."

Above, glass shattered. Shop's front window exploding inward. Shards raining across floorboards. Voices followed. Too many. Moving with purpose. Air tasting of wet iron.

Legs barely held. Krishtan pulled him toward stairs. Glyph pulsed against sternum. Second heart. Throwing violet light across stone that had absorbed three centuries of ritual. Each step upward made bones hum. Frequencies didn't belong to human flesh.

Behind them the basalt tomb sat empty. Three centuries of steady flame lived in him now.

Marisol followed close. Face pale. Academic composure shattered. Clutched gris-gris bag at throat. Lifeline. Lips moving in prayers older than city above.

Climbed in silence. Stone stairs exhaled cold. Breath misted despite heat radiating from chest. Each step heavier. Gravity multiplying with every beat of merged flame.

Krishtan's hand gripped his shoulder. Steered him. Rootworker's eyes held fear wrapped in reverence. Kind that came when prophecy stopped being legend. Started walking beside you.

"Flame ain't never chose nobody, Sam-eee," Krishtan whispered. Voice tight. "Three hundred years she burn steady. Now she inside you. Breathin' wit' your lungs."

Halfway up, Krishtan stopped. Head tilted. Reading vibrations through stone. Sam's altered senses could almost taste them. Above. Boots on floorboards. Heavy. Deliberate. Hunters had found the Hex.

"Dey close, Sam-eee," Krishtan murmured. "But dey ain't rushin'. Dey movin' smart."

He tilted his head, listening deeper. "Dey testin' da seams in da walls. Lookin' for weak places. Tryin' to push us right where dey want."

Sam felt it then.

Probes sliding through the stone. Sharp. Surgical. Little pulses of heat and cold working the wards like lockpicks. Not brute force. Pattern work.

They weren't guessing. They mapped him. Herding him toward the choke point.

Hunters who knew Dauvee magic well enough to unmake it.

Chest flared hot. Glyph responded to proximity of threat. Mapping space above through frequencies bypassing normal perception. Counted six bodies. Maybe seven. All carrying weight not just physical.

"Then we go back," Marisol said. "Find another way."

"No." Krishtan's copper rings clicked. Fingers moved to jacket. "We go through."

Pulled out small vial. Glass sealed with wax. Filled with powder glowing faint green in violet light bleeding from Sam's chest. Old glass. Imperfections carrying generations.

"Gran-Mé's dust," Krishtan whispered. "Made from graveyard dirt and her own blood. Opens what need openin'. Hides what need hidin'."

Uncorked it. Poured contents into palm. Powder moved. Memory. Particles arranging into patterns new vision could almost read.

Krishtan blew across palm. Dust scattered. Caught air that shouldn't move in enclosed stairwell. Drifted toward wall. Not stairs going up. Blank stone wall to left. Solid foundation.

Where dust touched, symbols appeared. Spirals. Intersecting lines. Protection. Passage. Carved so fine invisible without dust to make them sing. Stone shimmered. Not opening. Admitting it had been lying.

A door. Small. Narrow. Cut into stone in way not structurally possible. Beyond, darkness breathing cool and damp.

Secret door. Hidden passage. Glyph recognized something older. Not architecture. Root magic made permanent. Geometry bending space because rootworker who carved it made city agree.

"Tunnel goes under da courtyard," Krishtan said. Already moving through revealed door. "Through da building next door. Come out in my ward. Nobody know it exist 'cept family. Been keepin' us safe since before dis city had a name."

Above, front door of Hex splintered. Wood giving up. Force. Boots on floorboards. Moving toward stairwell.

Marisol grabbed elbow. Pulled toward opening. "Move, cousin. Now."

Stepped through. Passage swallowed him whole.

Stone walls pressed close. Slick with moisture. Air tasting of minerals. Deep earth. Floor smooth. Worn by centuries. From when this city was swamp and prayer.

Door behind shimmered. Vanished. Becoming wall again. Sealing them in darkness lit only by violet pulse of glyph.

Krishtan moved ahead. Sure-footed. Hand trailing along wall. Copper rings clicked rhythm against stone. Deliberate. Speaking language tunnel remembered.

"How far?" Voice hollow. Eaten by dark.

"Fifty feet. Maybe less. Built when my great-great-grandmother first came to dis city. She knew what it meant to need a way out nobody could follow."

Altered vision mapped space. Tunnel not straight. Curved. Dropped slightly. Following contours having nothing to do with buildings above. Old geometry. Knowing where earth wanted paths to go.

Behind them, sound. Muffled. Real. Hunters found revealed door. Found dust's trail.

"Dey followin'," Marisol whispered.

Krishtan didn't slow. "Don't matter. Tunnel got defenses past dis point."

Passage ahead shimmered. Shadows peeled from walls. Forming shapes testing edges of vision. Not solid. Not quite there. Guardians. Waiting for permission.

Glyph flared hot. Shadows pressed closer. Tasting what he'd become. Deciding if merged flame counted as intrusion.

Krishtan pulled copper coin from pocket. Kissed it. Tossed it forward. Rang against stone. Clear. True. Carrying prayer in echo.

Shadows paused. Considered. Then slipped back into the walls.

"Blood price paid three generations back," Krishtan said. "My Gran-Mé made sure we could always use dis path."

Behind them, scream. Cut off mid-breath. Silence. Erasure.

Kept moving.

Tunnel bent one more time. Ended at ladder. Iron rungs. Old. Solid. Climbing up through darkness into what smelled like cedar and sweetgrass.

Krishtan went first. Pushing open trapdoor hidden beneath floorboards. Light spilled down. Warm. Amber. Scent of candle wax. Old wood.

Sam followed. Muscle shaking. Glyph pulsing so hot thought it might burn through skin. Hands found rungs. Pulled weight rung by rung. Cells screaming with effort of containing what flame had made him.

Emerged into ward.

Not different building. Same structure as Hex. Higher. Top floor. Space didn't exist on blueprints. Room looking abandoned from outside but breathing with protection layered so deep it had own gravity.

Bare wood floors carved with spirals. Intersecting triangles. Candles burning without smoke. Photographs covering every wall. Faces watching with eyes present. Knowing. Windows shuttered. Painted with symbols hurting to look at directly.

Room older than building containing it. Existing in pocket of space city agreed to hide.

Made three steps. Legs gave out.

Not dramatic. Sudden. Done. Body carried him through escape. Transformation. Stairs. Tunnel. Now demanded payment.

Collapsed. Sliding down wall. Vision graying. Glyph pulsed irregular. Rhythm breaking. Consciousness trying to hold what it couldn't contain.

Krishtan closed trapdoor. Sealed with gesture making air hum. Beside Sam. Kneeling. Hands moving in patterns pulling heat away from flesh burning itself hollow.

"Let it take you, Sam-eee. Stone gon' hold what you can't. Tunnel sealed. Dat door don't open for shadows. You safe. Let da stone carry da weight, cher."

Tried to speak. Tongue wouldn't cooperate. Glyph flared white-hot. Vision whited out completely.

Falling. Not down. Inward. Into space flame carved in chest. Into place where gold and green spirals still learning to breathe as one.

Last thing heard was Krishtan's voice. Steady. Certain.

"We got you, Sam-eee. Blood holdin' tight."

Then nothing.

Ward held breath. Candles flickered once. Steadied. Protective symbols pulsed faint violet. Responding to unconscious man whose heartbeat carried frequencies they'd been designed to recognize.

Three floors below, Hex burned. Hunters torching what they couldn't claim. Destroying evidence of sacred flame. Ancient ritual.

But ward held. Hidden in plain sight. Protected by generations of root magic. Blood price paid long ago.

Krishtan and Marisol knelt beside Sam. Checking vitals. Reading signs written in sweat and heat. Breath shallow but steady. Transformation took him under. Wasn't killing. Teaching.

Marisol pulled something from inside shirt. Rosary. Bone-white beads strung on copper wire. One bead cracked. Pale green. Held it over chest. Feeling for right placement. Exact angle where Ama's protection would resonate with glyph.

"Dis gon' keep him tethered," she whispered. "Keep da light from eatin' him while he sleep."

Lowered it slowly. Reverently. Draping across sternum. Beads settled against skin. Weight deliberate. Sacred. Cracked green bead rested directly over glyph.

Moment it made contact, breathing eased. Heat radiating from chest dropped. Searing to steady. Rosary pulsed once. Acknowledging work. Went silent.

Krishtan exhaled. Shoulders dropping. "Ama's love still workin'. Even from da other side. Dat rosary been on her altar fifty years. Soaked in protection. Prayer. He safe now. For a while."

Marisol's own beads, ones at wrist, cracked. Three split clean through. Wood unable to handle proximity to what Sam had become. Didn't flinch. Pulled them off. Set aside. Reaching for new ones from bag.

"How long he gon' be out?" she asked.

Krishtan checked symbols on walls. Reading protective geometry like map. "Long as it take for da fusion to settle. Could be an hour. Could be till dawn. Body gotta learn what it is 'fore we can move him."

Stood. Joints popping. Moved to window. Through gap in protective symbols, watched Quarter. Streets different now. Not in structure. Awareness. City watching. Deciding what new power meant for her.

Streetlights flickered. Once. Twice. Steadied into rhythm matching pulse of sleeping man three floors above burning shop.

"We got maybe a day," Krishtan said quietly. "Maybe less. 'Fore da city make up her mind. 'Fore whatever huntin' him feel where he restin'. We move him to Ama's land soon as he wake, or we don't move him at all."

Marisol tied new beads at wrist. Darker wood. Stronger. "Den we wait. An' we pray she give us time."

Settled into vigil. Krishtan in chair by door. Copper rings still smoking on fingers. Marisol cross-legged on floor beside Sam. Close enough to touch if transformation turned violent again.

Candles burned steady. Protective symbols held. Outside, New Orleans breathed in rhythm with sleeping man. Learning frequency of merged flame and human will.

Waiting.

# Chapter 6

# Twin Helixes

Sam woke to the smell of candle wax and river mud. Underneath, the sterile absence of smoke. Three floors down, the Hex burned, but the Ward held the air clean. His chest pulled tight with every breath, ribs wrapped around a pulse that wasn't his. He sat up. The room tilted. Weight shifted against his chest, cool and unfamiliar.

Above him, photographs lined the walls. Faces that watched with eyes present, knowing.

He looked down.

A rosary lay across his sternum, bone-white beads strung on copper wire, resting over the glyph with clear intention. One bead near the center was cracked, pale green, catching the candlelight different than the others. The beads were warm where they touched his skin, alive in a way that made the glyph hum quieter, steadier.

Sam lifted it, confused, the beads pooling in his palm. He didn't remember putting this on. Didn't remember anyone giving it to him.

Marisol sat a few feet away, watching him with tired eyes. New beads at her wrist, bigger than before, carved dark wood almost black in the candlelight. The old ones sat in a small pile on the floor nearby, cracked clean through.

"What is this?" His voice was rough.

"Ama's rosary," Marisol said softly. "Laid it on you while you was sleepin'. You was burnin' too hot, twistin' like hands pullin' you under. Beads cooled you down, kept you tethered to dis side." She gestured to the cracked green bead.

"Dat one been on her altar for fifty years, homme. Soaked in protection and prayer. It know how to keep da light from eatin' you whole, homme."

Sam ran his thumb over the cracked bead. It pulsed faint, warm, resonating with his chest in a place that wasn't quite the glyph and wasn't quite his heartbeat.

"I didn't even feel you put it on me."

"You wasn't supposed to. Dis da kind o' protection dat work best when you don't know it's workin'."

She smiled, tired but real. "But now you awake, you feel it. Keep it on, Sam. Don't take it off. Not till we get you to Ama's land."

He lifted the rosary over his head, settled it back around his neck where it had been. The beads fell against his chest, the cracked green bead resting just above the glyph.

"Thank you."

"We family, cousin. Dat's what family do." Sam's hand went to his pocket. Empty. The instinct to check his phone, to ground himself in the ordinary, met only absence. "Your phone still in da Hex," Marisol said, reading the gesture. "If it ain't ash by now, cousin. Can't go back for it."

"My family." The words caught in his throat.

"We get word to 'em when we can. Right now, you callin' anybody just put a target on dey back. Krishtan say it plain before he left. We gotta keep you quiet till we know what you is."

His mother's face. Aunt Kay. His cousins. Couldn't risk drawing hunters to their doors.

He looked at Marisol. "Where is he?"

"Gatherin what we need to move you. He ain't far. Symbols still holdin', mean we safe enough for now." She glanced toward the door, toward the walls covered in symbols that pulsed faint violet in rhythm with Sam's chest. "City went quiet when you passed out. Streetlights stopped flickerin'. Dat huntin' we felt, it pulled back. She waitin' to see what you do next."

Sam pushed himself up on trembling arms. His body felt wrong, lighter and heavier at once, hollow in places that used to be solid. The glyph across his chest radiated steady heat, no longer the searing burn from before, but a constant presence that made his skin hum.

Hunger clawed at him. Deeper. His body burning fuel faster than he could replace it.

"There water?" His voice came out rough.

Marisol reached behind her, pulled a plastic bottle from a cabinet built into the wall. Distilled water, generic label. "Dat's all I found. No food, just salt and dried herbs. Dis place ain't for livin', Sam. It's for hidin'."

He reached for the bottle. His wrist throbbed. A dull echo of the brand. His fingers worked. He drank half in three swallows. The water was flat, chemical, but his body pulled it down desperate. When he lowered the bottle, his hands shook.

"How long till he's back?"

"Soon." Marisol settled cross-legged on the floor. Velvet pouch pulled from her shirt, wine-dark, edges frayed from years of handling.

She opened it slow. Bones poured between them. Small. Pale. Etched deep enough to outlive the hands that carved them.

Humming started.

Not sound. Pressure. A low tremor riding straight through Sam's ribs, making the glyph answer in rhythm.

One bone twitched. Rolled left. Stopped like it had found its mark.

Another spun once, slow circle, then pointed at the door.

Marisol's lips moved in silence. Old language.

The room watched her.

Sam swallowed. "Where?"

"Bayou. Old Dauvee property, passed down through da women. Ama carved protections into da ground herself, back when she first came to dis city. Veil thick dere, cher. It hold you while da flame learn yo' shape."

One bone rolled away from the pattern entirely, tumbling across the floor till it hit the wall. Marisol watched it go, face tight.

"Dat mean we out of time. Whatever quiet da city holdin', it won't last."

The door opened. Krishtan slipped in, bags slung over both shoulders, suit jacket rumpled and copper rings tarnished dark. He looked tired, older than Sam had ever seen him, but his eyes went straight to Sam with relief.

"Sam-eee... look at you. Breath back in yo' chest. City ain't sure if she gon' welcome you or spit you out, but you wakin'? Dat's somethin', cher."

He set the bags down, pulled out wrapped bundles. The smell hit first: beignets, still warm, grease bleeding through the paper. Then chicory coffee in a battered thermos, steam rising when he unscrewed the cap.

"You been ridin' dat spirit wave a long time, Sam-eee. Da sun done climbed da sky and slid back down while you was under. "It's evenin' again, cher. Quarter holdin' her breath, but she ain't holdin' long. Wind shift comin', Sam-eee."

Sam's stomach twisted with want, sharp and empty.

"Man," he muttered, voice thin, "I could crush a Lucky Dog right now."

Not craving. Memory. Something solid from the world he still hoped he belonged to.

Krishtan let out a laugh, sudden and raw, breaking the weight in the room.

"Sam-eee, you jus' swallowed three hundred years o' sacred fire and you thinkin' 'bout hot dogs from a cart."

Gold tooth flashed in candlelight. Relief more than humor.

"Dat's how I know you still in dere, cher. Still Sam under all dat light."

The laugh died. His face settled serious, eyes reading the tremor in Sam's hands.

"But we go slow now. Body gotta learn what it is 'fore we ask it to do more."

He pressed a beignet into Sam's hand. Sam took three bites, tried to force normal into a body that wasn't normal anymore.

Sweetness curdled to ash on his tongue. His stomach lurched hard.

He set it aside, reached for the coffee. Bitter. Scalding.

It stayed down. Held him in place. One familiar anchor in a room full of strangers.

Marisol showed Krishtan the bones, the one that had rolled to the wall. "Bones pointin' home, cher. Ama's land callin' him by name."

Krishtan nodded, no surprise in his face.

"Yeah, cher. Saw wrong cars circlin' da Quarter. Church folk, but not da prayin' kind. Suits too sharp, shoes too clean, eyes dat don't blink right. Been askin' quiet questions. Strange lights off Decatur. Who still walk in da Hex. Which families keep da old ways."

He crouched by the bags. Pulled out gris-gris pouches. Bone ash sealed in glass. Bundles of dried sage wrapped tight. Then something wrapped in red cloth, old and careful.

Marisol's breath caught. "Gran-Mé's mirror. You brought dat?"

Krishtan opened the cloth slow. Reverent.

Black glass. Obsidian. Edges worn soft by generations. Surface dead-dark, no reflection unless he angled it just right. And even then, only shadow looked back.

"Need to see what we dealin' wit', Sam-eee. Need to know what da flame made you into."

Krishtan's voice dropped low, reverent and scared together.

"Obsidian don't lie, cher. It show what's real, not what you want. Strip away da skin, show da soul underneath. Flame done changed you. We gotta know how, or we can't keep you safe."

Sam's pulse kicked. The glyph heated against his sternum.

"You want me to look in it?"

"Need you to, Sam-eee. Hold it steady. Look where da mark burnin'. Tell us what you see in dat glass."

He placed the mirror in Sam's hands. Cold. Heavier than it should be, carrying weight that felt older than the room.

Sam angled it down.

His reflection met him.

Skin.

Glyph lines, still as ink.

Then the mark shifted.

Moved.

Beneath them, deeper, two shapes twisted.

Helixes. Twin spirals turning slow, patient, alive.

One burned gold. Warm, molten, pulsing like small suns caught in metal. It moved with certainty, ancient and entirely his.

The other glowed green. Vivid. Electric. Breathing with its own cadence, separate at first, then adjusting, learning the gold spiral's rhythm and matching it beat for beat.

Where they touched, light flared violet white, too bright to meet even through obsidian's shadow.

They were not fused. Not yet. They studied each other, spiraling closer with every turn, practicing how to share a single shape, how to become one thing made of two.

Sam's whisper scraped out of his throat.

"There's two of them. Gold and green. They're moving."

He could not look away. The spirals pulsed with his heartbeat, slow and deliberate, older than breath.

"They're breathing together. Like they're learning how to be the same thing."

His chest tightened.

"The gold one. That's me, isn't it? And the green..."

"Da flame." Marisol's voice thinned, breaking on the truth. "Dat's her. She alive in you."

She dropped to her knees, hands pressed together. Prayer rose out of her in Creole, fast and sharp, a rhythm older than breath. Words Sam could not translate, but felt in bone.

"Kenbe li fò, mon chèr homme."

Hold him firm, my dear man.

The rest flowed as cadence and heat, the inheritance-language, the one spoken by hands lighting candles in dirt long before the city took shape. Her beads warmed against her wrist, faint glow catching the edges, answering what Sam had become.

Krishtan stumbled back three steps, hand covering his mouth. His rings smoked, copper blackening as he stared, eyes wide as moons. He started pacing tight, shoulders high, movement caged and panicked.

"Lawd have mercy. Lawd have mercy." The words leaked out of him, low and cracked, like he was praying to keep his own bones steady. "Gran-Mé told stories, yeah... flame takin' flesh, walkin' round in skin. I always thought she was rememberin' crooked, cher. Thought it was old women embroidin' truth in da dark."

He froze. Turned slow toward Sam. Hands shaking so hard the beads on his wrists clicked panic rhythm.

"Two spirits, one flesh, Sam-eee. Dat ain't how da world ever worked. You supposed to carry da flame like a torch, not bind wit' her. Dis somethin' else. Somethin' da elders feared an' da city ain't got a name for."

Sam dragged the mirror away, fingers trembling. His chest still burned, the memory of those twin helixes turning under his skin, alive and learning his shape.

"What does it mean?"

Marisol stayed bowed, lips moving, prayer wrapping tight around the room. Krishtan paced hard, copper beads on his wrists clicking a frantic beat.

Marisol lifted her head. "Not a vessel, homme. A union. You ain't holdin' da flame anymore. She woven into you. Spirit-twined. Like vows whispered where no light reach."

Krishtan stopped mid-step. Turned full toward Sam, eyes wide and scared in a way Sam had never seen.

"You ain't human clean no more, Sam-eee. But you ain't pure flame neither. You walkin' da seam between worlds now, somethin' da old powers and da new ones both gon' fight to claim. Ain't nobody ever born like you."

Sam looked at his hands, ordinary skin over somethin' that wasn't. The helixes moved inside him, gold and green, twisting closer with every heartbeat.

Krishtan wrapped the mirror in red cloth, hands moving quick, tightened by fear he wasn't botherin' to hide. "We move tonight, Sam-eee. Ain't no waitin'. Dat fusion inside you gon' settle or it gon' hollow you clean. Ama's land da only place wit' ground strong enough to hold what you becomin'. Quarter wards too thin fo' dis."

Sam pushed himself upright, legs unsteady. He needed to see the street. To know what waited.

He moved to the window, catching himself on the sill to keep from falling.

His knuckles brushed the casing of the old radio sitting in the dust.

The radio breathed awake under his hand.

Static rose, parted, a voice sliding through smooth and holy-soft.

"...Sovereign Hope Ministries invites believers to stand in unity tonight against the false light risin' in our midst. Join us as we..."

Krishtan tore the cord from the wall. Sparks spit. The voice cut off mid-breath.

Silence hit hard. Thick enough to make Sam's ears ring.

All three stared at the dead radio.

"You just woke dat up, Sam-eee." Krishtan's voice tightened thin. "Radio been dead six months. Tried it last week, got nothin'. No signal, no power, no breath. You touch it one time and it start preachin' 'bout false light."

He studied Sam, fear settling behind his eyes. "Cher... you ringin' like a church bell in a storm. Every spirit from here to Claiborne gon' hear you hummin' now."

Sam pulled his hand back fast. "I didn't mean it."

"Don't matter what you meant." Krishtan's face stayed grim. "You wakin' things now. Electronics, spirits, da city herself."

Outside, the sun slid low, light catching the symbols on the windows, turning them gold then blood-red. Krishtan moved through the room one last time, checking corners, tightening straps, settin' every bag where it needed to be. His copper rings clicked steady rhythm against wood and stone.

"We move at full dark," he said, voice low, certain. "Car three blocks down, close as I could get without drawin' eyes. We don't stop, we don't look back, we don't answer nobody callin' yo' name. Quarter might let us pass, might not. She still decidin' what you is to her. Either way, we gone fore she make up her mind."

Sam tried another bite of beignet. Managed to swallow, barely. His body burned fuel faster than he could replace it, the flame inside demanding more than food could offer.

Marisol gathered the bones, slipped them back into the velvet pouch, tied it to her belt with hands that shook once then steadied. Krishtan moved through the room in silence, sliding gris-gris into pockets, sealing jars of bone ash, working like a man who had done this run too many times and survived by inches.

The Ward held them, but only barely. Obscurity had limits. Not against what was waking in the city.

Outside, the light shifted. Purple first. Then deep blue. Evening settling like a veil pulled tight across the Quarter.

Krishtan parted a narrow gap in the symbols on the window and leaned in, breath held. He read the street the way his ancestors read river currents. Shadows. Stillness. The way noise paused in the wrong places.

Things Sam could feel now too, faint but rising.

"Clear enough fo' now," he said, stepping back from the window. "But we slip quick, Sam-eee. City holdin' her breath only long as she choose to, and she fickle when light start shiftin' her bones."

They stepped out into dusk, air thick as water, humidity pressing close. The Quarter was different. Too quiet. Too still. The streets held their breath. Shadows pooled in doorways, darker than the fading light could account for.

Sam's legs shook with every step, but he kept moving. Krishtan on one side, Marisol on the other, both close enough to catch him if he fell.

They passed a corner where a woman sat behind a card table, tarot spread before her. Tourist trap, usually. Painted sign and cheap velvet cloth.

Krishtan shifted closer, body angled between Sam and the open street. Not touching him. Guarding him. His eyes cut the Quarter clean, reading shadows, doorways, windows with curtains that breathed wrong. Reading the street the way a rootworker reads bone fall.

The woman at the table lifted her head like a hook caught her spine.

Her eyes went wide. Terrified.

The top card snapped off the deck. Not slid. Not dropped. Snapped.

It spun once in the air and hit the cobblestones between them.

Judgement.

The dead rising. Reckoning walking.

Her fingers jerked again, pulled by something wearing her skin.

The Tower.

Stone splitting. Bodies falling.

A third card.

Devil.

Chains. Covenant twisted.

Blood slid from her nose. Thin red line. Dripped off her chin. She didn't move to stop it. Didn't blink.

When she spoke, the voice came river-deep and older than her bones.

"You already burned once. You won't get a second mercy."

Krishtan stepped tighter to Sam, stance widening, blocking half the street without laying a hand on him. His voice stayed low.

"Eyes ahead, Sam-eee. Keep walkin'. She felt da helixes inside you. Dat sight carve through regular folk like blade."

They moved. Faster. The Quarter shrank with every step, shadows leaning inward like the whole street had an opinion.

Sam risked one glance back.

The fortune teller sat frozen. Cards scattered. Blood dripping onto Judgement. Eyes locked on him, wide and unblinking, mouth open like a scream stuck in her throat.

She didn't blink. Didn't breathe.

Krishtan pulled him around the corner, and she vanished from sight.

Every block stretched long. Wrong. Shadows moved half a beat ahead of the light. Sound carried too far, echoing like the Quarter was hollowing itself out around them.

The veil was thin here. Thin enough Sam could feel things watching from the other side, measuring his shape, tasting what he had become.

Then finally, the docks.

Krishtan's Cadillac sat under a dead streetlight, black DeVille with age in every dent, every scratch that had a story. The interior smelled of sage, old leather, tobacco. Talismans tucked in vents. Cross swinging slow on the rearview.

Sam climbed into the back with Marisol. Krishtan slid behind the wheel. Key turned. Engine caught on the second try, rumbling low, familiar, real.

Krishtan eased from the curb, smooth hands on the wheel, steady even though the dashboard light betrayed the shake in his fingers.

Behind them, the Quarter's streetlights flickered once. All of them. Together.

Then synced into a rhythm that matched the pulse burning beneath Sam's sternum.

Three blocks. Silent.

Shadows thinned. Pressure eased with distance.

Sam's hand moved on instinct, checking the glyph. Heat steady. Alive. His fingers brushed the rosary.

The moment intention touched the beads, they flared warm. Not fire. Recognition.

A single pulse that wasn't his heartbeat.

Krishtan and Marisol turned at the same breath, heads snapping toward him like the car itself had twitched.

"You feel dat," Krishtan said. Voice low. Eyes cutting to the mirror to lock on Sam.

Marisol's fingers pressed to her beads, the new ones at her wrist vibrating faint like they were answering a call.

"He touched it," she said. "With intention. Ama's protection just woke up full."

Sam looked down at the rosary. The cracked green bead glowed soft in the dim light, pulse nested inside its fracture.

"What just happened?"

"Rosary been workin' since I laid it on you," Marisol said, awe folded tight into her voice. "But you was too deep in da fusion to feel it. Now you awake. Now you reachin' for it with your mind behind da touch. Dat green bead mute yo' signal. Block what you is from whatever out dere listenin'."

Krishtan let out a slow breath, shoulders easing only a fraction.

"Dat's why we made it dis far without somethin' crawlin' out da dark for you. Ama's rosary been shieldin' you. Keepin' da light from ringin' through every street from Treme to Claiborne. But it don't hold forever, Sam-eee. Dat bead already cracked. Protection like dat got limits."

Sam closed his hand around the beads. The pulse under his palm answered him, quiet and sure. Protection he never knew he carried. Love set in motion long before he opened his eyes in this room.

"How long will it last?" he asked.

Marisol held his gaze. "Long enough to get you to da land if we move clean. After dat, we find somethin' else to hide you. But right now, cher, you keep it on. Ama's love still workin' through dat rosary. It da only thing standin' between you and every predator in dis city feelin' yo' light."

Sam looked through the rear window. New Orleans stretched behind them. Lights. Shadow. Old as scripture. The city watched him go. Measuring him. Deciding if she was letting him leave or waiting for him to come back changed.

# Chapter 7

# **The Crossing**

The Cadillac's engine died at the estate gates. Not mechanical failure. Decision. The hum that carried them through the Quarter's watched streets cut out clean. No sputter, no warning. Krishtan guided them off the road onto grass gone wild where wrought iron met cypress. Gravel crunched under tires rolling slower, slower, until the car settled into stillness.

Silence pressed in. No crickets. No frogs. Just the tick of cooling metal and swamp air thick as syrup. A watchful quiet, the kind that comes before a storm or a predator.

Krishtan turned the key. Nothing. He tried again. The engine gave one dry click.

"Ain't the battery." His rings caught moonlight as he gripped the wheel, knuckles loose, unbothered. "Ain't mechanical neither. Somethin' don't want us ridin' da rest of da way."

Sam's rosary warmed against his chest. The cracked green bead heated sharp, a point of fever against his skin. Warning written in temperature, not language.

Marisol leaned forward, palm on the dashboard, eyes closed. Reading the metal like scripture.

"Wards still holdin' on da car, but dey thinnin'. Whatever stopped us ain't here to wound. It testin', cher. Seein' if we turn back."

Krishtan opened his door. Humid air rolled in carrying rot, wild jasmine, and beneath it a faint medicinal sting, menthol and bitter root. The scent hit Sam's glyph hard enough to burn.

"Boat's two hundred yards through da grounds," Krishtan said. "Den we take water da rest of da way. We walk from here."

They took only what mattered. Krishtan slung two bags across his shoulders, the weight settling like something his blood already knew. Marisol tucked her bone pouch inside her shirt, checked the new beads at her wrist, and stepped into the night. Too warm. Too still. Air holding its breath.

Sam followed last. Legs unsteady but working.

The moment his feet touched grass, the world shifted.

Not vision. Not sound.

Memory.

Argyle. His childhood street at dusk. Wayne's truck in the driveway, ticking just like the Cadillac. Texas light smearing everything gold. Asphalt heat under his bare feet. Cicadas screaming. Motor oil. Fear.

He had stayed out too long. Wayne would be waiting. The belt already off the hook.

The glyph pulsed. The memory shattered. Swamp air rushed in, wet and heavy.

Krishtan studied him close.

"You runnin' hot, Sam-eee. Somethin' crawlin' under yo' ribs."

"Yeah." Sam wiped sweat from his lip. "Just tired."

Krishtan held his stare a moment longer, then nodded once.

They walked.

The path curved through live oak and palmetto. Spanish moss hung like torn cloth. Moonlight leaked through in shards, cutting the ground into silver and black. Every footstep sounded too sharp in the quiet.

To their left, ruins opened through the trees. Brick columns strangled by ivy. Roof collapsed inward. A grand staircase rising to nothing.

Krishtan flicked his chin at it.

"Da Big House. City tried makin' it a museum in da nineties. Water kept takin' it back. Folks walked in feelin' sick before dey even hit da stairs."

The smell of wet brick and old sorrow rolled toward them.

"Ama walked dis path every night," Krishtan said. "Old Jean Baptist had da rot chewin' him from da inside out. Money ain't do nothin'. Doctors ain't do nothin'. Ama da only one who shut his screamin' down."

His rings clicked once, sharp.

"She kept him breathin' long past his time. Fed him bitter root. Swamp water. Words dat ain't in no church Bible. When he begged her what she wanted fo' savin' his soul, she ain't take one dollar."

He tapped his chest.

"She took da dirt. Iron deed. Blood claim. He paid wit' soil."

They passed the ruin.

Krishtan's eyes narrowed at the brick.

"Walls kept sinkin'. Swamp took dat house back. But dis stretch right here? Ama carved it herself. Sang it solid."

Sam felt it under his feet. The thrum. The ownership.

Krishtan glanced over.

"She knew somethin' was comin'. Knew da flame gon' choose one of hers. Didn't know yo' name, Sam-eee, but she knew your weight. Built all dis fo' you before your mama ever carried you."

They walked deeper. The trees pressed close. Something moved through the water beside them, slow and deliberate, keeping pace.

The next memory hit hard.

Wayne's carport. Hot concrete. Diesel. Rubber. Tools lined in order. Sam small. Wayne's shadow towering.

"You ever gon' be worth somethin'? Your grandfather'd be ashamed."

The words drilled straight into marrow.

The glyph flared and the scene tore apart. Bark bit into Sam's palm as he caught the oak trunk.

Marisol stepped close.

"Breathe. Dat ain't da past. Dat da land draggin' your hurt up. Purge. Don't let it steer."

But the presence pressed again. Wayne's voice softer than it ever had been in life.

Turn back. Go home. Be small.

Sam shoved the whisper aside.

"I'm good."

He wasn't, but the land was measuring him, not asking for truth.

The dock rose ahead, wood lifting from black water like a spine. Barnacles crusted the pilings. A flat-bottom skiff waited, rope older than it had any right to be.

Krishtan stepped on first. The planks held without a sound.

"Ama's work. Wood listen when da right voice call."

They boarded. Sam took the middle. Marisol fixed her gaze forward. Krishtan steadied the tiller.

He flicked the motor. It answered with a low hum, vibration rolling through the hull like a borrowed heartbeat. The skiff drifted into the dark.

Cypress closed around them. Roots twisted thick. Shadows bent. Green shimmer rose from beneath the surface like sleeping breath.

Five minutes in, the motor died clean.

Silence locked down.

"Wards," Krishtan said. He lifted the dead motor clear and took the push-pole. "Technology don't cross dis line. From here on, we work wit' clay and breath."

Thump. Swish. The skiff moved again, muscle and intent carrying it forward.

The silence deepened until the water itself felt alert.

Sam touched the rosary. The cracked green bead had split wider.

Then the flash.

Argyle. Kitchen table. Fluorescent buzz. Wayne's hand on his neck. Newspaper full of futures that were not his.

"You ain't never gon' be nothin'. Quit pretendin' you special."

The hit landed too sharp to be memory alone.

The glyph ignited white. Pain tore through his sternum. Breath ripped out of him.

Ama had not crossed rivers at midnight so her line could fold in a boat. She had not carved wards into dirt only for her great-grandson to bow to a ghost wearing Wayne's voice.

Sam lifted his head.

Krishtan watched him from the stern, framed in cypress shadow. Waiting to see which way the fire would break.

"Somethin' tryin' to split you open, Sam-eee. It know if you step foot on Dauvee land, you ain't ever slippin' back to da man you was."

Sam steadied himself.

Krishtan planted the pole. Thump. Swish.

The skiff slid deeper into guarded dark.

Chapter 8

# Signal and Response

They stepped off the boat onto the dock. Silence pressed in from all sides. Nothing moved in the trees. No sound but their breathing and the slow lap of water against pilings worn smooth by time.

The land rose here, a dry back of earth where everything around it drowned. Cypress canopy locked overhead, dense enough to hide the cabin from anything flying above. From the air, this would look like unbroken swamp. Protected Louisiana ground, forgotten in old files, touched only by Dauvees and the elders who came to witness.

Sam's legs trembled but held. The dock boards felt solid beneath him, worn by Ama's footsteps and by every Dauvee who had walked here in need or duty. A path held firm by intention.

The cabin sat small and weathered in the clearing. Cypress siding gone silver. Tin roof streaked with rust and moss. Porch slightly sunken on one side. The bones were right. Ama's hand had put them down. Built to stand and stay standing.

They approached slow. Krishtan first, then Marisol, then Sam. Each step careful, reverent. A procession walking into a place that remembered them before birth.

Sam stepped onto the porch.

Inside, every candle sparked alive.

All of them. Same breath. Same instant.

Small flames at first, faint light sketching the room. Then they leaned. Not stirred, not swayed. Pulled.

Fire bent toward Sam the moment his foot crossed the threshold. Wicks strained in his direction. Green flames stretched long, reaching across the air toward the helixes turning under his chest. Every candle answered him like they had been waiting for this exact signal.

Krishtan and Marisol stopped dead behind him. Neither stepped forward.

Krishtan spoke low, steady.

"Dem bones didn't lie, Sam-eee. Family feel you here. Dey callin' you home."

The rosary warmed against Sam's sternum. A slow pulse. Recognition claiming him. His throat locked.

Krishtan unlocked the door with a key worn smooth by generations. The hinges made no sound. The door opened like it had been waiting.

They stepped inside.

The cabin was cramped with purpose. Shelves lined the walls, packed tight with jars of herbs, bones wrapped in cloth, oils sealed in dark glass. Nothing for show. Everything for work. Decades of Ama's preparation arranged with a precision that felt ritual instead of tidy.

Candles crowded every surface. Wax built up in layers thick as bark. Every flame burned high, steady, and all of them leaned a fraction toward Sam. Subtle, but real. A room of fire tilting its attention.

Tintypes watched from the walls. Dauvee women across generations, their metal-dark faces catching candlelight in ways that made the eyes look alive, reflective, alert. Not trapped behind glass. Present.

Marisol stepped into the center of the room and stopped cold. Spine locked. Shoulders tight. Head tilted like she'd caught a sound from under the floorboards or behind the walls or somewhere deeper than either.

The room held its breath.

Marisol's head snapped back. When her eyes opened, they were white. No pupil. No iris. Just blank fog rolling behind the surface like something ancient trying to see through her.

"Dey here," she said, and it wasn't her voice. It carried age. Weight. A chorus stacked inside one throat. "Dey waitin'. Dey comin' now."

Krishtan moved before the last word finished. No pause. No fear wasted. He dropped to his bags, pulling gris-gris, oils, bone bundles, laying them out with the speed of someone who had rehearsed this moment in nightmares.

Then he turned to Ama's shelves. His hands scanned jars and cloth-wrapped shapes with a craftsman's certainty, taking only what belonged to this moment, what Ama had left for a night exactly like this.

He crossed to Marisol and pressed a small pouch into her palm. The fabric was thin from age, the stitching old but unbroken.

"Ama's work," he said. "You wear dis now."

Marisol's eyes cleared, white draining out like tide retreating from shore. She sucked in a breath, nodded once, and tied the pouch to her belt beside her own.

Krishtan turned on Sam fast. No gentleness. No buffer. "You stay inside till I call you. Not one step out that door. You understand me, Sam-eee?"

Sam nodded.

Krishtan grabbed what he needed and moved, no wasted motion, boots hitting the porch boards like a warning shot. He descended the steps and cut across the yard toward the circle of white stones set into the dirt. The bone ring. Ama's line. The only thing between them and whatever followed them here.

He dropped to one knee and tore open his gris-gris bag. Ash hit his palm. He started retracing the sigils carved decades ago, reinforcing them stroke by stroke, voice low and hard as he worked. Not prayer. Command. Layering his authority over Ama's design.

Then the eyes opened in the trees.

Sam saw them first. Dozens. Then more. Pairs blinking into existence, catching candlelight like glass marbles catching fire. They didn't move. Didn't shift. They just watched him. Silent. Intent. Too many and too still to be anything natural.

Inside the cabin, the candles dipped. Flames bent sideways as if something sucked the air from the room. Wax crawled up the glass. The smell changed too. Burnt wire. Wet cedar. A static sting that prickled the back of Sam's tongue.

Marisol stiffened. "Krishtan."

He didn't look up. "I feel it." His voice had lost every trace of charm. Hard. Flat. "Dey close, and dey hungry fo' his signal."

Sam stood at the window. His shirt was burned open in jagged patches where the rosary had seared straight through cloth and into flesh. The skin beneath was blistered, angry red in the exact pattern of the beads. Some lay against bare skin. Others pressed through scorched fabric still clinging to his chest.

He looked wrecked. Nose had bled; he'd wiped it without noticing. His hands shook nonstop. Not fear. Electrical overload. Like his nerves were still catching current from something that should have killed him.

Outside, Marisol and Krishtan worked the bone ring. Their voices moved in and out of the fog, rhythmic, sharp, answering something Sam couldn't see.

The fog hadn't lifted. It held the bayou tight, thick enough that Sam couldn't see more than thirty feet off the porch. But he could feel what waited beyond it. Heavy. Focused. Watching him through the dark.

Sam moved from the window to the doorway, bracing one hand on the frame. The wood hummed under his palm, picking up the same rhythm that throbbed in the cracked green bead. The cabin wasn't shielding him. It was signaling back.

He stepped out just enough to see Krishtan's silhouette in the bone ring, and beyond that, the trees holding their breath.

Something was out there.

Close.

Listening.

He looked toward the water through the cabin's dirty windows.

The bayou had gone mirror-still. Black glass, reflecting nothing. Then the surface bent, warped inward, like something underneath was pushing the whole world out of shape.

His breath locked. He moved to the doorway, stepped out onto the porch.

Krishtan snapped his head around, voice cutting sharp. "Sam-eee, stay behind us."

Marisol shifted beside him, both of them forming a wall between Sam and the water. Their stance said everything they weren't willing to speak aloud.

From the porch, the thing resolved.

Not a shape in the water.

A shape where water should be.

The bayou had pulled itself aside, carving out a perfect cylinder of absence. No current. No ripples. Just a column of impossible air punched through twenty feet of depth, held open like a throat waiting to inhale.

Sam stepped off the porch and onto the packed earth, needing the extra angle, needing to see.

Krishtan's voice cut across the yard like a blade. "Stay close to da house, Sam-eee. Don't you wander no farther than dat shadow line."

Sam didn't answer. Couldn't. The thing in the water held him.

Arms crossed.

Eyes open.

Waiting.

The glyph flared hot under his skin. The rosary answered, the cracked green bead warming just enough to warn. The fracture had spread nearly three-fourths around, light leaking through the break with each slow pulse.

Steady. Dying.

Krishtan turned from the bone ring, body angling toward Sam even before his eyes did. Instinct, not sight. A man who felt danger before it spoke.

"What you see, Sam-eee?"

Sam's throat tightened. His mind kept trying to rewrite what he was looking at, make it human, make it possible.

He forced the words out.

"There's..." His voice scraped raw. "Something in the water. No. Under it. Standing there."

Krishtan rose slow, every joint deliberate, ash dusting off his palms in small gray clouds. His rings clicked once, sharp. Marisol froze mid-prayer, beads at her wrist rattling like teeth.

"Describe it," Krishtan said. The tone left no room to refuse.

Sam kept his eyes on the water. Looking away felt dangerous.

The thing had not moved. Not a breath. Not a ripple. It stood inside the column of exposed depth, the bayou pulled apart around it like something had parted the water by will alone.

Its chest did not rise. No bubbles climbed. The depth beneath it made no sense. Twenty feet down, maybe more, and still the bayou held open, refusing to close over it.

He felt its attention before it acknowledged him. A pressure on his spine, the sense of a gaze without motion, the way prey knows a predator is present even when nothing stirs.

"It is standing under the surface," Sam said. His voice scraped thin. "Arms crossed. Head up. Eyes open. They are not glowing... more like catching light. Yellow, maybe gold. Face smooth as clay until..."

He drew in a tight breath.

"Until it moved."

Marisol's voice lost its Oxford polish, shifting into something older that lived in her bones. "It moved how, cousin?"

"Turned its head," Sam said. "Slow. Like it already knew where I was. Looked straight at me."

His hands tightened at his sides, knuckles pale.

"Then it smiled."

The bayou fell still.

Even the frogs choked off their noise. Even the insects went silent. The whole swamp held its breath.

Krishtan and Marisol traded a look. Not confusion. Recognition. The kind of look passed through bloodlines that carried stories in whispers and warnings. They knew this shape. They had prayed never to meet it.

Neither spoke a name. Names had weight. Names traveled. The thing was still listening.

The water where Sam had seen it did not close. No ripples. No drift. Only the sense of something vast sinking back into depth that had no bottom. Waiting for the next summons. Or the next permission.

Marisol exhaled through her teeth, breath shaking. Her voice came out softer than Krishtan's, but marked with the cadence of her foremothers, vowels rounded, consonants slower and older.

"Whatever dat was, it older than dis land. Older than any tale we keep."

Krishtan nodded once, heavy, jaw set tight. "Older than memory."

He turned toward Sam, eyes sharp and scared in the same breath.

"Sam-eee, dat thing looked at you. It put its sight on you. Dat mean somethin'."

A ripple cut across the bayou. Black water pushed outward in perfect rings, centered on the far shore. Not the movement of something falling in. The movement of something rising.

The Observer Lieutenant climbed out of the shallows.

Sam saw him clearly now in the fog-thick moonlight.

Tall. Humanoid in outline only. His robes might once have been ceremonial, but the fabric had fused into his flesh, grown into it, seams tightening like thread pulled through wet paper. His face was stretched thin, colorless, glyphs etched just beneath the skin pulsing faint like a buried signal.

His eyes were wrong. One vertical. One horizontal. Both luminous. Both tracking Sam with the precision of something trained to gather and report, not question.

He stood on the far bank, water sliding off him in patterns that did not match gravity. The droplets drifted instead of falling. His movements slipped out of sequence, joints bending ahead of their turn, as if time stuttered around him.

He did not advance.

He did not threaten.

He held position, every inch of him tuned to a single purpose. Bearing witness. Marking what he had found. A thing built to rise, look, and carry truth back to whatever waited beyond the trees.

Marisol's beads vibrated. Not shaking. Resonating. A low tremor running through the strand like something had plucked a hidden nerve.

The creature crouched. One hand slipped into the bayou. The water around its fingers went black, thickening in an outward bloom, infection spreading like ink dropped in a lung.

He opened his mouth and screamed.

Not sound.

Signal.

The pulse ripped through the clearing. No air. No vibration. Just a force that hit Sam's chest like a fist from inside his ribs. His glyph seized. Light flared behind his sternum with a violent snap.

The rosary burned against his skin, each bead sparking hot. Krishtan's rings went bright copper, smoke curling off his knuckles. Marisol gasped, hand clutching the bone pouch at her throat as the resonance climbed her spine.

The scream left him. It rode the night on channels Sam could not hear, sliding out across the swamp and into distances the trees could not hold.

The creature straightened. Water dripped from its robes in steady lines. Its eyes held their unnatural glow.

Then it shot upward. No crouch. No coil. One instant on the shore. The next dragged skyward by a force that treated gravity like suggestion. The motion was clean and brutal, a body pulled along a line only it could see.

Fog closed around it. The shape vanished into the white.

The air soured. Ozone. Wet copper. The faint sting of something sacred twisted the wrong direction.

Marisol's fingers trembled around her beads. Her voice dropped into something older than fear. "He sent it. Da message gone out. Dey know we here now. Dey know what you carry."

Sam's legs felt hollow. "Where'd he go?"

Krishtan did not look away from the water. "Nowhere good. But wherever he headed, somethin' else already movin'. Feel dat air. World shiftin' underfoot."

The fog tightened around the cabin like a closing hand.

The night blinked.

## TULSA, OKLAHOMA - 2:29 AM

The sanctuary lights burned white and merciless. Marble floors polished to mirror brightness. Gold veins threaded through the altar like false holiness. Cameras washed the room in broadcast glow, each angle crafted to sell certainty to the faithful.

The Vigil of the Third Watch was winding down. Only a few hundred remained in the pews, bodies slumped in devotion or exhaustion. Enough to look respectable on a livestream. Not enough to notice when the temperature dropped a few degrees without warning.

The choir kept singing. The congregation kept swaying. The cameras kept rolling.

Only the stone felt it first.

Another fifty thousand watched through the livestream as the speaker delivered closing remarks on the cost of faith. His tone never shifted. His eyes never wavered.

Then the air shimmered.

Only for a heartbeat. A distortion at the corner of the frame, like heat rising off an August road. Impossible here. The sanctuary was climate-controlled so precisely that nothing should move except breath and song.

The cameras caught it. Thousands watching from home saw the flicker even if they didn't understand it.

The speaker touched the earpiece tucked behind his jaw. His face didn't change. His cadence did not break.

"Let us pray," he said, each word smoothed by rehearsal.

Six glass reliquaries lined the walls. Silent. Sealed. Meant to be symbolic more than functional.

A child somewhere in the far pews began to cry. Loud. Raw. Her sobs sharpened into high screams the hymn couldn't bury. The mother did not soothe her. No one turned.

The speaker lifted two fingers. A small gesture. Precise.

The crying stopped mid-breath.

The child sat rigid. Eyes wide. Throat moving with no sound.

The Lieutenant materialized above the altar. Suspended in air. Robes dripping bayou water that hissed when it struck consecrated marble.

Inside the reliquaries, the preserved bodies pressed against the glass. Faces slack. Mouths opening and closing in silent urgency, as if trying to warn or to welcome.

A man stepped forward from the platform steps. Not the preacher. Someone higher. Someone the cameras never lingered on. His suit caught the light in sharp angles. His expression never shifted.

He lifted his hand.

The Lieutenant reached out. Their fingers met. Violet spark. A flash that rattled every metal surface in the sanctuary.

The Lieutenant's jaw unhinged, wider than human bones should allow. Black water poured out, splashing across the man's face. It absorbed instantly, sinking through skin like a substance returning home.

His eyes rolled white. A tremor moved through him. The glyph-frequency carried from Sam, through the bayou, through whatever ancient channel the Lieutenant had opened.

When the man's eyes returned, they glowed faint gold for three steady seconds.

The Lieutenant collapsed. Bones folding inward. Robes empty. Only a husk remained, sagging into a wet heap on the marble.

A hiss swept the sanctuary. The sixth reliquary unsealed.

Inside each glass chamber, a husk waited upright. Former lieutenants who had not survived their reports, bodies slack, eyes forever open, faces pressed to the glass as if trying to witness the next arrival.

In opposite corners, two blind chantors knelt with heads bowed. Their lips moved in fragmented prayer-code that kept the chamber humming. Their voices drifted out of sync, producing faint harmonics that made the marble tremble underfoot.

## DAUVEE CABIN, LOUISIANA - 2:30 AM

Sam stiffened. His hand snapped to his chest. The glyph fired once under his ribs, white-hot, the light pushing through fabric like a star trying to break skin.

He sucked in air but could not move.

"Sam-eee." Krishtan turned from the bone ring, already coming toward him.

Sam's breath locked. Pressure pulled inward. His lungs tightened. His ribs cinched around something not human. It was not pain. It was a signal returning to the point it had come from. A long-distance hand closing around his center, pulling through channels he had never felt before tonight.

The rosary flared red under his shirt. Burned bright. Then dimmed in a single sharp pulse.

Marisol stepped in close, eyes narrow. "Sam. What you feel right now?"

He forced the words out. "Something far away. And it is coming back."

Krishtan's expression hardened. He looked at Sam, then at the bayou, then at the bone ring flickering weak under his boots.

"Dat pull you felt," he said. "Dat mean you tied straight to da same line dey reachin through. Steady up, cousins."

The air thickened. Metallic. Copper sitting heavy on the tongue.

The bayou moved.

Right where that ancient thing had sunk, the surface indented, then unraveled. Not water. Geometry. Ice crawled outward in spirals and hexagons, fractals locking into place like a code being written across the swamp.

The frost advanced slow enough to watch. Each inch carried a crystalline hum that made Sam's teeth ache. The bayou hardened under rules that had nothing to do with temperature.

Steam rose when the ice reached the bone ring.

Marisol's voice dropped to a whisper. "Look."

The ash symbols inside the ring pulsed gold. Heat rose off the ground in waves. The air shimmered like metal bent too far. Cedar smoke curled from nothing, Ama's scent rolling out of the soil.

Krishtan's voice slipped into an old prayer before he realized he was speaking.

The bone ring flared white.

The frost stopped one inch from the perimeter. Not melting. Not breaking.

Held.

Fifty years of Ama's protection locking the bayou out.

But the ice did not withdraw. It lingered at the edge, humming against the heat.

Waiting.

Alive.

Testing the boundary.

The three of them watched heat meet ice, silent forces grinding against each other in a war fought without sound. The air hissed where the two fronts touched.

Krishtan's eyes never left the bayou. "Dey comin. Not through sky. Through da roots."

The bone ring pulsed again, bright enough to sting. Frost thickened around the perimeter, spirals dropping into black water that looked bottomless, patterns rising from a depth that felt older than the land itself.

Sam's glyph burned hotter. The crack in the green bead spread another thin line.

Far from Louisiana, beneath a cathedral in Tulsa, something answered the Lieutenant's call. It clawed upward through marble and shadow with Sam's frequency woven through its core.

Night held its breath. Form shifting in the dark.

A voice not Sam's, miles away but tied to the same line, whispered the words he felt in his ribs.

"Found you."

The rosary's green bead split clean through.

# Chapter 9

# **The Siege**

Air tasted of burnt cedar and something colder, not ozone. The residue of whatever had risen through the water. Heat moved under Sam's feet in a slow pulse, the ground carrying old prayers and older bloodlines like a buried heartbeat.

He stood in the yard between the cabin and the bone ring. Shirt burned open where the rosary had fused cloth into flesh. The glyph beneath his sternum pulsed steady, light visible under skin, each beat moving on rhythms he did not recognize but felt in the base of his spine.

The rosary lay against his chest, beads warm. The cracked green bead leaked faint light. Dying. Holding on.

Fog clung to the bayou. Not drift. Placement. Thick enough to taste metal on his tongue. Ice geometry threaded beneath the black water, faint fractals glowing under the surface, cold mathematics waiting for instruction. Humidity pressed against his skin. Air moved like breath through torn gauze.

Night birds had gone quiet. Insects cut off mid-song. Even frogs held still. The bayou locked into a hush that felt chosen.

Behind him, the cabin watched.

Krishtan kicked off his boots. Bare soles hit soil. The ground answered at once. Warmth first. Then heat. Then something older than heat rising through the ley lines stitched beneath the cabin.

Lines that ran beneath states and rivers and old fields where nobody prayed out loud anymore.

He felt them wake. Gran-Mé Yvette. Maman Celestine. Names whispered when candles burned low. Hands settled across his shoulders. Breath slid into his lungs. Not burden. Appointment.

He stepped to Sam's left, planting himself like another post in Ama's fence. His rings caught ash-light, copper-bright, symbols etched into the metal glowing faint as they recognized work.

Marisol moved to Sam's right. Her hands shook as she unclasped the pendant at her throat. Resin, amber-colored, Ama's ashes sealed in the center. The glow sharpened in moonlight, as if recognizing it was needed.

She pressed her thumbs into either side.

The resin cracked.

Blue-white fire erupted between her palms, cold as winter stars, burning the frequency before it burned flesh. It hummed at a pitch that climbed straight into her teeth. Her skin blistered at once. Red welts rose where mortal bone tried to carry something that was never meant for bodies.

She gasped. Did not close her hands. Smoke curled from her wrists.

"Maman, garde nou," she whispered. Mother, guard us.

The bone ring flared gold beneath them. Ancestral wards answering living blood. The air thickened. Water shifted against the bank with the slow sound of something leaning closer to hear.

Then the bayou changed color.

Fractals lit up under the surface, bright now, ice-geometry spreading wider across the black water. Not weather. Code. Fog vented upward in slow breaths, carrying iron and candlewax, the scent of sanctified places that had been opened by the wrong hands.

Something old below the waterline turned its attention fully toward the yard.

The grinding began.

Low at first. Mechanical. Bone meeting metal. Neither side giving. The vibration hit Sam's molars, teeth buzzing like tuning forks struck wrong.

Shapes rose through the lattice.

Grindmen.

Two of them. Pale torsos dragged up out of the geometry, spines replaced with segmented augers ratcheting with every forward inch. Communion wafers replaced their teeth, shards soaked in dark ether clicking together in reversed prayer rhythms.

Their forearms ended in rotary joints. Fists spun. Not hands. Bits. Industrial. Hungry. The smell that rolled off them was burnt incense and hot iron and something like damp choir robes left molding in the dark.

They did not hiss. They did not breathe.

They advanced in silence, eyes fixed on the cabin, auger-spines ratcheting as they ground through ice and shallow water toward Ama's ring.

One reached the perimeter first. Its spinning arm struck invisible boundary. Sparks flew where corrupted metal hit blessed earth. The pitch climbed. Metal screamed. Bone dust shook loose from the circle. The dust drifted up instead of falling.

It floated toward the Grindman. Settled on its skin. Burned black spots straight through pale flesh. It did not flinch. Rotary joint spun faster, grinding deeper into the unseen wall.

Its partner fanned out, angling toward Sam.

Krishtan slammed his foot down.

The ground cracked. Red-orange heat bled up through thin lines, smoke rising from the fractures.

"Lwa leve, zansèt pwoteje." Spirits rise, ancestors protect.

His voice layered without echo, harmonics stacked, one man sounding like three. Each stomp sent pressure outward. Heat spread through the soil in rings, ancestral fire pushing back against the cold geometry crawling in from the water.

The Grindmen did not slow.

Wood creaked behind Sam. The cabin settled, timbers reacting to pressure. Candles inside flickered with no wind. The air felt crowded.

Fog thickened at the treeline.

Something stepped out.

It walked like a man and did not carry a man's life. Limbs too stiff. Head turning in small increments, like a puppet checking its strings. Skin gray as drowned stone. A dull glow flickered under its sternum, trapped signal pressed behind bone.

Lieutenant Husk.

Its breathing sounded wrong. Every inhale like air dragged through wet cloth. Eyes filmed over, irises barely visible beneath the cloud. From under its ribs, faint gold pulsed, fighting the flesh that held it.

A low hum bled into the yard. Subsonic. Climbing. It came from the Husk and from the bayou beneath it, one note shared between corpse and water.

The bone ring answered with its own vibration, gold flaring, ward-light stuttering off beat.

Marisol's flames lashed out in a blue-white arc. The fire snapped through fog, aiming dead at the Husk's chest.

Halfway there, the flame bent. Pressure pushed it sideways, as if something invisible cupped a hand and batted it away. Heat dispersed into mist with a sharp hiss.

Marisol swayed. Blisters climbed her palms. Skin split. She gritted her teeth and held her hands open anyway.

The hum rose.

Sam's glyph flared, hot enough to punch breath out of him. He grabbed his chest, fingers digging into scorched fabric. Light pressed against his ribs from the inside, too bright, too large for the cage that tried to hold it.

The Lieutenant's head tilted. Like listening to a far command. Like waiting for a cue.

Fog at the far edge of the yard folded inward.

The Eyehollow stepped through.

It moved in jerks, like a thing forcing itself into a film that could not carry it. Motion broke into frames. Limbs flicked forward in short skips that made Sam's stomach lurch.

Its eyes were gone. Stained glass filled the sockets instead. Fragments of saints and symbols from shattered windows fused into bone. Figures that should have worn halos now bent backwards. Crosses inverted. A serpent twist cut through what had once been an angel's wing.

Its mouth was sewn shut with silver thread, lips pulled tight over teeth, cheeks drawn in permanent strain. Every motion made the threads tremble.

It saw Sam. It did not need eyes.

The creature blurred. One frame on the ground. The next almost on him. Refracted edges cut light into wrong angles.

Sam stumbled back. Bare heels dug into warm dirt. No time to think. No space to run.

The Eyehollow lunged.

It did not strike to kill. Fingers hooked, reaching for his shoulder, for the center of his chest. Not claws. Hooks. Designed to drag. To lift. To carry. A courier that stole living bodies instead of letters.

Sam's hand rose without his consent.

His palm met its sternum.

The glyph detonated.

Light tore through his arm, white-gold and green, blasting out of his skin. For one stretched instant the yard became noon. No shadows. No mercy. Everything laid bare.

Time slowed.

The Eyehollow hung in the air, frozen between frames. Cracks crawled across its skin, glowing from within. Stained glass in its sockets spiderwebbed, shards drifting outward like they had been underwater the whole time.

Pain hit Sam's skull, not his hand. Not his arm.

Stone floor under knees. Incense thick enough to choke. A hymn caught mid-note, twisted sharp. The memory did not belong to him. It punched straight through the glyph, a borrowed suffering slicing across his nerves.

Three heartbeats.

A foreign pulse echoed in his chest, syncing to his own. Each strike weaker than the last.

A whisper slipped free from behind the sewn silver. He barely heard the word. Latin softened into gratitude.

"Gratia."

The Eyehollow's shell peeled away. Not into ash. Into light. A human silhouette formed inside the ruin, arms spread, head tipped back. For a blink Sam saw a man there, not a monster. A priest. Or a singer. Someone who had stood in front of an altar and meant it before someone else twisted his song.

The light unmade what had been built. Upward. Clean.

The body dissolved into frequency and vanished into the fog. Only silver thread hit the grass. It smoked where it landed.

The green bead on Sam's rosary split with a sharp crack. The halves vanished into luminous dust before they reached the ground.

The bayou responded.

Ice geometry under the water flared bright, furious. Fractals multiplied, racing outward in jagged spirals. Cold gripped the clearing. Heat under Sam's feet did not vanish; it locked, held in place, pressed by something that wanted to smother it.

Something deep below felt its chain tug.

Pressure rose from under the cabin. Older than the Lieutenant. Older than the Eyehollow. Older than the hymns that had twisted those creatures into what they were.

It pushed once against the underside of reality.

Boards in Ama's porch creaked like they carried more weight than three living bodies. The bone ring dimmed then flared back, straining. The air over the bayou dipped, as if a giant hand had pressed down on the world, testing the give.

A whisper slid across Sam's spine, not sound, not thought.

Free me too.

The words carried hunger. Loneliness. Fury.

Sam's stomach turned. His glyph snarled in answer, a low interior warning. Not yet.

The pressure below withdrew. Not gone. Waiting.

Fog above the water folded again.

The Hollow Seraph arrived.

Reality wavered. The creature hung twelve feet above the ground, suspended like a marionette held by strings that nothing in the yard could see. Wing-ruins spread wide, charred frame twitching against invisible bonds. Its bone mask had been carved in the rough shape of a face, caught halfway between rage and worship.

Green fire burned in its sockets. Not flames reaching out. Gravity reversed, pulled inward, folding all light back into its gaze.

The moment it manifested, every candle inside the cabin snuffed out. Not dimmed. Not wavered. Gone.

Darkness hit like a physical blow.

Only two lights remained.

The gold-white glow rising off the bone ash circle.

And the pulse under Sam's sternum.

The Seraph turned toward that light first.

Fog lowered, kneeling around it. Grass leaned. Water flattened to pure mirror. The Grindmen froze mid-grind, augers still ticking, eyes locked on nothing as the Seraph claimed all attention without moving an inch.

Sam inhaled. His pupils blew wide, swallowing his irises. The ash-light poured into his eyes, then squeezed down into vertical slits before snapping back to round. It happened too fast for anyone to see. The world saw it anyway.

Krishtan's next stomp shook more heat out of the earth than it should have. Marisol's flames brightened for a breath against her blistered palms. None of them knew why.

The Seraph spoke.

"Our Father who art beneath," it said, voice layered in chords no human choir could hold. "Hollow be thy grave. Thy kingdom fall. Thy will be broken on earth as it is in the abyss."

The corrupted prayer reshaped the yard.

Invisible pews flickered into place around them, lines of pressure folding the air into aisles and rows. The cabin timbers groaned under weight that did not come from wood. The sky itself seemed to press closer, starless, listening.

The Grindmen answered in reversed Latin, wafer teeth chattering on the consonants. Their voices rasped like broken organs.

"Dominus pascit me, et nihil mihi deerit..."

Sam's glyph responded like someone had struck it with a tuning fork. Heat climbed his chest, up his throat. Breath shortened. Somewhere far away, something listened along the same line, amused.

The Lieutenant Husk drank in all of it. Its chest glowed brighter, the trapped signal inside straining against bone. Its eyes rolled back until only white showed. The hum coming off its body climbed another octave.

Marisol wavered. Blood streamed from her nostrils. Her fire shook between her hands, guttering in and out. Her skin cracked open along her wrists, blackening where celestial voltage met human limitations.

"I cannot..." Her voice broke. "Krishtan, I cannot hold much longer."

He did not look away from the Seraph.

"You hold till we gone or we guarded," he said, jaw set. "Ain't no third option, cher."

The Seraph descended. Not falling. Lowering, drawn by a pull it did not control. Six feet off the ground. Then four. Its bone mask tilted. Green fire narrowed, focusing on Sam and nothing else.

It saw what had been watched on a monitor somewhere. A boy. A glyph. A possible instrument.

It floated closer.

Sam could not move. Knees locked. Lungs caught halfway through an inhale that refused to finish. His heart hammered once, then slowed, then fell into a rhythm that did not belong to his species.

His skin lit from underneath.

Veins glowed green on one side, gold on the other, meeting at the glyph, braiding their light into something the world did not have a word for. The air tasted metallic and sweet and burned-out all at once.

"Sam-eee." Krishtan's voice came from very far away. "You still wit' us?"

Sam did not answer.

The Seraph reached. One skeletal hand extended, fingers too long, joints wrong. It did not need to touch him. It only needed proximity. One brush would tag him, mark him, drag him later along a line only it and its maker understood.

Sam's hand rose again.

Not his choice. A compulsion older than his lineage moved his arm.

Palm up.

Green and gold burst from his chest, ran the length of his arm, and hit Krishtan square between the shoulders.

Not attack. Transfer.

Krishtan's back arched. His shout ripped out of him. His rings went blinding white, copper flashing through colors a human eye was never meant to see. The symbols etched into them woke fully, each rune an eye, each eye a small door.

Power flooded his frame. Not heat. Current. Solar, wild, uncontained.

He stomped.

The shadow under him did not stretch. It detached.

A wave of pure dark blasted out from his stance, a sheet of black so complete it made the night around it look gray. It moved in a straight line, skimming the ground, blade-flat and liquid at once.

It hit the first Grindman.

There was no impact sound. No explosion. The creature just stopped existing. Rotary joints ceased. Auger-spine froze. Body folded inward, erased from the world like someone had scraped it off the film.

The wave took the second Grindman a moment later. Same result. There. Then not.

The darkness snapped back to Krishtan's feet, whipping under him like an obedient dog that had just bitten through steel.

He staggered. Smoke curled from his shoulders. His lungs dragged at the air. His eyes did not feel like they belonged to him anymore.

"That ain't mine," he rasped. "That was not mine."

The Seraph recoiled. Not in fear. In recognition. That frequency was not supposed to be in human hands.

It turned on Sam fully, bone mask split by cracks of light that crawled across its surface. Green fire flared, then guttered. Another color fought to replace it.

Sam's eyes went white. Light poured out in steady beams. Not reflection. Emission.

The glyph under his ribs flared brighter than any candle Ama had ever lit.

For a breath, the Seraph remembered.

Not Louisiana. Not Tulsa. Not whatever basement they kept its vessel chained in.

Sky. Choir. Fire that did not burn. The weight of a Name spoken without corruption.

The harmonic that rose from its chest now was not the same prayer it had spoken minutes before. The words were twisted, but the interval landed true. A fragment of an old hymn forced through a throat that had not used it in centuries.

Bone split.

The mask shattered. Wings tore free of invisible bonds and flared once, wide enough that the whole yard felt smaller. Gold brightened where charcoal had sat dead.

For a single note, the Seraph was what it had been before anyone ever learned its title.

Then it unraveled.

Light took it cleanly. No ash. No body. No fall. It went upward, frequency slipping out of the yard, out of the swamp, out of the reach of the man who had learned to use it like a knife.

Somewhere far away, someone lost his prize and did not yet know why.

The last gold bead on Sam's rosary cracked and fell away, turning to dust in the air.

Silence hit so hard the yard rang.

The Lieutenant Husk shuddered. Signal inside it surged. Its chest glowed brighter, ribs lit from the inside like the creature had swallowed a furnace. It turned its head toward a point that did not exist in the clearing. Listening.

Then its body folded at the joints. Knees buckled. Spine bent. Not collapse. Bow.

Geometry opened under its feet, small and exact. A perfect circle of nothing cut through grass and dirt in the space of a heartbeat. The Husk dropped through, yanked back along whatever line had birthed it.

Courier recalled. One witness returning to tell a story its maker would not like.

The circle snapped shut.

Sam's knees gave. He hit dirt hard, hands digging into Ama's yard. Steam rose from his skin. His breath rasped like he had swallowed fire. The glyph beneath his sternum pulsed once, then dimmed to ember.

The bayou seethed.

Ice patterns raced under the water, bright with fury. The thing below had felt all of it. The Eyehollow freed. The Seraph released. The Grindmen erased. Its chains untouched.

It pressed one more time against its cage. Harder.

The ground under Sam's hands jumped. The air over the bayou dipped again, then snapped back into place.

A voice brushed the inside of his skull. Older than their tech. Older than Sovereign Hope. Older than the churches they corrupted.

Free me too, thief.

Sam's vision went black around the edges.

The bone ring answered instead of him.

From the scorched places the Grindmen had chewed, white dust rose. Luminous. Green and gold flickered inside each grain. Rosary and glyph and Ama's old work braided together. The dust settled into every crack in the ring.

It hardened. Brightened. Veined with new light. The circle stood whole again, stronger than it had been when the night started.

Ama's wards took Sam's offering and made it permanent.

Sam drew his next breath.

It did not sound like it came from this world.

# Chapter 10

# Ashline Fog

Sam hit the earth hard.

One moment he stood in the yard, steam rising from skin cracked by divine voltage. The next, the cabin reached for him. The cypress boards stretched as if space bent inward to claim him. The doorframe widened, swallowed distance, and pulled him forward without touch.

Fifteen yards vanished between heartbeats.

The ground caught him. Dirt, heat, cedar smoke. His chest struck the threshold before he slid across it, carried on a breath that did not belong to the outside world.

Silence followed. Thick. Absolute.

Fog pushed through the floorboards in thin threads, tasting the air for intent.

Krishtan dropped beside him, breath broken, hands hovering above the burning glyph. Light pulsed steady under Sam's skin, a second heart beating through bone.

"Li pa mouri." Not dead.

Relief hit him with heat.

"Li nan jan nou gen bezwen li." He is in the state we need him.

Marisol knelt on Sam's other side. Her palms were blistered and split, weeping clear fluid that hissed against the boards. Pain sat behind a curtain of shock. The air tasted of cedar and iron, the moment before lightning writes new law in the sky.

"Kisa nou fè kounye a?" What do we do now?

The fog thickened. Slow. Intentional. Mapping the room the way water finds its path home. It carried the scent of old cypress water and earth prayed over by women whose names the world never learned.

Krishtan's fingers moved without thought. Blood memory guided them. Shapes he did not remember learning shaped themselves in the air. The marrow remembered even when the mind did not.

"Nou kite l vin." We let it come.

His voice sank into the wood. The cabin answered.

The walls hummed. Low. Resonant. Cypress planks breathed instead of creaked. Angles softened. Corners widened. Space shifted to cradle the wounded thing it had chosen to shelter.

The cabin was not changing. It was waking.

The waking carried weight.

The floor no longer felt flat beneath them. Grain lines in the cypress shifted, subtle as muscle under skin. What had been wood took on resistance, as if the cabin decided how much of their bodies it would allow inside itself. Sam's weight pressed downward, yet the boards bowed just enough to hold him without complaint.

Marisol's breath caught. Her ears rang, not loud, not painful, just full. As if something inside the room had begun to listen. She tasted metal and river water. Her vision narrowed, colors sharpening until the edges of objects bled faint light. When she blinked, the walls were closer than they had been a moment before.

Krishtan felt it in his knees.

The house did not recognize them equally.

Where his bare feet touched, warmth gathered. Not heat. Welcome. The same warmth he remembered from candle rooms sealed against storms, from floors scrubbed with salt and prayer before rites no one wrote down. His pulse synced to the hum running through the boards, slow and deliberate.

Sam shifted once, unconscious, and the cabin answered.

A low note rolled through the structure, too deep to be sound. Nails tightened. The doorframe contracted by a finger's width. The windows clouded, not with fog, but with reflection, as if they had turned inward.

Outside pressure vanished.

Inside, the room decided its shape.

Fog curled along the floor and climbed the walls. Its movement was not random. It followed currents woven through the bayou long before boundary lines were carved through stolen land.

Marisol felt the frequency in her teeth. Colors sharpened. Shadows moved on their own. Her broken necklace scattered prismatic light that bent around the new geometry forming in the room.

"Krishtan." Her voice was thin, scraped raw by the current running through her teeth. "What happenin' to dis place?"

He did not answer at once. Bare feet pressed into warm boards. Ash clung to his ankles. The symbols he traced outside glowed beneath the floorboards like coals remembering heat. The cabin absorbed them and claimed them.

"It not breakin'." His voice was quiet. "It rememberin'."

Fog rose higher until the world shrank to a small circle around them. Everything beyond dissolved. The air rearranged itself into a veil.

Time loosened.

Marisol blinked. The blisters on her palms boiled over, healed by the cabin's grip, then ripped open again in the same heartbeat. Her shadow-work rejected the light, and her flesh paid the tax for the conflict. She was a wire carrying too much voltage, kept from melting only because the house refused to let her break.

Krishtan felt the shift in his bones.

Gran-Mé Yvette stood behind him. Warm breath touched the back of his neck. Maman Celestine crossed the room, her presence trailing fog and starlight. They did not speak. They rarely did. Dauvee dead needed no words to be understood.

Sam's glyph pulsed again. Light pooled under his ribs and spread outward. The copper rosary chain glowed faintly, each empty link holding memory of the beads that were now dust.

Marisol leaned close to his cheek. His breath came slow. Calm. His lips moved in languages that predated the land beneath them.

"He somewhere else," she whispered.

"He everywhere," Krishtan answered. His voice sank into the foundation and made the boards tremble. "Body here. Spirit walkin' roads we not allowed to step on."

The cabin's hum deepened. Bass rolled through the spine of the building and made the fog ripple. The air folded around Sam, becoming a cradle instead of a room.

Outside, the bayou held perfectly still. Water froze mid-ripple. Night creatures vanished into silence. Even the wind waited.

Inside, time shifted into Kairos. Duration measured by meaning rather than seconds.

Krishtan inhaled. Ancestral weight settled across his shoulders. The cabin's pulse merged with his own. The voices of the dead pressed close but left space in front of them, clearing the way for something else.

The fog shifted in the center of the room.

Not retreat. Revelation.

A corridor formed. Straight and narrow. Walls of vapor held their shape as if carved from stone. Light moved inside it, first faint, then sharp. Silhouettes approached with wings kept close to their bodies. Limbs bent in patient anticipation. Light wrapped each form in a radiance that did not belong to man or the Watchers.

Even the ancestors stepped aside.

Gran-Mé Yvette faded toward the wall. Maman Celestine withdrew with a slow nod.

Sam's glyph brightened. His sternum became a lantern. Ribs glowed from within. Light cast long lines across the floorboards.

The corridor brightened further.

Krishtan's chest tightened.

He did not know its name. Only the truth settling over his skin like cold water.

"Yon bagay ap vini."

Something is coming.

Silence followed, complete and sacred.

The kind of quiet the world makes when eternity arrives and the living must decide whether to kneel or stand.

Chapter 11

# Kairos

Silence held weight. Not absence. Presence packed too tight to move. Dust hung motionless in amber air. Time kinked sideways, edges misaligned.

Sam lay on cypress planks. Warm from voltage. Palm pressed flat where heat pulsed through grain. Chest rising. Shallow gasps synced to the glyph's rhythm beneath his sternum. Sweat beaded on his forehead, evaporated before it could run. Steam drifted into the seams between the boards, thin as breath.

Krishtan and Marisol knelt at the cabin's edges. Bodies locked in witness. Wards pulsed faint beneath their clothes, answering frequencies conscious minds could not name. Blood recognized. Air tasted of charged cedar, metal, consecrated earth.

Mist held a faint reflective shimmer.

Three harmonic overtones rose. Pressure in bone before sound. Six candle flames leaned toward Sam's prone form, wax dripping sideways. Nine motes of light hung suspended, catching illumination from nowhere. Motionless. Then they snapped into spirals.

Light bent wrong. Heat refracted around the glyph. Arcs drew symbols in empty air. Ancient sigils formed from bent atmosphere, patterns older than carved stone, older than clay. Each configuration built on the last until the interior became a lattice of living pressure.

Air inverted.

For three heartbeats, no sound. Only vibration through marrow. The room hummed. Harmonics layered until a single tone swelled against dimensions too narrow to hold it.

Patterns collapsed inward.

The radiance from the yard had not left; it waited.

She condensed.

Light pulled itself into shape. One instant, swirling fog. The next, complete. Body caught between film frames, reality stuttering around her, existing in several states at once and refusing to choose.

High cheekbones. Bronze skin carrying sunlit stone's luminescence. Alive. Etched with fine runic filaments that moved beneath the surface like slow lightning. Hair fell to her waist in obsidian strands threaded with thin currents of pale light, each strand carrying its own pulse.

Eyes pale gold, halos violent at the edges. Pupils dilated until starfields flickered in depths that did not belong to human anatomy. She breathed once. Color deepened. Light shifted through the spectrum of stars forming and collapsing in the space of a blink.

She wore no fabric that cloth-makers understood. Layered mesh of translucent gold draped her frame, moving like water and metal at the same time, humming as it caught the light in fractal shards. Beneath it, skin carried markings that rearranged with each breath, mathematics older than any word for number.

Her feet were bare. Each step left a brief flare of symbols beneath her soles, glowing and fading like cooling metal. Footprints pressed into reality rather than wood.

At her throat, a torque of luminous bronze. Three inset glyphs: heart, spiral, star. Each pulsed in rhythm with the cabin's hum.

Weapon and sanctuary in one shape. Power that did not need to threaten. Existence alone carried weight.

Sam's body responded. The field around her dragged him upright. Vertebrae straightened as if caught by invisible hands. He propped on one elbow, dazed, vision locking on her face when she knelt beside him.

Heat radiated from her. Not comfort. Calibration. Adjusting his frequency to match hers. Circuits pushed past design limits. Bones rang.

Voice came first as pressure in his skull. Words bypassed his ears, resonated directly along his nervous system.

Stabilize. The vessel leaks.

Fingers settled over the glyph. Heat evened. Wild surges smoothed into a steady pulse. His breathing synced with hers in three measured beats. Each inhale drew air that tasted of cedar, mineral, strange metal. Atmosphere thick with presence. Skin prickled.

She spoke aloud. The sound rode air this time, layered with a faint harmonic undertone that did not match her volume. Dampened enough for his mind to catch.

"The veil is not a wall. It is a lung. You are the breath."

Sam's throat worked. Vocal cords remembered their job.

"You..."

Hoarse. Half question. Half recognition. Waiting for this moment across lifetimes without memory for why.

Her expression shifted. Not a smile. Acknowledgment. Tempered steel.

"Debt is a circle. I close it here."

She studied him. Pale gold eyes reading the signals his body threw off. Thumb traced from his sternum to the hinge of his jaw, finding the pulse point beneath his ear.

Pressure spiked. Static before lightning. Warmth surged through him, deliberate, precise, like tools entering an engine.

Nerves realigned according to blueprints written before his lungs ever learned air.

"The seal opens. Qibītu builds worlds. They feed on the scream. You will become the silence."

Sensation rolled through him in waves. Each pass rewrote one more connection his nervous system had forgotten it could make. Conditioning, the logic of the cage, all of it hit and burned away.

He saw the mechanism.

The trauma was not an accident. It was architecture. Wayne's hand. Janet's silence. The erosion of Charles and Pat. The slow rot Brownlow coaxed through his line. Not bad luck. Harvest.

They ate the suffering.

Heat gathered under his ribs, pulling memory into focus like iron filings dragged to a magnet.

He looked at her. Realization landed like impact.

"I chose this," he whispered.

Her eyes intensified. Halos swelled, gold consumed by storm-bright white at the edges. When she spoke again, her voice dropped into a register that made the floorboards vibrate.

"You chose the cage to learn where it breaks."

Tone shifted. Not mercy. Not comfort. Battle-hardened steel that remembered what it felt like to die and stand up anyway.

"Memory returns when pain remembers its purpose. Not before."

Her hand lifted from his jaw. Connection severed. Cold rushed in where command had sat.

Air fractured. Heat bent around edges that should not exist. She rose in one fluid motion, mesh mantle catching light from inside her instead of the room.

"Go," she said. Voice calm, perfectly controlled, threaded with that faint harmonic that made the walls shudder. "The path is already cut."

Glyph beneath his sternum detonated.

Light exploded. Concentric bands folded space around his body. Not slow. Instant. Air compressed inward. Force slammed Krishtan and Marisol to the floor, hands flying up to shield their eyes. Eardrums strained.

Candles imploded. Flames collapsed into hard points, burned too bright, then vanished. Cypress grain bent around Sam's center mass, wood warping in spirals. Ley-line mathematics took over where physics quit.

Light wrapped him. Bands rotated faster. Compression built until reality groaned under strain.

A single tone pushed through him, breath remembering its source. It climbed higher than hearing. Glass threaded with hairline cracks. Windowpanes shivered.

One heartbeat he was there, body solid, glyph blazing like a sun dying backward. The next, he became a column of refracted air and sound. Matter translated into frequency. Flesh became signal.

Gravity stopped meaning anything. He did not fall up or down. He fell in. Into the grain of the world.

The floor beneath him turned transparent. Soil opened. Dark and teeming. Cypress roots grasped like pale fingers in the deep. He saw them, not with eyes but resonance, sensing sap, the slow life of things that grew in drowned silence.

He sank past the water table. Cold and black. Taste of minerals. Iron. Limestone.

Speed increased. Frictionless. He was a note sliding down a guitar string.

Bedrock rose and blurred. The crust's slow pulse thudded through him. Tectonic plates ground past one another with a sound like history breaking.

He reached for the pattern. Tried to read the syntax of the travel, the way the corridor nested through the ley line. How it moved, where it bent. He reached to classify the weave.

Too much. Too fast. Data poured through him like floodwater. A newborn thrown into open air. He could not map it. Only endure it.

Vertigo clawed at him. Sensation of being unmade and poured into a new mold mid-fall. North slid sideways. Down became in. Up was nowhere.

She did not travel with him. Her absence was clean, deliberate. She had loaded the round. He was the shot.

Forward. Through dark. Toward the city's glow.

Forces older than continents gripped him and pulled.

Above, the column collapsed. Thunderclap blew ash off the altar. Dust exploded outward in a perfect sphere. Shockwave rattled every surface, made glass sing, metal ring, pressure rolling through the cabin like the world's lungs had emptied in one exhale.

Silence rushed back.

Krishtan uncovered his eyes. Ears rang. Dust drifted down in slow spirals, each particle catching light that had no source. Where Sam had lain, sigils glowed faint orange, pulsing in rhythm with an absent heartbeat. Marks scattered like a choir grid. Ember points arranged with intent.

He blinked. Hand rose to his chest without his say-so. Rosary chain lay at the center of the sigil grid, copper links warm, bare of beads. He reached for it, fingers closing around metal that had sat under Ama's hand for half her life.

He lifted it. Felt the weight of a job finished. No protection left to give. No barrier left to hold.

"She ain't let him go," he whispered. "She sent him."

Voice came rough. Awe sat inside it like gravel.

Marisol lowered her hands. Breath came in quick, shaky pulls. Beads had fallen back to her wrist. Tiger's eye stones dimmed, still warm, holding leftover heat from contact with something Oxford had never prepared her to name.

The cabin felt empty and full at once. Sam gone. The visitor gone. Presence printed into the air. Frequencies that would take hours to bleed out.

Krishtan pushed to his feet. Legs unsteady. Rings back on his fingers, cooler now, copper etched with new symbols that had not been there an hour earlier. Lines precise, cut clean. Work of a hand that knew what every mark meant.

He crossed to the place where Sam had disappeared and knelt. Pressed his palm against the sigils. Heat rose through his skin. Gentle. Undeniable. Translation, not death.

"Dat was no loa," he said. Voice low. He flipped the lamp's switch. Darkness settled. In it, faint footprints glowed across the boards in front of where she had stood. Symbols held shape for three breaths, then faded. "Dat was light wit' a name."

Marisol pushed upright. Body moved on habit while her mind tried to reconcile every academic frame she had ever trusted. None of it held. What had touched her nerves had bypassed theory and gone straight to blood.

Blood remembered what it had been forced to forget.

She crossed herself with fingers still dusted in ash. Gesture automatic. Motion altered. Less begging, more acknowledgement.

"Archivist fires do not burn clean," she said quietly. "You can smell da glue centuries later."

She spoke toward the ashes, not to him.

Krishtan nodded. Standing. On the altar, blown ash had settled in a spiral that kept trying to turn. Particles shifted by fractions, following commands written in frequencies too low for ears.

"Dey covered da lines. Buried da veins. Put concrete on top." He watched the slow turning dust. "Ground still remember."

He did not check his phone. Did not need to. He felt the grid through the soles of his feet. Substations twitching from Miami to Memphis. Instruments chirping at observatories. Solar readouts matching no known cycle.

The world was waking up. And it was not calm.

He gathered what they had brought. Movements slow, deliberate. Sudden gestures felt wrong in a room still rearranging itself around a new memory. The cabin hummed underfoot. Frequency had shifted. This house would never be only wood again.

Outside, the boat waited. Rocking gentle on water gone mirror-still. They walked without speaking. Footsteps echoed longer than they should have. Air hung thick with what had just happened.

At the water's edge, Krishtan paused. Turned back. The cabin leaked light through its seams, faint, persistent. Glow that would take days to dim.

"Eyes gon' turn dis way," he said. "Military. Gov'ment. Folks wit' badges an' no sense. Dey gon' come sniffin' like dey own dis dirt."

Marisol's jaw set. "Den we make sure da right people here first. Elders in da parishes. Root workers who remember da old ways. Dey need to feel dis, not just hear story."

They climbed into the skiff, taking their positions without thinking. Krishtan at the stern, hands on the pole. Marisol near the bow, fingers trailing in water that carried currents older than every man-made canal.

They moved through darkness that reflected no moon, following waterways mapped in bone long before charts existed.

Behind them, Ashline's changed ground kept working. Signals climbed through soil and stone, out beyond atmosphere. Networks that had slept jolted in their sleep.

They did not speak again until the dock came into view. Morning mist clung low. City scents floated thin on the air: coffee, fried dough, river. New Orleans waking. Ordinary to most. Singing to those who could hear the new harmonics under everything.

They tied off. Knots precise. Final. At the bank, they looked at each other. Understanding crossed without language.

Krishtan nodded toward the Quarter's cluster of roofs and neon ghosts. "Quarter gon' shake when da strangeness hit. Folks gon' need a hand holdin' dey sanity. Dat's mine."

Marisol turned her gaze west, toward parishes where old women would be rising from dreams that did not belong to sleep. "An I got calls to make. Dis not for text messages."

They separated without looking back. Each carried a different shard of what had happened. Dawn touched the water. Somewhere between gulf and hills, the translation that had ripped through the grid kept echoing.

Geometry continued its work under perception. Ley lines hummed. Current threaded ground to networks that did not care about borders.

Sam hit the Quarter.

One instant he rode the deep black under the continent. The next, his shoulder slammed into a cast-iron lamp post on Royal. He staggered, sucked in air, tried to remember how to breathe like someone who had not just been poured through the earth's veins.

The bricks under his hand radiated heat. Steady. Real.

Copper still warm in a cabin framed by cypress. Boards still singing to anybody with the ears. Proof enough.

Some ground never heals.

And some battles follow you home.

# Chapter 12

# 3:03

GOOSENECK BEND, MUSKOGEE, OK

Her knees were already on cold concrete. That was the first wrong thing.

Audrey knew the texture. Pitted. Damp. The smell hit next. Mildew. Rust. Burned plastic. Not her bedroom. Not her life.

She tried to move her hands.

Rope bit into someone else's wrists.

Awareness sat behind another woman's eyes. Vision tunneled. Dark walls closing in. Stone slick with condensation. Air so stale it tasted gray.

A breath scraped raw through a throat that had begged for too long.

"God protect my children."

The sound was not hers. The prayer felt like it came from the marrow of the body she was pinned inside.

Copper thickened the air. Rot sat in the corner. Animal, human, both. Hard to tell. Harder to look.

The woman turned her head.

Eyes met hers across a distance that was not distance at all.

Eyes Audrey had not seen since childhood.

"Audrey."

The name came out fractured. It still hit like a thrown stone.

Something struck the base of Audrey's skull. Not impact. Frequency. A high, thin ring drilled through bone. It felt like a scream too sharp to hear, compressing into a single note that set every nerve on edge.

The world tore sideways.

She jerked awake. The room inhaled around her. Curtains sucked inward toward the glass, then sagged.

Her chest heaved. Tongue tasted like tinfoil. The air felt wrong, charged and metallic.

Hal snored beside her, heavy and oblivious.

The ring in her head did not stop. It sharpened until it became a whisper hiding inside the sound, like someone breathing through the frequency itself, close enough to fog her ear.

Her right ankle caught fire.

Not the skin. Deeper. Bone. The hidden mark she had been pretending was nothing lit up like a brand pressed from the inside out.

She threw the covers back. Feet hit carpet. The room tilted once, like a boat hitting wake.

Clock: 3:03.

She stumbled to the bathroom. Shut the door quietly so she would not have to explain. Light on.

Humidity hit her face like a wall.

It was wrong. Too dense. Too heavy. Condensation did not sit on the mirror. It pushed out. Beads of water formed under the glass, as if the thing on the other side was sweating into this room.

The ring in her skull climbed higher. The whisper under it shaped itself around her name without fully forming it.

She gripped the sink.

"Stop," she whispered. "Just stop. Stop it."

The mirror rippled.

Not imagination. The whole surface moved like disturbed water. Her reflection smeared. Eyes, nose, mouth, all dragging sideways for a heartbeat.

Smoke curled behind her mirrored eyes.

Not steam. Smoke. Black against the fogged glass.

For one blink she was not looking at a tired woman in an Oklahoma bathroom.

She was staring through her own face at a sky the color of open flame. Armor caught the light. Rows of figures in formation. Heat. Shouting. The clash of weapons. A line of warriors braced against something marching out of the fire.

Her own mouth moved. Another voice rode her tongue.

Not English. Not anything she had learned.

Her bones understood every word.

*Remember who you are.*

The command vibrated through her teeth.

Audrey slammed her eyes shut.

"No."

The ringing popped. Pressure snapped.

She opened them again.

Plain mirror. Condensation running in thin streams. A pale woman stared back, shaking, hair stuck to her forehead.

Her phone lit up on the counter. Message banner. She could not bring herself to read it yet.

The ankle burn throbbed once, then dropped to a steadier ache.

She lifted the hem of her sleep pants. Skin looked normal. Nothing to explain. No mark visible.

Her pulse did not care.

She edged around the phone as if it might answer questions she was not ready to ask. Turned the light off. Stepped back into the dark bedroom.

Hal rolled over and snored louder.

The ring had gone, but the silence it left felt like a held breath.

LUKE'S HOUSE, GOOSENECK BEND, OK 3:04 AM

Luke woke with his heart already racing.

The bed frame shuddered under him. Nails creaked in the wall. The house flexed like something huge had leaned on it from outside.

Temperature jumped. The air turned thick with cedar.

Not air freshener. Not sawdust. Real cedar. Resin and sap and fresh-cut boards. Dad's shop. Summers spent sweeping the floor. Splinters in hands and no complaints.

For half a breath he was twelve again.

Then his back lit up.

Two points burned between his shoulder blades. Half circles, hot and precise. The heat bit straight into muscle, then settled on bone.

He sucked air through his teeth. Hands flew back to claw at the spot. Skin felt normal. The burn lived under it.

"Dad?" The word came out reflex. Empty room answered.

The pitch rolled in next.

It did not ring in his ears. It lived in his bones. A low, rising tone that made the fillings in his teeth itch. Like the house itself was humming.

Every loose thing lifted.

Coins. Pencils. Bookmarks. All floated a few inches above where they had been.

His blueprints slapped flat against the far wall. The lines on the page jittered, then aligned along one clean angle, all pointing to the same direction.

Southeast.

Curtains drew tight, the fabric pulled toward the same point.

The smell of cedar thickened until it felt like a third lung.

Luke sat very still.

Nothing held the things up. No wires. No draft. Just that tone climbing.

His hands shook. Not fear. Adrenaline. Every muscle coiled tight. His father's voice, uninvited, slipped into his head.

*When the angles line up, boy, you pay attention. That is the world telling you something is about to move.*

The pitch peaked.

Then everything rotated. One clean, perfect turn. Clockwise. Coins, pens, books, keys. Everything.

Rotation finished.

Gravity snapped.

Thump. Thump. Thump.

Objects hit floor, desk, nightstand.

The blueprints peeled off the wall. Drifted down onto the chair.

The curtains fell limp.

The cedar remained, woven through the air.

Luke swung his legs out of bed. The carpet under his feet felt faintly warm, like someone had been walking there all night.

He crossed to the window. Pushed aside the curtain.

Black Oklahoma sky stared back. No sign. No figure in the yard. No headlights on the road.

Still he knew.

The pull in his chest pointed the same way as the blueprints had.

Southeast. Like a hook sunk behind his sternum.

Sam.

He turned away from the glass. Grabbed his phone.

Thumbs moved.

Luke: I had a weird dream last night. It was of Dad and when I woke up my bedroom smelled like cedar.

He watched the message leave.

He hesitated only a second before opening Sam's thread.

Luke: You up? Had the weirdest dream about Dad. Call me when you can.

Send.

The bar crawled halfway. Hung.

Red.

Not delivered.

A cold feeling slid under the cedar.

Luke stared at the screen until it dimmed. Then tossed the phone back onto the bed.

The burn between his shoulders had not faded. It had settled into a steady throb that pulsed with his heartbeat.

He went to his closet. Turned his back to the mirror. Lifted his shirt over one shoulder. Held his phone up behind him. Took a photo.

Checked it.

Skin. Freckles. Old scar from a linebacker hit in high school. No new mark. No reddening.

He deleted the photo anyway.

Something had touched him. Something had rearranged his room like a diagram and then walked away.

He sat on the edge of the bed. Elbows on knees. Hands dangling. Breath coming slow now.

Under the weight of the house and the smell of cedar, the hook in his chest tugged again.

Southeast. Toward a city with too many ghosts.

## MUSKOGEE, OK 3:05 AM

Kay did not wake so much as surface.

One moment, sleep. The next, awareness snapped on like a light.

The pitch in the floorboards had changed.

It rose through the bed frame. Up her spine. Into her teeth. The taste came with it. Sharp. Metallic. Like she had held a nine-volt battery on her tongue.

She sat up.

The room leaned left for one second. Righted itself.

She was in the hallway before her mind caught up.

Carpet heated under her socks as she walked. Air growing thicker. A pressure in the house she recognized from tornado seasons and hospital calls. The moment before bad news.

She passed the entertainment room.

The doorway shimmered. Air inside bent light slightly. As if she were looking through rippling water.

The living room pulled her like a tide.

Celine stood at the front window.

Sleepwalking. Eyes half-open, not quite focused. She faced the glass with her palm flat against it.

Steam rolled off her bare arms. It hit the cool pane and turned to condensation in clouds.

The window itself bowed outward, breathing against the night.

A sound vibrated out of Celine's chest. Not quite voice. Not quite song. A low note that matched the pitch drilling behind Kay's ears.

Her fingers moved.

Curves and angles traced through the fog. Not random. Not doodling. A pattern looping back on itself. A circle intersected with a line. A shape too close to the rough sketches Sam had made in a notebook he thought no one had seen.

Kay took a breath that felt too hot.

"Celine."

No reaction.

She stepped in. Laid her hand gently on the girl's shoulder.

Heat hit her palm hard enough to make her flinch. Not fever. Furnace.

She held on anyway.

"Celine. Honey. Come back to me."

The sound in Celine's chest stalled.

Her fingers slowed.

The window shuddered. Glass snapped back flat.

Celine blinked. Pupils adjusting.

"Mom?" Her voice sounded scraped. "Why is it so hot in here?"

Some part of Kay cataloged every detail. The rest moved on instinct.

"You were sleepwalking," she said. Kept her tone level. "Let us get you some water and put you back to bed."

In the kitchen, the air already felt cooler. The pitch in the boards dropped.

Celine drained a full glass without stopping. Lowered it. Frowned.

"It tastes weird," she whispered. "Like... metal. Like when you bite foil."

Kay's own tongue still tasted the same way.

"New filter," she lied. "We will change it in the morning. Lie down."

She tucked Celine in. Smoothed hair back from her forehead. Watched her breathing until it slid into deeper rhythm.

Then she walked back into the living area.

The heat had leaked away but left a residue. A prickle on her arms. Every framed picture felt like it was watching.

The pull at her sternum drew her toward the console table.

She knew that feeling. It lived in the same place as the warnings that had saved her life more than once.

She opened the top drawer.

Menus. Scattered mail. Old keys.

And an envelope that did not belong.

Plain, sealed. No stamp. No date.

Her mother's handwriting across the front.

Sharp. Slanted. Unmistakable.

Four words:

If the mirrors speak.

Cold settled under her ribs. Pauline had never said that phrase to her once. Kay would have remembered.

She picked the envelope up. Turned it over. No seal broken. No sign it had been handled in years.

How long had it sat here? Waiting for this exact night.

Instinct stopped her from opening it. That same Velstra instinct that tasted storms days before radar called them.

This was not for panic.

It was for when the floor dropped out a little further.

She slid it into her robe pocket.

Her phone buzzed on the counter.

Luke.

Luke: I had a weird dream last night. It was of Dad and when I woke up my bedroom smelled like cedar.

Another buzz.

The envelope felt heavy in her pocket.

Kay: Everyone ok?

Dots appeared. Vanished. No response.

She stared at the screen for a long moment, then locked the phone.

The house groaned once. Settling.

Under the quiet, the ring in her skull shifted. Not gone. Retuned. Like it had found a new note to rest on.

Somewhere, something had moved. And whatever had touched her niece and her nephew smelled just like the thing that had kept her up for years when Sam was little and she could not name why she was afraid he would not make it to adulthood.

## NEW ORLEANS, LOUISIANA 3:06 AM

Sam hit cobblestone like he had fallen out of the sky.

Knees cracked against stone. Hands slapped wet pavement. The air punched his lungs empty.

The French Quarter snapped into focus around him. Balcony railings. Gaslight halos in fog. Distant brass. Laughter pouring out of doorways. The usual chaos, wrapped in night.

None of it felt usual.

The lamp post under his palm hummed. Not from electricity. From him.

The glyph under his sternum stuttered, then locked onto a tempo the rest of him scrambled to follow. His inner ear flipped twice. Gravity pointed sideways for a blink.

He breathed through it.

In. Out. One beat, then another.

The ground caught up.

He pushed himself up to standing. The lamp post stayed warm under his hand, picking up the rhythm of the pulse in his chest.

The signal he had become was not contained. It pushed outward. Through metal. Through stone. Through the wet air. A broadcast he did not know how to shut down.

Three steps toward Lafitte's.

The world stopped.

Sound froze. A trombone note hung mid-swell. A laugh stuck in a stranger's open mouth. Fog stopped moving, turned into carved glass.

Sam's breath came in. Went out. No one else's did.

Directly in front of him, a tourist stood with a bright green Hand Grenade drink in one fist and a ghost tour brochure in the other.

The man's eyes went black.

Not pupils. Not dilation. Solid. Oil-deep.

His arms snapped stiff. Fingers clenched. Drink slipped. Hung in the air beside his leg, liquid caught mid-splash.

The ring that had harassed his family gathered itself all at once at the base of Sam's skull. Climbed forward. Sat behind his eyes. It was not a sound so much as a pressure that wanted to become word.

Something inside the man's chest exhaled.

The voice that came out had been dragged across stone.

"Ego sum via. Et mors. Et mendacium."

I am the way. And death. And the lie.

Frost crawled along the cobblestones. Up the lamp post. Across the tourist's shoes.

"Nemo venit ad gloriam," it hissed, "nisi per submissionem regi vero."

King. True king.

Bones popped. The man's fingers bent backward, joints reversing with small cracking sounds. His head tilted sideways. Farther. Farther. Past anything that should have kept him breathing.

Sam's skin crawled. Hair rose on his arms. The glyph flared.

Heat rolled through him, then shot out, washing the street in ghost-light only he seemed to notice. Jazz froze mid-note against the brightness.

The thing inside smiled through borrowed teeth.

"Stirps tua bears the signum. Thief's blood. Fire stolen from its owners. You will kneel when called, son of…"

The refusal rose from somewhere behind his spine.

"No."

He did not push the word out. It shoved past his teeth on its own. Old. Final. A decision his blood had made before he was born.

The sound hit the thing like impact.

Its head jerked. Smile split wider, past the edges of its cheeks.

It bit down on its own tongue.

That tongue tore free. Hit the cobblestone. Did not look like anything that had ever lived inside a human mouth. Black fluid spilled. Thick and tar-like.

The creature swallowed the taste of itself.

Then grabbed its own skull with both hands and twisted.

The neck broke with a loud, flat crack.

The body did not drop.

It folded.

Hands slapped stone. Broken head hung at the wrong angle. The body scuttled backward, then ran up the wall in a crooked climb, limbs jerking like bad film.

Halfway to the roofline it twisted the ruined neck so the black eyes could still face Sam.

"Children of Marduk rise," it grated. "Your light is stolen. We come for reclamation."

The last word scraped against the air and did not fade.

Then it vanished over the lip of the roof, leaving a smear of drying black where brick met sky.

The image rippled like heat haze, then snapped. The figure on the roof vanished.

Time lurched back.

The drink hit the street. Liquid splashed. The guy behind Sam swore and jumped back.

"What the hell, man? Watch it!"

The tourist stood. Mouth open. Eyes normal brown now. Brochure in hand. No idea his body had already died once today.

Jazz stepped back into the measure like it had never stopped. Conversations resumed mid-sentence. Fog resumed its slow creep.

Sam's heart hammered once. Twice. Then steadied.

The glyph did not dim.

Instead, as his breath slowed, the signal wrapped tighter around the beat. Tuning itself.

Something eased behind his eyes.

Her presence. Not as sight. As countertone. She took the outer edge of the broadcast, the wild noise bleeding off him, and curved it away. Whispered it down into different layers so it did not drag every watcher within range to his location.

He felt it then.

Three answering pulses.

One in Gooseneck Bend. One in Muskogee. One in the same house as the second.

His family.

The glyph under his sternum beat once in recognition. Their own marks, still hidden from them, had flared through the same moment he had been pushed through the earth.

Same minute. Same note.

The Quarter breathed around him, unaware it had almost hosted a very public execution.

He turned toward Lafitte's.

The doorway glowed warm. Low light. Shadows moving inside.

Every step he took hummed up through the brick. The city heard him. The bayou behind him remembered. The land between started to pass the news along.

The Split had put a pin in his chest.

The other side had just tugged the string.

# Chapter 13

# Lafittes

Sam hit the doorframe. Shoulder first. Wood split under the impact. The world lurched sideways. Gravity slipped its anchor. His legs staggered across a floor that refused to stay flat.

The transition still clung to him, heavy, long past when it should have burned off. Part of him was trapped in bedrock. Part of him was suspended in the ley line. Part of him was here in Lafitte's, where air thickened around his skin and refused to let go. Body reassembled in pieces. Bones catching up half a second late.

Heat rolled off him. Metallic. Copper-bright. The smell of scorched earth from the cabin carried into the room.

Inside, Lafitte's shifted. The jazz blurred. Laughter warped. Glasses on tables vibrated. Light from the brick hearth bent toward Sam, flames leaning with a strange intelligence, as if recognizing what flared behind his ribs.

Above the churning row of neon slush machines, the mounted television screamed catastrophe. Chicago burning. Riot lines breaking. Smoke swallowing the Loop. The patrons turned their backs to it, clinking glasses and chasing the night, happily ignoring the apocalypse playing out right above the 'Purple Drank' sign.

He pushed through the crowd. None of them noticed him. Or maybe they refused to see him. Ash clung to his shirt. Static crawled across his arms. The glyph under his sternum pulsed in a rhythm his lungs tried and failed to imitate.

He saw her before the room noticed it had gone quiet.

Corner table. Deep shadow. A place the light avoided. A pocket of stillness in a building full of noise. The shadows around her were not absence; they were attention, drawn in tight.

Sam crossed the room. Every flame in the hearth leaned toward him again. He felt their heat glide across his ribs, reading the pattern beneath the skin.

He reached the table and sat. Hard. Muscles misfired. Nerves jolted. His hands betrayed him with a tremor.

A sharp throb hit his wrist. A memory. No. A mark waking up.

He pulled his hand into the lamplight.

The preacher's grip had not faded.

The handprint burned in his skin. Fingers wrapped around bone. Thumb pressed to the pulse. Not a scar. A signature. Territory claimed. Hours old yet aged like it had lived there a lifetime.

A dormant frequency inside it stirred when he looked at it. A second heartbeat under the first.

She studied the mark. No shift in expression. No softness. Just precise attention.

"Flesh remembers contact," she said. Voice low. Controlled. Words carrying weight without force. "Memory sits deeper than the mind."

Sam swallowed. Throat raw. Ribs ached where the glyph had flared too hard in the cabin.

"Am I losing it?" His voice scraped thin. "Tell me what's happening to me."

A pressure touched the air behind his head. Cold. Heavy. Familiar. Wayne's voice threaded up from memory like poison gas.

You're not special. You imagine things. You break things. You always have.

A geometric weight pressed against that thought. Something old. Something that did not tolerate lies.

Her eyes flicked once to the space beside him, seeing what whispered there. She acknowledged none of it. Returned her gaze to him. Pale gold. Steady. Measuring his fractures.

"You are not breaking," she said. "You are waking."

She lifted a hand from the table.

The bourbon bottle didn't move. The liquid inside did.

Amber rose in a slow spiral, drawn upward like metal filings chasing a magnet. Gravity forgot itself. Pressure did the work. The bourbon arced into two glasses. Three fingers deep. Smooth. Controlled.

A sharp crack. Ice formed inside the tumblers, fractures blooming outward.

Sam reached for his. His hand trembled. He lifted it. The burn hit his tongue first. Cedar. Smoke. Something older than flavor.

Heat spread through him. Up his spine. Into his skull. Vertebrae clicked into rhythm. The glyph under his sternum pulsed five times in a star pattern he didn't recognize but somehow matched with his breath.

She watched the pulse. Her gaze sharpened.

"The fire finds its path," she said.

Sam gasped. Gripped the table. Wood creaked under his fingers.

Heat settled at the base of his skull. Coiled tight. Waiting.

"Why my family?" he said. "Why us?"

The room shifted.

Jazz slowed. The bartender's motions blurred. Every flame leaned horizontal, pointing toward him. Above the bar on the TV,

Chicago froze mid-collapse, a riot held in place by a force no one else could see.

Her gaze turned upward, past the ceiling, past the Quarter, tracking something circling above the city.

"A bloodline is more than lineage," she said. "It is assignment."

She looked back at him.

"And you were born into a contract older than language."

A cold shiver carried down his spine. Not fear. Recognition. Something inside him leaned toward the truth like a plant toward sunlight.

He tried again. "Who are you?"

"You already know."

He shook his head. "I don't."

She didn't answer.

She waited.

Pressure built behind his eyes. Not pain. Memory. Something sliding out of the dark. A brightness he could not hold. Gold flared across the edges of his vision. A chord he had never heard vibrated through his chest. Air thinned until every breath felt like a secret.

The name rose through him.

It didn't come from thought. It came from the marrow.

"Inanna."

The sound emptied the room.

Every bulb in Lafitte's flickered. The hearth collapsed into coals. Glasses rattled. The screen above the bar cut to static. The floor tilted half an inch and corrected. Reflections in the bar mirror lagged a moment behind the bodies casting them.

Her eyes brightened. Not pride. Recognition.

"That name will do," she said.

Sam's pulse hammered. His ribs expanded too far. The glyph under his sternum pressed outward, answering something only she could hear.

She stood.

Light did not touch her. It avoided her edges like a hand recoiling from heat.

"You remember enough for now," she said.

A shift rolled across the bar. Not sound. Pressure. Chairs trembled. Shadows folded in toward her feet. The temperature dropped until Sam's breath misted.

She turned. Walked once through the static-split light.

The shadows followed.

Then she was gone.

Silence filled the booth. Not empty. Dense.

The glyph steadied. His breath found a rhythm that didn't tremble. Muscles remembered how to hold him.

He stood. Hands braced against the table until his balance caught up. Each inhale tasted of cedar and cold stone. Each exhale carried the echo of a name older than the city outside.

Sam pushed out into the Quarter. Amber streetlamps flickered. Fog curled around his feet. Music from the bars wavered in strange harmonics.

He pressed a hand to his chest. Felt the glyph pulse once. A vow. A warning. A signal.

Her name settled behind his ribs like a blade and a lantern at the same time.

Inanna.

The war had found him.

And for the first time since the preacher grabbed his wrist in the church basement, he understood the truth:

He was not prey.

He was being summoned.

# Chapter 14

# Vault of Echoes

Sam opened his eyes. The Vault blurred at the edges. Obsidian walls breathed around him, dark glass alive under its own pulse. Heat climbed his spine from wherever Inanna's gesture had dragged him.

Sconces dimmed. Green-gold flames stretched thin, pulled low under a weight the air had no right to carry.

The first memory surfaced.

Eight years old. Kitchen table. Sixty-four Crayola crayons scattered around a sheet of white paper. The house quiet except for the tick of the wall clock and the lawnmower humming through summer heat. Afternoons silent. Solitary. Except when his cousins came. Then anything felt possible.

Waxy scent thickened the air. Too sweet. Heavy.

He drew monster trucks with fire shooting from the exhaust. Superheroes holding back impossible collisions. Paper shifted under his small hands as if breathing with him. Edges curled. Heat rose. Reds too red. Blues electric. Colors refusing to behave.

In the Vault, Sam's breath caught. Something off. Something wrong.

Inanna stood in the doorway.

She hadn't been there. Couldn't have been there. Yet her shadow fell across the kitchen floor with ancient patience. Witnessing what the child couldn't understand he was shaping. A thin stream of gold ran down her side, dripping onto the obsidian. She did not acknowledge the wound.

The Vault wasn't replaying memory. It was letting him see what had always watched from beyond the veil.

Fire traced the wax lines. Images lifted from the paper. Young Sam laughed, reaching for flames dancing just out of reach, unaware his loneliness was bending reality into form.

Temperature spiked. Sam pressed his palm against the obsidian table. Warmth spread beneath his hand, answering him.

The clock ticked louder. The lawnmower's drone sharpened into a frequency that made his teeth ache. Wonder in the boy's face wavered, fragile as glass. Magic happened only in isolation. Meaning required witnesses. Childhood had neither.

The scene dissolved.

Another rose.

The Schwinn wobbled once, then steadied under him. Sam stood on the pedals, driving the bike forward. He never sat. Never tired. Bare legs pumping with relentless instinct. Audrey sat on the bike seat just behind him, her hands on his waist. Behind her, Celine balanced on the flat metal rack above the back wheel, arms around Audrey's hips, laughter shaking her whole frame.

Luke perched on the handlebars, leaning forward into the wind, knees bent, arms stretched wide as if daring gravity to disagree.

Sam stood and pushed harder. The bike rattled but never failed. They flew past Farley's tomato plants. Green scent heavy in the heat. Dust rose behind them as Hyde Park roads stretched ahead, carrying them toward the Catfish.

Four kids. One rhythm.

Audrey's steady hands.

Celine's breathless laughter.

Luke's fearless wingspan.

Sam's legs turning the world beneath them.

A single heartbeat riding on steel and summer.

In the Vault, tears pricked. This one was whole. Pure. Before Wayne. Before fractures. Before childhood learned how to brace for impact.

But the memory warped.

Sunlight bleached to white. Laughter echoed half a breath late. Celine's shriek came after her mouth had closed. The road stretched too long, distances bending out of sense. Sam kept pedaling. Effortless. Endless. The bike suspended between places, refusing to let them arrive.

Time held its breath. The afternoon caught on the rhythm of four hearts.

Even then, they were aligning.

Even then, they were tuning themselves for what they would one day carry.

The Vault reacted first.

A shudder passed through stone. Frost feathered across the floor. Breath left Sam's mouth in clouds. His hands lifted from the table. Obsidian held their prints in crystallized moisture.

The memory fractured. Shards hung in the air. Luke's face in one. The smell of tomato vines in another. The feeling of pedals under his feet in a third. Warmth with nowhere to go inside the sudden cold.

Heat returned. Violent. Immediate.

Back of Wayne's pickup. Camper shell shut tight. Eleven years old. Sitting on a plastic crate meant for Coke bottles. Vinyl burning his bare legs. Sweat-soaked shirt sticking to skin. Bottles clinking when the truck hit bumps. Air thick enough to chew.

Burnt vinyl. Stale sweat. Gasoline that lived in Wayne's fingerprints.

Through the small window, Wayne's hands on the wheel. Janet beside him, shoulders tight. Most days Sam rode alone back here. When Luke and Audrey visited, he rode up front. Today the verdict was clear. Shell closed. No appeal.

Wayne's boots paced circles outside. Not to calm down. To keep rage from turning inward enough to recognize itself.

The truck stopped. Gravel crunched. The shell opened. Janet stood there. Eyes wide. Concern too late. Her gaze flicked toward Wayne's silhouette in the cab. Measuring the cost.

"Baby, it's too damn hot back here." Voice soft. Practical. Survival framed as kindness. "Get up front."

Her hand swept hair from his face. Tender. Automatic. But her eyes stayed locked on Wayne.

He climbed into the cab. Air conditioning hit like forgiveness he hadn't earned.

In the Vault, Sam understood what the boy could not. Janet wasn't cruel. She was exhausted. Every act of love a calculation. Every silence a survival strategy. Two truths living in her body.

The table heated beneath Sam's palms. Frost veined over the warmth. Memory arguing with itself. Mercy or abandonment. Always both.

Gravity flickered. His hand passed through the solid table as if matter remembered being fluid.

Inanna's shadow appeared at the edge of the light. Not in memory. Here. Watching him watch his own history. Parallel grief in her stillness, carved from betrayals far older than his.

The memory collapsed.

Another rose.

Winter. Wayne's garage. Fifteen. Concrete cold through socks. Bell found on the fence. Sam sanding rust for hours. Steel wool tearing skin. Copper and dust thick on his tongue.

Three coats of red enamel. Same color as Wayne's Chevy. Gleaming under the garage light. He tapped it once. Pitch almost right. Almost true.

Wayne came home.

Sam waited by the kitchen table. Bell set on a paper towel. Hope a dangerous glow under his sternum.

"I fixed this for you," Sam said.

Wayne picked up the bell. Turned it over once. Approval flashed across his face. Rare. Real. Gone too fast.

"Well look at that." Smooth voice. Oil on water. "We've got a painter in the family."

Smile forming.

Died.

"And he ruined what wasn't his."

Bell flew.

It struck Sam's chest. Hollow clang cutting through bone. Air left his lungs. Spine hit counter. But his hand flew to his side, not his chest. A phantom puncture wound throbbed there, wet and hot.

The bell hit linoleum. Paint chipped.

"Janet," Wayne called. "Your kid ruined my bell."

Through the doorway, his mother sat on the couch. Hands twisted in her lap. Lips parted as if to speak his name. She didn't stand. Didn't move. Eyes fixed downward. Survival measured in silence.

The bruise on Sam's chest lasted three weeks.

In the Vault, the memory stayed whole. Unbroken. A pillar.

Three anchors now orbiting him.

The crayons.

The truck bed.

The bell.

Repeating. Overlapping. Laughter bleeding into metal. Wax into vinyl. Sweat into enamel fumes. Time folding in on itself.

The Vault wasn't replaying memories. It was showing the pattern.

His heart thrashed against the glyph beneath his shirt. A second heartbeat aligned with it. His chest glowed faintly through fabric.

Gravity failed.

He lifted six inches off the floor. Kneeling in midair. The three memories circled him, bright as moons around a dying world.

You are not safe.

You have never been safe.

Love is conditional.

Conditions shift without warning.

Inanna stepped closer. Eyes holding recognition. She had lived her version. Bound by her sister. Betrayed by blood. Fate repeating itself across divine lines.

The Vault built itself from his pulse. Cracks spread across the floor in sync with his heartbeat. The walls wept liquid silver. Rivulets pooled into shapes that wanted to become words older than language.

Everything loops.

Lifetimes stacked too close. Bleeding through.

His breath broke. Childhood wreckage around him. Man kneeling inside the ruins, holding together the contradictions of a life lived under conditional love.

Light pushed through his sternum. Spiral after spiral widening beneath the skin. Depth forming that shouldn't exist in flesh.

The chamber trembled. Sconces guttered. Mist churned overhead, revealing shapes neither angel nor monster. Watching him without flinching.

A word rose from somewhere below speech.

Again.

Not despair. Recognition.

He had broken here before. Forgotten it. Been forced to break again because forgetting was the only way to survive remembering.

"Not again," he whispered. Barely a sound.

The Vault heard him.

Obsidian cracked deeper. Molten tears ran faster. The ripple spread to the walls. To the ceiling. The chamber preparing to rupture. Destroy him. Remake him.

Three anchor memories froze mid-orbit. Waiting for judgment.

Inanna stood unmoving. Witness. Not savior. Not shield. The one who knew what it meant to survive the shattering.

The Vault went silent.

No heat. No cold. No gravity. Just the pressure of silence folding around him like a closing hand.

The glyph at his sternum answered first.

And somewhere far beneath the chamber, something ancient and patient lifted its head.

It had heard its name.

# Chapter 15

# The Unraveling

Silence pressed in. Not peace. Pressure.

Sam stayed seated at the obsidian table, but his body felt an inch out of phase with the chair. Like someone had traced him in light and shifted the outline half a step to the left. The Vault pulsed around him, glass and stone breathing in a rhythm that did not belong to lungs.

His chest answered.

The glyph under his sternum beat harder, a second pulse riding the first. Two hearts arguing inside the same cage. Heat ran up his spine in a steady climb, vertebra by vertebra, like someone lighting a fuse with invisible hands.

He tried to breathe slow. In through the nose. Out through the mouth. Counting without sound. One. Two. Four. Eight. Numbers slid away. The air did not care about his counting. It weighed the same no matter what he called it.

The Vault dimmed.

His depth perception slid. The table felt closer than it looked, farther than it should be. His own hands seemed a fraction delayed from where his eyes saw them.

Green-gold fire thinned to threads. Sconces stretched into vertical smears, each flame a line dragged down by gravity that no longer agreed with itself. The shadows they cast gathered in corners, too thick for absence, too dense for smoke.

Sound arrived first.

Not memory. Not yet.

A bell rang somewhere he could not point to. A single lonely chime, metal on bone. The tone carried the weight of a bruised sternum, the shape of a kitchen, the silence of a woman staring at her own hands. It hit his nervous system like it was happening now.

He flinched.

Another sound, low and mechanical, the burnt-plastic whine of a toy motor punched too hard. No room, no truck, just the pitch. The guilt baked into it. The knowing, even then, that joy could be a trigger.

Heat washed over his face. At the same time, cold crawled under his skin. Two climates living in the same body.

The Vault did not show him pictures. It whispered frequencies.

A soft scuff of vinyl on the back of his thigh, the weight of a camper shell's air, the taste of stale sweat and gasoline. It rose through his bones in a wave, then dropped away before the image could fully form.

Sam gripped the edge of the obsidian table. Fingers dug in. The surface flexed, not stone for a moment, not liquid either. Something that remembered being both.

His knuckles blurred.

He looked down. His hands were there, but not entirely. Edges fuzzed, like bad reception on an old TV. For an instant, he could see three sets of fingers layered on top of each other, all his, all at different ages, all reaching for something that never stayed.

The Vault took that uncertainty and magnified it.

Obsidian panels along the walls shifted. Lines of ancient geometry rearranged themselves, sliding with the soft grind of planets changing order. Patterns he had no words for emerged, held, then broke apart again.

He was not just sitting in a room.

He was sitting inside a diagram.

His diagram.

Something in the stone recognized him and was forcing him to recognize himself.

The bell tone returned, low enough to vibrate the roots of his teeth. Not once. A sequence now. Three strikes, spaced like a heartbeat that could not decide whether to stop or sprint. With each ring, his sternum tightened under his palm. The skin there burned cold.

His chest lit under his shirt, a faint glow leaking through cotton, then skin, then bone.

The Vault leaned in.

He felt it. The whole chamber drawing closer without moving, the way a crowd can close ranks without a single footstep, just a shift in intent. The air crowded his throat.

"You are in the seam," Inanna said.

Her voice came from his right. Not loud. Clear enough to cut through every echo.

He turned. She had moved closer to the table, but he had not seen her move. Her face remained unreadable. Her eyes did not.

They held recognition and something worse. Recognition and grief.

"Between what?" His throat tightened. He had not been speaking aloud, but his voice still came back hoarse.

"Between the wound," she said, "and choosing."

For a blink, her outline doubled, then snapped back into place.

He swallowed. The words slid down into a place already crowded.

The Vault answered her with another shift.

Obsidian beneath his elbows rippled. Reflections of his face broke into stacked versions, young, older, older still, all sharing the same eyes, the same tightness around the mouth. All layered over the present him, like the stone was running a scan and refusing to pick a single frame.

His stomach lurched.

For a heartbeat, he knew what it felt like to be nine and eleven and fifteen and thirty at the same time. Not as memories, but as simultaneous processes. Every age running in parallel, each one braced, each one waiting for impact.

A static headache bloomed behind his eyes, the kind that comes not from pain but from too much truth trying to occupy too little skull.

The nervous system was never meant for that kind of concurrency.

His vision went grainy at the edges. Not dark. Pixelated.

Light in the Vault shifted. Green-gold fire turned thin and white and then something beyond even that, a color his mind could not file. For a second the walls were not stone at all. They were overlapping diagrams of him, traced in thin lines of light, each outline a different posture, a different era, all stapled to the same coordinates in space.

His body trembled.

He let out something that should have been a laugh and was not.

"Feels like a distinction without a difference."

She watched him. The corner of her mouth almost moved. Not quite.

"Madness drifts," she said. "This is too exact."

The bell tone swelled. Turned into the soft hollow boom of a slammed door. The pop of gravel under bare feet. The buzz of a fluorescent light in a classroom where everyone stared. The scrape of a hook through divine flesh in a place that was not here, not now, but lined up clean with the rest.

The Vault fed him no images, only the residue of what those moments had carved.

His body felt every cut.

Shame hit first. Hot, fast, almost welcome. Familiar poison. The voice of the bruise under the bell. You should have known. You should have stayed quiet. You should not have needed.

Behind it came grief. Slow and heavy, like water rising at the bottom of a well. It brought Janet's face with it, not the details, just the ache shaped like her. The shape of "I love you" spoken into a world where he had forgotten to answer.

Anger followed, not fire at first, but pressure. A hand on the back of his neck pushing his face toward concrete. An invisible weight that said this is how it is, boy, and you do not get a vote.

His chest tightened as if a rope had been pulled through all three feelings at once, knotting them behind his sternum.

They did not take turns.

They arrived as one.

The glyph beneath his hand burned brighter. Light climbed his spine again, this time less like a fuse, more like something waking vertebra by vertebra, claiming each bone.

The pressure was wrong in a way human harm never managed. It pressed from above and inside at the same time, a shape without a face, interested only in shrinking whatever light it found. Not as a vision, but as a pressure in his skull, a static that tasted like church basements and sermons about worms and worthlessness. About heaven as a gate with a clipboard. About love as a test he had already failed.

Words he had heard in a hundred rooms, through a hundred different mouths, began to echo in his ribcage. Not in English now. In the feeling behind them.

You are broken.

You must be fixed.

The ones who hurt you stand between you and God.

His jaw clenched. Teeth ached.

The Vault harmonized with that lie at first. Then it rejected it.

Obsidian cracked again. Thin silver light bled from the seams. The chamber shuddered the way a body does when it has decided finally, fully, that it will no longer carry someone else's story.

"You feel them." Inanna's voice barely brushed the air. "The ones who fed on your fear."

He nodded once. Could not trust his throat.

"Call them," she said.

He started to say Wayne. Janet. Ms. Kathy. Pastors. Everyone who had turned away or turned on.

What came out instead was a single word.

"Liars." The word left his mouth like it had been waiting decades.

The Vault reacted as if he had spoken a true name.

Silver veins in the floor flared. For a moment the entire chamber lit from underneath, every crack a river, every river a script written in some pre-human hand. The light did not burn his skin. It burned something under it.

Programs.

He could feel them now, woven into reflex. The flinch. The apology. The half-step back from his own power. Every time he swallowed a truth to keep someone else comfortable. Every time he chose exile over conflict so no one would have to see him.

He saw none of the scenes.

He felt all of the cost.

"Who taught you you were dangerous?" Inanna asked.

"Everyone," he rasped.

"Who benefited from that belief?"

Not him.

The answer rose hot and fast. Not another name. A sensation. A curtain. A hand behind the hand. Something that had been fed with every small betrayal, every quiet surrender, every sermon that insisted he was dust and someone else was the gate.

The Vault trembled as if he had pointed at the right shadow even without a word.

A low hum started in the walls, deep enough to vibrate his molars. It was not sound in the usual sense. It was the frequency of something that had always been there, now exposed.

A pressure older than men.

He did not see faces. He saw effect.

Families held in cages of fear. Children trained to doubt their own seeing. Men who hurt so they would not have to feel. Churches that preached a heaven outside to keep people from finding the one already burning inside their ribs.

His heart pounded. The second pulse kept pace.

The two rhythms began to match.

He put both hands flat on the table.

"I do not belong to them," he whispered.

The words scared him more than anything he had seen.

They did not sound like him.

They sounded like something using his mouth to remember itself.

Inanna's eyes brightened, reflecting the silver veining through the obsidian. She said nothing. Not praise. Not warning. Only watched.

The Vault reacted.

For the first time since he sat down, gravity remembered itself long enough to slam him back into the chair. All the floating, all the near-weightless drift, ended in a single crushing pull. His bones complained. His muscles trembled.

Silver lines on the floor converged beneath his feet, tracing a slow spiral that matched the one under his skin.

His body hurt everywhere. Not sharp pain. The ache of being used past capacity.

"I cannot do this," he said, barely a breath. The truth of a boy on a porch. The truth of a young man in a Red Lobster parking lot. The truth of every lifetime where he had walked away from his own fire because the world told him it was wrong.

Inanna tilted her head.

"That is the only doorway that works," she said. "The one where you stop pretending you could carry it alone."

He shut his eyes.

Behind his lids, colors surged. Not memories. Forces.

Pressure behind his sternum built toward something that felt like failure and birth at the same time.

Fear rose like a tide. What if he broke and never came back together. What if there was nothing on the other side of this except madness. What if the Vault finished the work Wayne started, and there was nothing left of him but light and ash.

Another voice moved beneath those fears.

Quieter. Older.

What if that was the point.

His throat tightened.

He did not want to be brave. He did not want to be holy. He did not want to be chosen or central or anything with a capital letter. He wanted a mother who lived. A family that stayed. A childhood that did not need a Vault to make sense.

He did not get that.

He got this.

The table warmed under his hands, heat growing until his palms should have blistered. They did not. Instead, sensation inverted. It was not the stone heating his skin. It was his skin heating the stone.

Light pushed outward again.

Inanna leaned forward, elbows resting on the obsidian, eyes never leaving his.

"You are not being punished," she said. "You are being unbound."

He had no answer.

The Vault went utterly still. No hum. No crackle. No flux in the sconces. Even the mist above froze, frozen waves of not-cloud caught just before breaking.

Sam sat in the center of it, every nerve lit, every emotion bare. Shame, grief, anger, fear, all stripped of story, all condensed into a single unbearable now.

His jaw unclenched.

He let one breath come exactly as it wanted. No control. No count. Just air moving however a body about to break needed it to move.

It shuddered through him.

Something deep inside, something that had believed for decades that it had to hold everything together alone or the world would end, finally admitted the truth.

He could not.

He could not fix it.

He could not earn it.

The belief cracked, fine and sharp, like a bone finally setting in the right place only after snapping the wrong way first.

He could not apologize enough for being born into the wrong house with the wrong man and the right amount of light.

The admission hurt worse than any blow.

It also loosened something around his heart that had never been loose before.

Dread stood on one side of that realization.

On the other, something that was not quite hope. More like a decision.

He did not know what waited past this breaking, but he knew one thing.

If this was the only road out of the cage, he would rather step into the fire than spend another year decorating the bars.

He opened his eyes.

Inanna watched him, expression unchanged, but the set of her shoulders softer. There was a question in her gaze. Not will you survive this. Something sharper. Will you stop lying to your own light.

His voice came out rough.

"Do it." The words shook, not from fear, but from the cost of telling the truth aloud.

He did not know who he was talking to.

The Vault.

The glyph.

Whatever old patience waited below.

All of them.

"Then let it take what it needs to," Inanna said. "There is nothing here worth saving that the fire can kill."

The words settled in his chest like a seal.

The silence in the Vault thickened. Heavy. Absolute.

The pressure climbed toward breaking.

The next instant would hurt. He knew that much.

He let his hands stay on the table. Let his spine stay straight. Let his fear stay exactly where it was instead of reaching for some lie to cover it.

The Vault leaned closer.

Air thinned. His lungs tightened as if the chamber were waiting to inhale him back.

The glyph under his sternum flared.

And somewhere beneath the chamber, in the dark architecture under all things, something vast and patient pulled its attention fully toward him and waited for the signal it had been listening for across lifetimes.

The world held its breath.

# Chapter 16

# Blood Remembers

Silence shattered. Not sound. Absence. A vacuum pulling air from his lungs and replacing it with pressure. Eardrums bowed inward. The Vault convulsed. Obsidian walls rippled like water struck from impossible heights. Cracks spider-webbed, geometry twisting hard enough to hurt.

Temperature collapsed. Frost and heat occupying the same molecular space. Conditions rejecting human flesh. Breath left as steam, froze mid-air, shattered into crystals that sang as they fell.

Gravity failed. Five chairs drifted in slow orbit, cutting faint arcs through green-gold light. Constellations he had never seen, but recognized. Sconces guttered. Reignited. Colors without names. Shadows moving without sources. Whispers older than speech.

Five anchor memories hung suspended. Crayon heat. Truck oppression. Bell impact. Porch exile. ICU flatline. Each one fracturing.

The storm opened its mouth.

Memories poured in.

Travel trailer. Thin carpet under knees. Diesel and old smoke in the cushions. A black-and-white Army TV humming in the corner, picture rolling like it didn't belong to a single world.

Nine years old. Christmas morning. Gray light through blinds. Cold drafting under the door.

Wayne grinning down at him, a grin that tried on kindness like borrowed skin.

"Here you go, bud. Saw you looking at this in the store. Figured Santa might've missed it."

Warmth. Safety. Hope trying to return.

Bright yellow Playskool Bigfoot Monster Truck. Oversized tires. Switch on the roof. Ran it over carpet. Engine noises in his throat. Wayne laughed. Honest. Almost human.

"Me and your mama are gonna lie back down. You stay quiet."

He nodded. Tried. Slipped. The motor erupted. Loud, too loud. The trailer shrank around that sound.

Wayne appeared like a verdict.

"Quiet means quiet."

Second mistake. Engine roared again. Two strides. Truck snatched. Door opened. Cold swallowed it.

Plastic shattered on frozen ground.

Sam curled on the couch. Trying to become quieter than noise.

Janet emerged ten minutes later. Face neutral. Mercy reduced to calculation.

"Sam, go outside. You can turn your truck on as much as you want."

He obeyed. He found it broken. He sat beside it. Never turned it on again.

The Vault looped the ache. The smaller heartbreaks hurting worse because they had nowhere to go.

Trailer dissolved.

Fluorescent lights. Ms. Kathy's remedial class. Tenth grade. Rows of desks. No talking here. Finished quiz early. Newspaper folded on his lap.

"You think you're slick, Sam Howardson?"

He looked up. Heard the verdict before the accusation.

"Principal's office. Now."

Hallway stretching forever. Footsteps echoing. Innocence irrelevant.

A crack formed in the idea of fairness. It never healed.

Scene dissolved.

Night air. Cicadas. A single-wide mobile home Wayne called an "upgrade." Seventeen now. Worn sneakers. Soles peeling. Friday night pretending life wasn't already weighted.

Wayne's new Reeboks beside the door. Spotless. Sam slid them on. Perfect fit. Bring them back perfect. Clean them. Invisible.

Home late. Door locked. Porch lights dull. Shoes dusted. Set neatly aside.

Door yanked open.

"Where are my shoes?"

"I borrowed them. They're fine."

Wayne turned them in his hands like evidence.

"Get the fuck out of my house."

Sam looked at his mother. Searching for anything. The woman who once tucked his hair behind his ear.

"Mom?"

"You put me in a tough spot, Sam. You took what wasn't yours."

Bolts sliding. Chain dragging.

Porch. Gravel under socks. Pot roast drifting from the window. A warmth he would never sit down to again.

Love choosing sides.

The Vault shuddered. Trauma overlaid itself with myth.

Hooks. Celestial hooks. Inanna hanging in darkness. Ribs torn. Throat slit shallow. Displayed. Abandoned by those sworn to her. Ereshkigal's laughter slipping through Wayne's voice.

The door slam became a hook through the shoulder.

Janet's silence became a hook through the ribs.

Pot roast continuing without him became a hook through the throat.

Two truths.

You are loved.

You are cast out.

Both real. Both permanent.

The overlay dissolved. The pain did not.

Next memory surged.

Antiseptic. Fryer oil. Bleach. Red Lobster kitchen during dinner rush. Twenty-two. Exhausted. Refilling water glasses.

Jen touched his shoulder.

"Sam, someone called. Said your mom was in a bad accident."

The world narrowed. Glass slipping. Water spreading. He was in the car before thought caught him.

JPS hospital. ICU humming like artificial noon. Machines breathing for Janet. Tubes branching from her like roots searching for soil.

Wayne slumped in a chair. Face gray.

"She's in bad shape, bud... they don't know when."

He left at dawn. Sam stayed.

Day blurred into day.

Machines breathed.

Janet drifted.

She woke on the second night.

Bruised. Fighting for air.

She wrote on a small pad with shaking fingers.

Still got it.

A fragment of the mother who once folded laundry during late-night game shows. Love trying to surface through exhaustion.

"Go shower, Sammy."

Voice almost steady.

He kissed her forehead. She touched his hand. Small. Real.

"Hey, Sam."

She studied his face.

"I love you. See you tomorrow."

He didn't say it back.

He went to Red Lobster instead.

Two beers. Three.

Laughter he didn't hear.

Vigil guilt pounding between ribs.

Then the phone call.

"Sammy... I'm sorry... Your momma passed away tonight."

Parking-lot lights.

Hands gripping the wheel she taught him to hold at ten and two.

She died waiting to see him tomorrow.

He was drinking when her heart stopped.

The Vault made him feel all of it. At once. Without mercy.

Flashes hit hard.

The truck.

The classroom.

The porch.

The hook through Inanna's ribs.

The ICU flatline.

Five memories collapsed inward, fitting into the space where safety once lived.

Pressure built behind the glyph.

Pain reframed itself as fuel.

Rejection turned to tinder.

Grief turned to voltage.

His body lifted from the floor. One inch.

Back arched. Fingers clawed at nothing.

Time froze on the exact second before surrender.

Light erupted.

Not blood.

Radiance.

Silver leaked from his nose and ears.

The glyph exploded in his chest.

Fire outlined his ribs.

Organs visible through skin.

Not burning.

Revealing.

Inanna stood in the edge-light.

Witness.

Unflinching.

Survivor of her own eternities.

"Every creation remembers the cut that shaped it."

The words struck him as truth, judgment, and blessing in equal measure.

Light compressed inward. Dense. Heavy as collapsed stars.

He wasn't dying.

He was becoming the wound itself.

The Vault held its breath.

Then it happened. The Vault ignited.

And the man who had spent a lifetime apologizing for existing was burned out of his own body, making room for whatever answered his name next.

Chapter 17

# **Supernova**

The Vault had changed.

Onyx curved where stone had been flat. Hematite veins throbbed through the black walls, faint red blooming each time the air shifted. The floor, polished jade dark as drowned glass, reflected the chamber with a half-second delay as if reality had to think before it followed.

Sam lay crumpled at the center.

A thin outline hovered beneath him, a ghost-shadow drifting half a breath out of sync. The table hung an inch above the jade. Its surface, volcanic glass threaded with living silver veins, pulsed like a creature trying to decide whether it should wake.

Air tasted metallic. Rain on cold stone. Copper wire struck against iron. Pressure gathered behind his teeth, across his sinuses, and inside the hollow of his throat where words formed before becoming sound.

He had not moved in seventeen minutes.

Then his eyes opened.

Pupils dilated. Irises rimmed gold and silver. Not glowing. Carrying light they could not fully hold. The whites were backlit like thin paper stretched over a candle. Something shifted behind them. Galaxies flickered. Then vanished. Human again, almost.

Pain detonated inside his skull.

No thought. No memory. Just sensation. Sunlight driven through bone. Heat rising where nerves were never meant to fire. Beneath agony, something else worked its way through him. Recognition. Not of power. Of origin. A pull toward a place he had forgotten until this second.

The glyph beneath his torn shirt flared once. White. Violent. A lattice surfaced across his sternum. Lines chased along the collarbones and down the ribs, not breaking them, illuminating shapes carved long before birth. They shimmered, dimmed, then waited.

Light ran through his veins for six seconds, silver and gold threading through blue. Bright enough to see through skin. Then it sank into marrow and into the empty pockets between atoms where identity had slept for lifetimes.

His bones hummed. Frequency shifting. Matter adjusting. Human shape protesting. Holding him small because it did not know what else to do.

Memory slammed into him without order.

Lapis walls. Sand drifting outside. A woman singing a language he had never learned yet understood in the chest. A crown of light pressing down until the neck remembered how to carry it. Sun-baked stone. Wine. Fig skins on warm fingers. A hand reaching toward him.

He jerked.

Now. Vault. Jade. Sconces burning green gold. His name is Sam. His body aches. His mother is gone. His past is real even when this is more real.

Utensils lifted from the table. Orbiting him in ragged arcs. Ash spiraled upward. Gravity stalled. Sound stretched thin. Every second arrived late. Heartbeats echoed half a breath after they landed in the ribcage.

Stone walls rippled like black water. Rings moved outward from his body. Hematite veins brightened and bled red into fractures that had not existed until he breathed.

Chairs sagged at the edges. Wood softening, dripping toward the floor like cooling metal.

The table dropped two inches. Stabilized. Shivered.

Reality thinned.

The street above flickered into view. Gas lamps. Royal Street. Wrought iron shadows. A balcony superimposed over the Vault's curvature like a memory caught between inhalations.

Beneath it, tunnels lined with bone. Catacombs. Water dripping. And beneath those, something older. A submerged temple buried under sand long before the first Creole stone was laid in the Quarter.

Time folded. Past. Present. Three futures. All bleeding through the same tear. The edges transparent. His breath echoing through versions of himself that had lived different days.

His body refused conscious commands.

He was dissolving. Not dying. Not disintegrating. Dissolving the lie of shape. Cells opening like doors. Frequency widening. Volume expanding. Human architecture bending to contain something too large for its frame.

If it continued, the frame would fail. No body left to hold him.

She watched from the edge.

Silent. Braced.

Not soothing. Not saving. Not instructing.

Witnessing.

Her posture carried the weight of someone who had survived this once and carried scars she would never name. Eyes tracking the exact second a soul stops fleeing itself.

Sam burned.

Light struck through his chest from within. Skin thinned. Ribs outlined in white gold fire. Breath staggered through lungs fighting to anchor him to a name, a memory, a body.

The glyph ruptured its boundary. Fractal lines mapped across his torso. Lines older than bone. Too fast for flesh. Too much for cells that had never been designed to carry this pattern.

The Vault groaned. Jade cracked. Fractures crawled outward like roots searching for light.

Sconces flared. Flames sharpened into ultraviolet.

Dimensional rifts opened across three walls at once. Through them he saw:

the catacombs,

the street above,

the ancient temple.

All existing now. All claiming him.

Too fast.

If nothing grounded him, the expanding pattern would tear the room open and pull half the Quarter with it.

She stepped forward.

Pain twisted and folded inside itself. Returned as totality. Every nerve firing. Pleasure tangled with agony until the distinction disappeared. Spine aligned. Vertebrae clicked into a configuration that belonged to him once, long ago.

Air scorched down his throat. Copper. Ozone. Breath stoking the furnace burning through his chest.

Perception broke open.

The city intruded.

The street above pulsed through him. Every heartbeat within three blocks struck his ribs. The Quarter pressed into his body, its ley lines humming under pavement, its rot drifting along ancient waterways, its dead leaving their footprints in stone. The city was no longer outside him. It moved inside his marrow.

A hand pressed against his sternum.

Cool. Solid. Anchoring.

One word reached him. Low. Resonant. A description, not a title. The name of what happens when wounded frequency finds itself again.

A return.

It struck like a stone dropped into water. Ripples moved through bone. Slowed the tear.

Not yet.

Her palm pressed harder. Energy bleeding out of him poured into her. She siphoned it, redirected it, grounded it through her body and into the Vault. She took more than she should have been able to take. Enough to kill anything mortal.

It did not kill her.

Her eyes flickered gold. Veins lit under skin. Mirroring his. Closed circuit. His fire. Her bridge. The room their vessel.

Breathe, she whispered. Voice thin. Trembling from the weight she carried. Hold the shape.

Air clawed into lungs. Light compressed inward. Not extinguished. Concentrated. Heavy as the heart of a collapsing star.

Dimensional rifts sealed.

Walls solidified. Hematite veins dimmed to ember. Jade cracks retreated. The table steadied. Chairs reformed. Reality folded back into a single layer.

Gravity returned.

His body struck the floor. Hard. Breath broken into three stuttering pulls. Light sank beneath skin, leaving faint radiance clinging along vein edges.

His eyes still burned.

Gold silver rim, permanent.

Blink. Only the Vault remained.

One room. One time.

She withdrew her hand. Staggered half a step. Sweat gathered along her temples. Fingers trembled from absorbing what he could not hold.

What happened? His voice was gravel.

She watched him with the patience of something ancient, something that had known him long before this life gave him a name.

Ignition, she said. Quiet. The first return.

He pushed up on one elbow. His body felt aligned. Not stronger. Not larger. Simply correct. As if something inside him had been set in place after years of tilting sideways.

The walls looked different. New veins. New pulse. New angles. The Vault had changed its skin. Not for him. For what survived inside him.

Can you stand?

He tested his weight. Knees cracked. Legs shook. He rose slow. The world swayed. Settled.
His palm found the iron railing, cold enough to bite, and the city stopped tilting.

Above him the city pulsed. Every heartbeat. Every secret. Every buried memory threaded through concrete and water.
He tried to speak.

You are still drifting, she said. It will take time to stabilize.
How long?
Longer than we have.
She lifted her hand.

Air peeled open. Light folded outward like petals. A corridor revealed itself, shaped by a law older than human time.

It is time.

Sam stared into the aperture.

His legs moved. Three steps. No hesitation. No thought.

At the threshold he looked back.

Hematite veins flared once. Red. Faint.

Not invitation.

Not approval.

Not destiny.

Warning.

He stepped through.

The aperture closed behind him.

The Vault settled. Walls shifting into a configuration drawn from a memory it had never been given. A skin altered forever by what it had contained.

Then stillness.

Chapter 18

# The Cathedral

Jackson Square held its breath. Fog clung to cobblestones, drowning every stone edge until the ground felt submerged. Sodium lamps flickered in rhythm with Sam's pulse. Air tasted of copper and rain-soaked stone, thick enough to chew.

His shirt hung torn at the shoulder. Ash streaked the fabric. Dried blood darkened the collar. Gold veins traced along his forearms in dim pulses that shifted beneath skin too thin for what lived inside it. His steps stuttered. He moved because stopping meant thinking. Thinking meant the Vault. The Hex. The sound of stone screaming.

The square stood empty. Bells echoed faintly somewhere beyond the mist, counting hours that belonged to no clock Sam knew.

At the cathedral steps, a figure stirred.

A homeless veteran hunched against the iron railing. Blanket pulled tight. When his eyes lifted, they flashed amber once. Not reflection. Recognition.

"The blood remembers," the man said. Voice scraped bone. No breath behind it.

Sam stopped. The words hit his chest like heavy stones dropped in deep water.

The amber faded to human brown. The veteran pulled the blanket tighter and turned away.

Sam climbed the steps. His footfalls echoed wrong, bending around the cathedral's mass as if the building listened. Bronze doors stood shut, saints and martyrs carved across their surface. Their faces shifted in lamplight. Not illusion. Attention.

The doors breathed open.

Warm air brushed his face. Beeswax. Frankincense. A space that held its breath too long and finally exhaled.

The nave stretched vast and silent. Shadows pooled in alcoves. Statues watched with eyes that held more than stone. Candles lined every surface. Flames leaned toward Sam, each wick turning like a compass needle searching for true north.

Brother James moved along the outer wall. His hand pressed the stone, fingers testing its integrity. His jaw tightened. A soldier reading stress before it became rupture. His eyes flicked once to the glyph beneath Sam's shirt, then back to the wall.

Marie emerged from the apse.

She carried decades in every movement. Grace shaped from discipline. Her hands trembled slightly. Age near eighty. Skin thin enough to show light beneath it. A silver braid hung over her shoulder. Indigo habit marked with gold-thread spirals. Carpenter's hands. Callused. Built for work that left marks.

Her gaze reached the glyph through his shirt. Recognition struck her first. Then grief. Then resignation. The frequency she had heard once before in a place without time.

"Filius." Her voice caught. The next word trembled on her lips, a prayer mixed with confession. "Child of the Line."

Air shifted. The word carried apology.

The glyph pulsed once beneath Sam's sternum. Violet-gold. Smoke settled in the hush that followed.

On the altar lay a reliquary. Inside, a shard of bone. Joan of Arc. The relic vibrated faintly. Sam felt it in his molars. Next to it stood a lightning-etched chalice and an iron key. All hummed in restrained harmony.

Brother James approached the altar. He touched each relic. Adjusted the chalice three degrees clockwise. Reading coordinates burned into memory.

Four candles stood in a perfect square. Two lamps hung above. Two sconces glowed on the floor. Six points. The geometry waited for the seventh.

When the glyph pulsed again, Marie shifted the chalice aside. She knew lightning amplified fire.

She led him past the altar into a small chamber.

A brass vial sat beside three censers and a bronze font. The air smelled of iron and old prayers.

Marie opened the vial. Dust rose in a thin stream. Myrrh. Moonflower. Relic ash. Salt ground to starlight. She flicked it into the air. Particles hung suspended.

Sam inhaled.

Light threaded through his lungs. Cold. Sharp. Electric burn scrubbing from the inside out. Static crackled along his ribs with the taste of winter storms and metal. Teeth ached. Copper bled into iron on his tongue.

The censers ignited without flame. Myrrh. Juniper. Red salt. Magnetite. Smoke rose white-gold, streaked with green filaments. Symbols formed in the air. Dissolved a moment later.

"Respira, et tace," Marie said. Breathe, and be silent.

She began the breath cycles. Two seconds in. Two held. Two out. Two empty. Her fingers counted with liturgical precision. The pattern moved through him like rotating wheels. Air flowed clockwise on the inhale, counter-clockwise on the exhale. The rhythm felt older than lungs. Older than blood.

Fourth cycle. His breath caught. Lost the count.

Marie lifted a hand. Held it until he found the rhythm again. Her knuckles whitened. A memory flickered behind her eyes. A hand on her own shoulder once. A voice calling her name. She steadied him without a word.

The glyph folded inward. Gold veins dimmed. Light sank deeper. Roots seeking depth. Sam's eyes shifted back to gray-green. Like deep water beneath a winter sky.

Geometry rose around him.

Two interlocked pyramids. One ascending with fire. One descending with shadow. Both spinning in opposite directions. Wheels within wheels. Frequencies made visible. Latin letters curved along edges. Hebrew script intertwined. Symbols older than either. Circuitry carved from the first stories spoken into the world. The structure held him steady. Not summoning. Not binding. Aligning him between worlds without burning him apart.

Ten cycles passed. At the end, Sam whispered a sound. Not a word. Something deeper.

Marie's pupils reflected the spinning geometry. Her voice faltered once. A crack in bedrock.

"Chariots of light always return to their source."

She moved to the bronze font. Water lay black as winter midnight. She pricked his finger with a silver needle. One drop fell.

Violet flame rippled across the surface. The scent of copper and distant storms lifted with it.

"See yourself," she said. "No more. No less."

Sam leaned over the water.

At first his reflection appeared normal. Exhausted. Pale. Shoulders carrying weight too old for him.

The surface shifted.

A man in linen robes looked back. Halo of clean, sterile light. Kneelers whispered. Their hands reached for him. The reflection smiled with gentle emptiness.

"Let them worship," it said. "It keeps them safe."

Breath stayed steady.

Water warped.

Ash-black armor formed next. A glass crown of jagged edges. A burning city behind it. Collapse and flame. This version stood untouched. Eyes cold.

"Rule them before they ruin it again."

Sam's hands trembled. He pressed them against his thighs. Breath steady.

Water churned.

A scarred version knelt amid bodies. Lips moved with a whisper only Sam knew.

"You already chose this," the broken reflection said. "You chose survival over love. You will do it again."

The surface flickered, as if the water itself recoiled from the truth it carried.

Breath wavered. He forced it back into rhythm.

The water darkened.

A hollow version appeared last. A transparent chest. Empty space where heart and lungs should be. Light passed through it without resistance. A warning. A cost.

It raised its hand. Mouth moved in silence.

Breath stayed steady. Barely.

The mirror rippled. Broke. Light rose in thin streams. Dissolved into air.

The water cleared. His face returned. Human. Tired. Present.

Marie's hands trembled. Not with awe. With dread.

Every candle died.

Darkness slammed into the room. Total. No shapes. No edges. Air grew cold enough to burn. Sound muffled into nothing.

A voice rose from the black.

"He shall give His angels charge over thee."

Street-preacher cadence. Smith's emissary. Distorted. Wrong.

"He shall cover thee with His fea-"

The word fractured. Consonants dissolved. Meaning melted into white noise. The voice carried no breath. No body. Not a presence. A signal. A probe sent down a conduit older than scripture.

Cold wrapped his chest. Crushed inward. The glyph wanted to ignite. Burn back the dark. Burn everything.

Brother James moved through the dark without hesitation. His hand trailed the wall. The cross at his wrist pulled toward the center like a compass dragged by unseen force.

Heat crawled up Sam's throat. Copper on his tongue. His hands glowed faint gold beneath the skin. Fire begged release.

The voice in the dark laughed. Pressure tightened.

Marie stepped back. Brother James reached for the cross at his neck.

So easy. Let fire burn. Cleanse everything. Erase hurt. Erase weight.

Salt cracked beneath Sam's feet.

His mother's face. Not memory. Presence. If he burned now, she vanished forever.

"I trust the silence," he whispered.

The words cut his throat like broken glass.

Light guttered in his hands. Died. The glyph pulsed once. Furious. Contained itself.

Minutes stretched.

A single candle relit. Blue. Steady.

Another followed, gold.

One by one, the flames returned. Colors shifting like dawn through stained glass.

Cold lifted. Pressure eased.

Marie exhaled. Not relief. Duty swallowing fear.

"Right hand on the glyph," she said. "Left above it."

For one breath she hesitated, the way someone touches the cradle of a weapon they swore never to use again.

Sam obeyed. His palm flattened over his chest.

"Three circles. Counter-clockwise."

He moved slow. On the third circle, something inside clicked. A memory of sound before names.

Marie lifted a beeswax seal. Amber disk carved with a spiral and cross inside a triangle. Forbidden law. Her hand shook. She pressed it to his chest. Direct contact.

Heat flared. Sunk. The seal fused into skin.

"Not again," she whispered. Prayer or promise.

Brother James closed the salt circle with reverence. When it sealed, the air snapped. Frequency vanished. Ley lines severed. Silence deeper than absence.

Sam reached inward. Nothing answered.

Marie stepped back. Breath unsteady.

"I can no longer feel you."

Softer. To herself. "Perhaps this time it will be enough."

Brother James heard the tone. He had heard it once in Kandahar when the sky opened wrong.

"The bloodline's Smoke walks free," he said. He did not know it was codename. He spoke truth written into him years ago.

Sam pressed a hand to his chest. The glyph throbbed inward, boxed behind beeswax and salt.

Beneath his feet, faint scorch lines formed. Six points. A star visible only from above. Geometry marked the stone. Waiting.

A vision struck him. Not his.

Desert sand. Endless night. Inanna's voice singing while chains cut her wrists. Grief older than cities. Fire she refused to abandon.

Marie staggered. She felt it too. She crossed herself by reflex. Hands shaking.

The vision vanished.

Marie walked him to the threshold. Bronze doors opened to fog thicker than before. Bells tolled through the mist.

She touched his shoulder briefly. "The seal will hold. Until you break it. And you will."

She pressed a small cloth bundle into his palm. Warm. Three objects inside. He pocketed it without opening.

"When that day comes," she said, "find the catacombs beneath Lyon."

No explanation. Prophecy did not need one.

Sam stepped outside. Air tasted metallic. Sharp as stone against a blade.

Somewhere in the city, a hum rose. Searching. Casting wide for a signal that no longer existed.

Sam paused at the gate. Fog wrapped around him like a second skin.

He walked forward. Mist swallowed him.

At the bottom of the steps, Brother James paused. He nodded to the veteran. Guardian to guardian.

The veteran's eyes flashed amber once. Faded.

By the time the bells finished tolling, the square stood empty. Only the veteran remained. Blanket pulled tight. His gaze followed the fog where Sam vanished.

Across the city, something stopped listening.

The hum that tracked Sam since birth fell silent.

Not because he vanished.

Because he no longer played their note.

For the first time since birth, the world had to find him without a map.

## Chapter 19

# Signal and Smoke

Rain beaded clung to the iron lattice on the rooftop.

Cavendish crouched low, breath steady, the heavy glass resonator balanced in his hand. The tungsten thread inside glowed a dull amber, sputtered, then died.

Dead air.

The gauge needle dropped to zero. No resonance. No trace of the subject's hum.

He tapped his iron receiver against his throat. "Subject's signal has gone cold."

Static answered. A voice followed. Clean. Surgical. "My Liege."

Then a second breath that did not belong to human lungs. "Then find what killed the note."

Cavendish adjusted his grip. Jaw set. He angled the resonator toward Chartres Street where fog swallowed everything down to the cobblestones.

In his coat pocket something vibrated. Not the primary scanner. The void coil. A heavy glass tube wrapped in iron bands, humming uneasily against his hip. It was not tracking a signal. It was tracking the hole where one used to be.

His hand pressed the pocket still. The coil steadied to a low, nervous whine.

On the street below, Sam turned a corner.

Fog swirled around him. His shirt hung torn at the shoulder. Dried blood traced his collar. Gold veins pulsed faint under the skin, shifting like molten metal behind a thin sheet of flesh.

He moved because stopping meant remembering. Remembering meant the Vault, and the Vault still lived under his ribs.

Krishtan walked at his side. Slow. Loose. Eyes reading everything the fog tried to hide.

"Sam-eee... dat bundle weighin' down your pocket." Krishtan shook his head, a small, sharp movement. "It hummin' heavy, cher. Smell like Sister Marie tryin' to bottle Sunday mornin' and lightnin' in de same jar."

Sam said nothing. Language had not settled back into him yet.

On the bench near the cathedral steps, the veteran stirred. Blanket tight around his shoulders. His eyes lifted once. Amber flashed. Not reflection. Recognition.

"The blood remembers," he said. Voice scraping bone.

Fog licked the wrought iron fences. Lamps flickered violet. The Quarter felt older than it had an hour ago.

Something reached for Sam from beneath the street. A hum that once hunted him, now lost in its own confusion. The seal kept him hidden. The silence itself became a signal.

The air bent.

Traffic noise stretched thin. Footsteps muffled. A shadow pooled between the lamps, rose upright, stepped through the veil of condensation.

It stood seven feet tall. Humanoid in outline. Limbs wrong. Joints bending past human tolerance. Skin translucent with molten copper veins scrolling like code.

Its head twitched. Jaw flexed open, then snapped shut like something remembering a shape from a book it had never read.

Time lagged a half second behind its body.

The relics in Sam's pocket flared hot. He stumbled, hand pressed against his sternum.

The creature's head tilted toward him. Drawn not by presence but by absence. By the void where Sam's frequency had once burned bright.

Krishtan drew his revolver. Short barrel. Iron worn smooth. Rounds carved with candle-script older than the city.

His voice deepened, dropping into the river-bottom rhythm of the rootworker. "Feu san fèn, pa touche mwen." Fire without end, do not touch me.

He fired.

The report cracked too loud for the street. Salt and sigil tore through the creature's torso. Copper light erupted in fractal bursts. It screamed in a frequency that made Sam's teeth ache.

The seal dampened ignition. Power wanted to answer. Could not.

The creature folded in on itself. Reassembled. Ribs knitting. Face reforming from static.

Sam reached for the glyph. Nothing answered.

His panic opened the bundle.

The cloth at his hip heated. Geometry ripped through the air. Two pyramids interlocked. One of fire rising. One of shadow descending. Wheels within wheels.

Light spun outward. The creature lunged and hit the field.

It ignited bright white. No time to scream. Ash scattered like metallic snow.

The geometry collapsed back into the bundle. Sam's knees buckled. Krishtan caught him under the arm and steadied him.

"Signal tryin' t' go home, Sam-eee," Krishtan murmured. "Seal tell it no."

Sam's breath came shallow. Something inside him hollowed further. Silence pressed deeper than absence. A wound shaped like a missing voice.

On the rooftop, Cavendish saw the flare. Saw it die. The void coil flared hot against his hip. Then went dark again.

He spoke into the receiver. "Brief ignition. Wrong frequency. Something blocked the read."

My Liege answered. "He is leaving New Orleans."

"Yes, sir."

"Then follow the silence."

The receiver clicked off. Cavendish slid the glass resonator into his coat and stepped back from the roof's edge.

Below, fog dragged low across Jackson Square.

Sam and Krishtan walked.

The air seemed to grow teeth. The light bent at its edges. Sam felt pressure behind the seal, a soft thrum like someone knocking inside bone.

Krishtan lifted a hand. Stopped Sam with a touch. "You hear dat, cher? Dat quiet dat hurt da air?"

"I don't hear anything."

"Dat da problem."

Something brushed the space behind him.

He turned.

Inanna stood near the curb. Not formed. Not fully here. Fog building her shape from the inside out. She looked at him. Not with eyes. With recognition.

A scent hit him hard.

Cedar smoke rising from damp Oklahoma grass. Pond water warming under dawn. And beneath it, the sharp, sweet bite of hickory smoke from My Place BBQ.

The smell of a booth in Muskogee. The sauce his grandfather used to wipe from his chin with a laugh that made the whole world feel safe.

Memory and place braided into one pull.

Home.

His ribs loosened. His breath tightened. His chest knew where to go before thought returned.

Krishtan watched the flicker in Sam's posture. Saw the decision land. "You headin' back to de mud, Sam-eee."

"Yes."

"Good."

He poured a line of rum on the street for the ancestors, then handed Sam a cup. "Road ain't kind to us, cher. But you walk it anyway."

They drank. Rum burned clean.

Inanna drifted backward. Fog folded around her. Her hand lowered in a silent command. Not a direction. A recognition of the path already chosen.

Krishtan leaned in, the smell of rum and ozone on his breath.

He gripped Sam's shoulder. "Anyting reachin' for yo now gon' meet my blood first. Dat all you need know. Marisol know her part. Da old ones do too."

He gestured toward the Quarter, fog curling around wrought iron like memory.

"Dis city? She older dan gods who forgot how t' bleed. Built on graves an' old promises."

He released him slow.

"So go do what you gotta do, cher. And hear dis part clear. When you gone, I'ma hold da line my blood been sharpenin' for since da first Dauvee foot touched dis shore."

Sam stepped into the street. He did not vanish. He walked.

Past the cathedral. Past the benches. Past the square waiting for sunrise.

Krishtan watched until the fog swallowed him.

"Walk good, cousin," he said, voice low. "Silence walkin' wid you now."

He lifted his cup to the empty air where she had stood. Then turned toward the Quarter. Toward the war he had always known was coming.

Across three states the cousins woke at the same moment.

Luke shot upright in bed. Chest tight. Air filled with the smell of campfire and hickory smoke. "Sam," he whispered.

Across the hall Audrey jolted awake with the taste of pond water in her mouth. She shoved off blankets and ran to the window.

In Aunt Kay's guest room Celine rolled over and pressed a hand to her inner left wrist. Her skin warmed for no reason she understood. "Sam," she breathed. Not fear. Recognition.

Miles away Loyd paused mid-step in his dark kitchen, hand braced on the counter. Something old moved through him. Slow. Heavy. "Boy's home," he murmured. "Finally."

Not one of them knew how. All of them felt it.

The moment Sam stepped out of New Orleans the bond inside the bloodline woke like something stretching in its sleep.

A tether pulled tight across the dark, dragging them all toward the same fire.

Fog thickened around Sam as he walked. Streetlights blurred to soft gold. His breath hitched once. The seal throbbed under his shirt.

The world leaned.

A pulse ran up his spine. Warm. Familiar.

Oklahoma air slid under New Orleans fog like two tides crossing. Cedar. Pond water. Horses.

The ground trembled.

His vision blurred.

Something opened beneath him.

A light not meant for streets or cities rose through the soles of his boots.

He reached for balance.

Missed.

The street fell away.

Chapter 20

# Gooseneck Morning

Palms hit wet grass. Cold shock. World finished drawing itself.

Sky purple. Bleeding into blue. Firepit stones black. Last summer's cookouts. Past the barn, tin roof catching first light.

Lungs pulled Oklahoma air. Tasted wrong. Too clean. No salt. No Quarter heat pressing down. Earth. Dew. Cattle smell drifting from across the road.

Knelt there. Trying to remember breathing. Before the fold. Before the heat took him. His mind couldn't map distance. New Orleans to here. Just heat. Pressure.

Inanna's hand at shoulder. Tethering.

Stood behind him in fog. Felt warmth. Turned. Already fading. Translucent as breath on glass. Making sure his heart remembered rhythm.

Eyes met his. The seal under his torn shirt pulsed once.

Gone. Retreating. Air shimmered. Hum stayed in bones.

Pushed up. Knees buckled. Locked. Blood dried at neck. Ash streaked across his forehead. Patterns deliberate. Random. Hoodie hanging in shreds. Undershirt torn at shoulder. Knee exposed. Skin raw. Left bootlace melted to eyelet.

Looked like he crawled out of a burning building.

Crickets started up. Hesitant.

Took a step. Porch light cut through fog. Yellow. Steady. Past the barn, pond caught dawn.

Under his feet, ley line pulsed wrong. Faint. Fractured.

Across the field, on the porch of the small guest house, Luke stopped.

Coffee cup halfway to mouth. He didn't see the light first. He smelled it.

Ozone. Burnt copper. The sharp, electric scent of air being torn open.

He dropped the cup. Ceramic shattered. He was running before the shards hit the wood.

Barefoot. Cutting across the yard. Straight through the brush where the gravel road bent away in an L. Wet stems slapped his shins. Roots grabbed at his feet.

He stumbled once, caught himself, kept running.

Fog parted ahead. The field glowed faint at its edges.

Sam stood near the firepit. Wrecked. Clothes torn to hell. Skin streaked with grime. Dried blood. Thing on chest glowing steady through fabric. Gold lines tracing patterns through scar tissue.

Luke skidded to a stop. Chest heaving. "Sam."

Head turned slow. "Luke."

Crossed distance. Grabbed him. Arms locking around shoulders. Body trembled. Forehead dropped against Luke's shoulder.

Pulled back. Saw it better. New Orleans hadn't just marked him. Changed him.

"Man. You look like hell."

Mouth twitched. "Beignets might've been..." Stopped. Shook head. "Can't tell when."

"Where's your phone?"

"Don't know. Burned maybe. Can't..." Eyes lost focus. "There was fire."

"Your car?"

"New Orleans." Words flat.

Studied him. "You folded here?"

"Yeah."

"Alone?"

Hesitated. Eyes flicked past shoulder. Shimmer fading in fog. "Something like that."

Felt it then. Echo. Not Sam. Something older.

Clapped shoulder. "Come on. Audrey's inside."

Back door of the main house banged open.

Audrey. Rinsing mugs. Glow caught eye. Window. Field shimmered. Figure took shape near firepit.

She knew.

Mugs hit counter. Shoved through screen door. Socks. Oversized flannel. Braid coming loose.

Audrey slid to a halt in the wet grass.

Clothes shredded. Skin marked. Ash. Blood. One eye swollen.

"Sam." Voice cracked. "What on earth? You look like you got rode hard and put up wet."

"Audrey."

Pulled him into hug. Hands checking shoulders. Ribs. Winced when she pressed near chest.

"Sorry." Pulled back. Eyes caught on glow beneath shirt. Stayed there. "What is—"

"It's a long..." Swayed. Luke caught elbow.

"Coffee first," Luke said.

Looped arm through his. Walked him toward house. Skin gray in porch light.

Inside. Smelled of coffee. Biscuits. Hal at stove. Undershirt. Pajama pants. Spatula in hand.

"Blessed be, Sam!" Set spatula down. Crossed kitchen. "When did you..." Grinned. "I swear the house IQ just shot up ten points."

Hug quick. Real.

Managed tired smile. "Sorry for just—"

"Just what?" Luke snorted. Pouring coffee. "Man, I've been calling you for days."

"Phone's gone." Wrapped hands around mug. "Everything's been..." Stopped. Couldn't finish.

Audrey pulled out chair. "Sit."

Sat.

Moved to counter. Loading plate. Biscuits. Sausage. Eggs steaming.

Stared at food.

"Eat."

Picked up fork. First bite tasted like salt. Butter. Body remembered hunger. Ate without stopping. Barely tasting.

Hal leaned against counter. Watching. "You okay, Sam?"

Swallowed. Nodded. Words wouldn't work yet.

Luke pulled up chair. "Mom's gonna want to see you."

"And Uncle Loyd called her," he added. "Said he's driving here."

*Loyd.*

Throat closed. Set fork down. Hands wouldn't stop shaking. Stared at table. Last time he saw his uncle. Grandma's funeral. Standing at back. Leaving before reception. No goodbye. Eyes burned. Blinked hard. Jaw locked. Turned toward window. Before face cracked.

Audrey's hand found shoulder.

Kitchen quiet. Refrigerator hum.

"Tomorrow morning," Luke said. Voice softer. "Mom said he sounded different."

Nodded. Couldn't trust voice.

Window. Dawn spreading across pasture. Turning fog bright.

Hal glanced at clock. "I gotta get ready for work." Looked at Sam. "You staying put?"

"Not going anywhere."

"Good." Squeezed shoulder.

Movement upstairs. Water running. Dresser drawers. Hal back down. Water plant work uniform. Plate finished. Staring into second cup.

Grabbed thermos. Keys. Paused at door. Looked one more time. Left. Truck started. Gravel crunched. Pulled away.

Luke stood. "I'm calling Mom."

Stepped onto porch. Phone. Voice low. Urgent. Audrey refilled coffee. Sat down across.

"You scared us."

"I know."

"Luke's been calling for days."

"Phone burned in..." Stopped. Memory fractured. Pieces missing. "There was a fire. Hex. I think I..." Shook head. "Can't remember all of it."

Didn't push.

Luke came back. "Mom's on her way. Be here in thirty minutes."

Nodded. Eyelids heavy. Adrenaline draining out.

"When's the last time you slept?"

Tried to count backward. Couldn't. Days had no edges. "Don't know."

"You need to lie down."

"After Kay gets here."

"Sam..."

"I'm fine." Head nodding forward. Caught himself. Blinked hard.

Audrey stood. "Guest room's ready. Clean sheets. Bathroom attached."

Wanted to argue. Body shutting down.

Kay's car pulled up twenty minutes later. Door slam. Quick steps. Screen door banged open. Purse on shoulder. Keys in hand.

Stopped.

Sam stood. Her face complicated. Relief. Fear. Twisted together. Crossed in three steps. Hug lasted too long.

"Sammy." Voice cracked. "You scared us to death."

Held onto her. Smelled like her house. Perfume worn since he was little. Ten years old again.

Pulled back. Hands to face. Checking. Eyes caught on glow beneath torn shirt. Went wide. Reached toward it. Stopped. Hand hovering.

Body changed. Tension rising. Breathing shifted.

"It's okay, Aunt Kay." Caught her hand. "I'm fine. I'll share everything later. All of us together."

Nodded. Eyes kept going back to seal. Working behind them. Memory. Recognition.

Swayed.

Luke caught elbow. "You need rest."

"Yeah." Looked at Kay. "Grandma's baked beans tonight?"

Blinked. Question pulled her back. "Sure, honey. Of course."

"With..." Voice thick. "The way she used to make them."

Eyes watered. "Yeah. Exactly like that."

"Good." Turned toward hallway. Stopped. "Thanks for coming."

"Always."

Audrey walked him to guest room. "Bathroom's through there. Towels in the cabinet."

Nodded. Left. Door closed.

Stood in middle of room. Trying to remember what came next. Shoes. Sat on bed. Pulled off boots. Left one melted lace. Sole coming apart. Set them by door. Lay back. Still in torn clothes.

Pillow best thing ever touched.

Sleep took him.

Kitchen. Kay sat gripping her mug with both hands. Luke and Audrey watched.

"What is it?" Luke asked.

Shook head. "That mark on his chest."

"You know what it is?"

"I don't know. But my mother..." Stopped. "She told me things when I was little. About the family. Why we had to remember certain sayings. Symbols." Looked at them. "I thought it was just stories."

Audrey leaned forward. "What kind of stories?"

"Later." Set down mug. "When Sam can tell us himself." Stood. "I'm going with you to get him clothes. And we need groceries for tonight."

Luke grabbed keys. "What else besides beans?"

"Charlie's chicken," Kay said. "The bucket. And everything for pink stuff."

Quiet for a second. "For Sam."

"Yeah," Kay said quietly.

Audrey set down mug. "He's too thin. Did you see him? His face is all hollowed out." Worry only Oklahoma women get. Someone they love not eating right. "I'm making pasta salad. And cookies. The chocolate chip ones he used to steal off the cooling rack when he was little."

Nodded. "He needs fattening up."

"Way too thin," Luke agreed. Felt it when he hugged Sam. All bones and angles. Muscle gone.

"We'll get him right," Audrey said. Not hope. Promise.

"Let's go."

Headed for door. Kay paused. Pulled out phone.

Sam's here. He's okay. Looks rough, but he's home. See you in the morning.

Three dots appeared immediately.

Thank God. Driving straight through. Be there by 7 AM.

Pocketed phone. Followed Luke to truck.

Woke to late-day golden light slanting through blinds. Didn't know where he was. Then came back. Gooseneck. Home.

Sat up slow. Body ached everywhere. Different than before. Less damage. More exhaustion. Work done.

Stood. Bathroom door caught eye.

Counter. Folded clothes. Black jeans. Creased from package. Plain black shirt. New boots. Fresh laces. Hoodie. Picked it up.

More in closet. Stacked on shelf. Enough for a week.

Oklahoma Sooners. Zip up. *Boomer Sooner* across front in crimson.

Got everything right. Sizes. Colors. Held hoodie to face. Smelled new.

Turned on shower. Stripped off New Orleans clothes. Hot water swirled brown down the drain. Ash. Blood. Hand to seal on chest. Gold lines raised slightly. Warm. Traced them.

Mirror. Saw full pattern first time. Language. Circuitry burned through scar tissue. Traced lines with finger. Collarbone to sternum. Pulsed faint beneath touch. Warm. Alive. Not ink. Him now. Skin. Blood. Heartbeat.

Didn't know if he could ever take it off. Wasn't sure he'd want to.

Dried off. Dressed. Everything fit. Boots solid. Hoodie soft. Zipped halfway.

Looked like Sam again. Just Sam.

Found Aunt Kay in kitchen. Working at stove. Turned.

"Feel better?"

"Yeah." Poured iced tea from pitcher. Leaned against counter. Looked at Aunt Kay. Baked beans. Grandma's way. Bacon. Brown sugar. Molasses. Mustard underneath. Like mashed potatoes.

Pushing down center with spoon. Butter lake. Could see hands working. Hear laugh. Trying to drink it straight.

"Thank you for the clothes." Paused. "And I was glad to see you didn't get me leopard bikini briefs like before."

Spoon stopped. Looked up. Grinned. "You used to wear those all the time, Sam."

"I was nine."

"Before that it was Underoos. Batman. Spider-Man. Whole set. Then you discovered the colorful bikini briefs. Wouldn't wear anything else."

Celine's voice carried from the living room. "Yeah, why leopard? That's weird, Sam."

Face went hot. "I was not right in the head back then." Looked at Aunt Kay. "And I don't think I am now, but I have changed and don't wear those horrid bloomers anymore."

Squeezed arm across bar. Smiling. "Luke picked most of it. I just made sure he got the sizes right. And yes, honey, I got you boxers and socks and everything you need. Plain black. No leopards."

Back to stirring beans. Sipped tea. Looked past her through window. Ridge rose in the distance. Late afternoon sun.

"Your uncle called while you were sleeping."

Stomach tightened. "What'd he say?"

"He'll be here in the morning. Around seven." Looked at him. "He sounded worried."

"I haven't seen him since..." Couldn't finish.

Set down spoon. Came around counter. Pulled Sam into hug. Hand on back of head. "I know, honey." Voice soft against shoulder. "He's been worried about you. Calls me sometimes to ask how you're doing."

Didn't know what to do with that.

Front door opened. Voices filled house. Celine's laugh. Luke's rumble. Audrey giving instructions. Bags rustling.

Celine came around corner. Library bag on shoulder. Stopped. Face lit up.

"Sam!"

Dropped everything. Hugged him hard. "You scared us half to death."

"I know. Sorry."

Pulled back. Looked him over. "You clean up nice. Luke did good."

"He did."

"I'm making pink stuff," Celine announced. "The good kind. Like Aunt Janet used to make."

Throat went tight. Nodded.

Patted shoulder. Headed for kitchen. "Where's the Cool Whip?"

Audrey came in. Grocery bags. "Fridge. Bottom shelf."

House filled with noise. Bucket of Charlie's chicken. Smell hit hard. Celine mixing Cool Whip. Pineapple. Cherries. Kay sliding beans into oven. Cutting fruit.

Watched them move around each other. Ease of long practice.

Hal came home at 5:30. Tie loosened. Grinned. "There he is. Thought you'd sleep till tomorrow."

"Almost did."

"Good. You needed it." Grabbed beer. Popped it open. Tossed one to Sam.

Caught it one-handed. Hal laughed. "Still got it."

Celine telling Audrey about library. Luke and Hal arguing about Sooners. Kay arranging dishes. Silverware. "Sam, honey, help me set the table?"

Kitchen warm. Loud. Chaotic.

Leaned against counter. Beer in hand. Something loosened in chest. Tight since New Orleans. Before that maybe. Since Janet died.

First time in years. Felt normal. Not Nexus. Not marked. Just Sam.

Ate around big table. Passing dishes. Talking over each other. Charlie's chicken perfect. Crispy. Salty. Way Grandpa used to bring it home on Sundays. Baked beans exactly right. Bacon on top.

Pink stuff came out. Looked away. Mother's favorite. Making him help back in Texas. Measuring Cool Whip. Teasing him about gangly hands. Laughing. Pecans scattering across counter.

Took a bite. Thirteen again. Mom's laugh. Hand on shoulder. World still whole.

Celine watching. Looked away fast. Nobody said anything. Just ate.

Cleared plates. Coffee. Moving slow. Full. Content. Sun going down.

Audrey set down mug. Looked at Sam. "Let's go out to the campfire." Gentle but firm. "You can tell us what's going on. And I want to know about that thing on your chest."

Nodded. Waiting for this.

Filed out. Firepit. Luke got it going. Pulled up chairs. Evening warm. Fireflies in grass.

Sat with back to house. Fire caught. Luke sat down. Watching him.

Opened mouth. Stopped. Looked past Audrey's shoulder. Shadows.

Inanna stood there. Translucent in dusk. Only he could see her. Nodded once.

Everyone turned. Saw nothing.

"Sam?" Audrey's voice sharp.

Looked back. Faces in firelight. Celine leaning forward. Eyes bright. Aunt Kay hands wrapped around mug. Worry lines deep. Luke calm. Alert. Audrey frowning. Impatient.

Sam took a breath.

# Chapter 21

# The Circle

Night settled deep.

Air cooled over the pasture. Cattle shifted against fence lines. Insects faded to a low, steady hiss. The fire in the ring of stones had burned down to coals and short tongues of flame.

Sam sat closest to it. Hoodie half-zipped. Heat on his face. Chill on his back.

Kay and Hal sat to his right. Audrey, Luke, and Celine rounded the circle. Half-moon of Howardsons around the fire.

No one spoke.

Questions hung between them. Static before lightning.

He watched the coals breathe. Orange. Red. Orange again. The pulse in his chest beat to that same rhythm. Had been since New Orleans. Maybe before. Maybe the hum had always been there and he was finally out of excuses not to hear it.

"Started in New Orleans," he said.

Voice came out smaller than it sounded in his head.

"With a mark. Wouldn't come off."

Five pairs of eyes lifted. Firelight caught them. Reflected back quiet, waiting.

"Rain," he said. "Preacher in a doorway. Some little church out past the Quarter. I was just walking. He stepped out like he had been waiting on me."

His fingers curled around the arms of the chair. Knuckles white.

"His eyes went black while I watched." He touched his throat. The memory made it tight. "Ink came out of his mouth. Not blood. Ink. Like someone tipped over a bottle inside him."

Celine leaned forward. "Ink?"

"Yeah." He swallowed. "He spoke a language I shouldn't understand. But I did. Every word. Asked where the Nexus was."

Kay squinted. "Nexus like the shampoo?"

The line tried to wear humor, but the sound behind it was wrong. Old recognition moving under the joke.

Sam looked down at his hands. Scar along the knuckle. He could still feel bone against bone.

"I hit him," he said. "Hard as I could. The way Grandpa taught me when I was small. Hit first or you don't get up."

The fire popped. No one moved.

"My word," Kay whispered.

"He got back up," Sam said. "Face wrong. Bones moving under the skin like something was trying to wear him. I ran."

He let out a breath that had been stuck in his chest a year.

"Went home. That night the mark burned into my chest. Felt like hours. Might have been seconds. Passed out. Woke up and it was there. Like it had been waiting on an excuse."

Luke's voice came low. "What mark, Sam?"

Sam's hand went to his sternum. The seal warmed under his palm, like it heard its own name.

"This one," he said. "I think."

"You think?" Audrey's tone sharpened. Scripture lived behind it, waiting its turn. "Sam, you either know or you don't."

"I know now." He kept his eyes on the coals. "Back then I just knew it was there and nothing could scrub it off."

He breathed once. Twice. Made himself keep talking.

"Friend texted me after. Krishtan Dauvee. Runs a shop in the Quarter. The Hex. I did tech work for him sometimes. He started calling me cousin. Said his people had been seeing me for years."

Kay's cup shifted in her hands. Porcelain clicked against her ring.

"Seeing you how?" Luke asked.

"In visions," Sam said. "Walking through fire. Standing in places they only go in dreams. They knew things I never told them. Knew I was marked before I knew what that meant."

"Visions," Audrey said. The word fell flat. Heavy.

"That is what they called it."

"Bible warns against false prophets," she said. "Signs and wonders from the enemy. People seeing things doesn't mean it's God."

"I know what the Bible says," he answered. "Sat in the same pews you did. Listened to the same sermons."

"I believe you." Celine said.

The sentence cut across the circle like a clean line.

Everyone looked at her. She did not look away.

"I believe you, Sam," she said again. "I don't know why. I just do."

Something loosened in his chest and hurt worse for it.

Luke nodded once. "Yeah. Me too."

Audrey's jaw tightened. Kay's eyes moved between them, weighing something, remembering something else.

"They took me to the cathedral," Sam said. "Krishtan and his cousin Marisol. St. Louis. Side chapel off the nave. Sister Marie and Brother James waited there."

He could still smell the wax. The stone. The faint bite of old incense ground into the floor.

"They did a ritual. I guess that's what you call it. Marisol drew something on the floor. Marie put a rosary on my chest. The light split. Not like a spotlight. Like somebody took scissors to reality and bent it."

Images flashed. The Vault. The thing in the stone. The first time his body unthreaded and rewove through a leyline.

"Burned through the skin," he said. "Through bone. Nothing left but current holding the pieces in place. I should have died. I didn't."

Hal cleared his throat. "Son, that sounds like you got into something serious Catholic folks didn't put in the brochure."

Sam let the corner of his mouth twitch. It died quick.

"People are hunting me," he said. "Sovereign Hope."

Hal snorted softly. "That big prosperity campus out by the highway? TV lights and fog machines folks?"

"They burn anyone like me," Sam said. "Anyone who can touch leylines."

Audrey flinched at the word.

"Leylines," she repeated. "That is witchcraft."

"Currents," Sam said. "Running under everything. Under the ground. Under us." He looked up. "Maybe it's all the same power and y'all just named it different."

"No power but God's power," Audrey said on reflex.

"Maybe that is what this is," he said.

The words dropped into the circle like a stone.

Audrey sat straighter. "Do not say that lightly, Sam."

"I'm saying it lightly," he answered. "I'm saying I do not know. That is the truth."

He drew a breath.

"I can feel them. The currents. When I am still. If I lean into it I can follow them. Sometimes the body goes with them. Folds. Ports. Whatever word you want."

Luke frowned. "Port. You mean teleport. Like you did this morning."

"I didn't decide to," Sam said. He stared at his hands again. The faint tremor there. "My body did. Same as it did when that thing came at me in New Orleans. The creature in the fog. By the cathedral. I didn't think. I panicked. Whatever Marie and Marisol did. Whatever was already in the blood. It answered before I could."

Kay whispered something under her breath. A phrase that did not belong to English. He had heard the echo of it in the cathedral. In Marie's tired eyes. It vanished as soon as it came.

"Hunters found me after the ritual," he said. "Krishtan was there. He helped. Stood between me and them like it was nothing."

The memory sharpened. Rum on the tongue. Ozone. The quiet promise in the man's eyes.

"He calls me cousin. Says his people and ours tied up farther back than anybody wrote down."

He exhaled.

"Next thing I remember clear is waking up in your field, Luke. Palms in the grass. Inanna's hand on my shoulder long enough to make sure my heart remembered what beating was."

Celine watched him the way someone watches the sky right before the storm hits. Open. Expectant. Ready.

Luke sat a little forward in his chair. Hands loose, but not relaxed. Audrey held herself as if something might break loose if she did not stay tight. Kay's lips moved in a silent pattern. Hal stared at Sam like a puzzle that should not exist but did.

Hal let out a breath. "Well. Either that's the craziest thing I ever heard or the Lord has a sense of humor way outside my pay grade."

The corner of Luke's mouth twitched. Tension cracked for half a second.

Audrey did not smile.

"You expect us to just take your word for all this?" she asked. The words vibrated between plea and accusation. "Show us, Sam. If this is real. If it's from God and not from..." She bit the rest off.

Not cruelty. Desperation.

Every eye turned back to him.

"Don't know if I can," he said. His voice wanted to break around it.

"You said you ported here," Audrey said. "You said you feel these currents. If this is truly of God, He would not ask us to walk blind. Test the spirits. Show us."

Celine reached toward him. Hand hovering. "You don't have to prove anything to anybody."

"Yes I do," he said. It came out harsher than he meant. He softened it. "To myself. As much as to you."

Luke shifted like he wanted to reach for him and did not. "Sam. You don't owe us a show."

"I owe you something," Sam said. He pushed himself to his feet. The world tilted. Fire blurred at the edges. "I dragged you into this without asking. Least I can do is not leave you in the dark."

He shrugged out of the hoodie. Warm air hit scarred skin. His fingers found the hem of his shirt. For a heartbeat he hesitated. Once it was seen there was no going back.

He lifted it.

Gold light spilled into the circle.

The seal blazed across his chest. Lines burned into scar tissue, not on top of it. Circuitry and language braided into each other. Spirals curling out from the center. Fine strokes anchoring the whole thing to bone. It pulsed with his heartbeat. Each throb sent a faint wave of heat across the clearing.

The air changed.

Kay gasped. Not church-Kay. Not Oklahoma aunt. The sound came from somewhere older. "No power but what is given."

The words came out in her mother's cadence. She froze like she heard it the same moment they did. Her hand went to her mouth.

Celine's breath hitched. She rose half out of her chair, eyes wide and wet, not in fear but in a bright, stunned kind of wonder.

Luke stepped toward him. One step. Then another. Drawn to the impossible thing on his cousin's chest.

Hal stood up slow. "Good Lord," he whispered. Not as a joke this time. As confession.

Audrey went white. Fingers digging into her knees. "That isn't possible."

"Scripture says nothing is impossible with God," Celine said softly.

Audrey snapped her head toward her. "Don't throw scripture at me like that, young lady."

"Then don't use it like a weapon," Celine answered.

The seal pulsed brighter. Responded to the heat in their voices.

The ground answered.

Sam's vision blurred. He was not pushing anything. He was trying to stay upright. The power did not feel like something he grabbed. It felt like something that had grabbed him a long time ago and was finally tired of pretending.

The hum rose in his bones.

Words scraped up his throat. Not English. Not anything he wanted. Syllables that felt like dragging a plow through stone. Ancient shapes of sound his conscious mind did not know but his blood did.

They tore out anyway.

The fire stilled.

Flames that had wavered in the breeze lifted straight up, stiff as if some invisible hand pinched them and pulled. Heat surged up his spine. The seal burned hotter. Not outward, inward, like it was soldering something in place.

The flames climbed. Five feet. Eight. Ten. Their edges turned blue.

"Sweet Jesus," Hal breathed. His voice broke on it.

Kay leaned forward in her chair. Her eyes went distant. Not in shock. In memory. Something in the sound of the rising hum pried at doors she had closed after her mother died.

Celine stood all the way. Hands out, fingers spread like she could feel the current in her palms. "Do you feel that?"

"Yeah," Luke said. His voice dropped. "In my teeth."

Audrey's lips moved. Prayer or curse. They sounded the same in that moment.

Birds lifted from the tree line at the property's edge. Dark shapes against a darker sky. No wingbeats reached them. The wind flattened. The night held its breath.

The fire was just the fuse.

The ward rose.

It was not a wall of light. No special effects. It came as pressure.

A ring expanding outward from Sam's body, pushing the air aside in a way no one could see but everyone could feel. Fifteen feet high, at least. Invisible. Humming at a pitch that threaded itself between thought and bone.

The circle of it snapped into place along the property lines. Past the garden. Past the ditch. Fence post to fence post. Oak at the north corner. The old well. Henderson's cattle pressed together on the far side of the fence as the vibration brushed them. They lowed once, uneasy, then settled.

Celine shivered. "That sound. Can you hear it?"

"Feel it," Luke said. "Like biting on tinfoil."

Audrey trembled. Her eyes shone too bright. "Sam..."

Outside the circle of protection, something else moved.

His awareness stretched without asking permission. It skimmed over highways and back roads, through hospital wards and alleys. Cold hands of intent. Sovereign Hope's hunters, sweeping outward from New Orleans. They did not know his name, but they knew the taste of what he was. Their devices listened for that old frequency.

They hit the edge of the ward and slid off like oil on glass. Their search patterns bent, paths nudged sideways by something they could not see and would not believe in if they did.

Sam did not know if he pushed them. Or if the leylines themselves, offended at being used as snares, decided to protect their new conduit.

The light from the seal dimmed.

His knees went out from under him.

Luke lunged and caught him before he hit the dirt. "I got you," he said, breath close and solid. "I got you, Sam."

Sam sucked in air. It scraped going in. The flames dropped back to a normal burn. Smoke drifted up like nothing had happened.

"What just happened?" he whispered.

No one answered for a moment.

Normal night sounds seeped in around the edges. A dog barked two houses over. Crickets started their song again. Henderson's cattle grumbled. The wind found its way through the trees.

The hum of the ward stayed. Softer. Like a second heartbeat buried under the first.

Hal walked slow to the edge of the firelight. Stopped halfway between the chairs and the dark. Put his hand out like a man feeling for a doorway in a cave.

His palm hit something that was not air.

His fingers flattened against it. He pushed. It pushed back just enough to let him know it was there.

He pulled his hand back. Looked at it. Then at Sam.

"Well," he said. "If that is the devil, he has a real interesting understanding of property lines."

Celine laughed once. Shaky. "Hal."

"I am just saying." He spread his hands. "Never read that part in Sunday school. Might have paid more attention."

Luke eased Sam back into the chair. Celine dropped to one knee beside him. Her hand rested on his forearm. Warm. Grounding. His pulse climbed toward hers and tried to match it.

Audrey stared at him as if she could see straight through his skin, through bone, to the thing beating underneath. Her hands shook.

"You really did that," she said.

He nodded. "Did not feel like I decided to." His throat scratched raw. "Felt like it decided to use me."

"Then who is using you?" Audrey demanded. Voice sharp with terror. "If that was not you, what was it? Because there are only two kingdoms, Sam. You know that. That is what we were taught."

"Don't know," he said. "That is the only answer I have right now."

"Not good enough," she whispered. But it sounded more like she meant it for the sky than for him.

Luke's hand tightened on his shoulder. "The heat was controlled. It did not burn the chairs. Did not jump the grass. Whatever it was, it knew what it was doing."

Kay had not taken her eyes off the dark beyond the fire. Her voice came low. "I heard it in my bones. Same as when my mama would hum under her breath in the kitchen. I never could catch the tune. Just the way the air felt around her when she did it." She blinked, pulled herself back. "That hum tonight felt like that. Same frequency."

Everyone turned to her.

She looked startled by her own words. "I don't know why I said that."

Sam did.

"The ward is still up," he said. The knowledge sat in him as simple as knowing his own name. "I can feel it. Property line to property line. Anything tries to come through, I think I will know."

"You think or you know?" Audrey asked. Hands digging into her knees again. "Hope is not a plan, Sam."

"Then call it hope for now," he said. "I'm not going to lie to you and pretend I have a manual for this. I don't. Body just did it. Like muscle memory for something I never learned."

The silence that followed was different than the one before. Less doubt. More fear. More possibility.

Something else stirred.

Luke's hand drifted to his upper back. Right between the shoulder blades. He pressed his shirt against the skin. Two curved lines burned there. Mirrored arcs. Like the roots of something that had been clipped off or hadn't dared to grow yet.

Celine traced her left wrist. An old faint shape there warmed. She frowned at it, then at Sam, then smiled like getting an inside joke she had not known she was part of.

Audrey shifted in her chair. Her hand went to her right ankle. A deep ache she had blamed on an old sprain flared hot, then settled into a steady thrum against the bone.

Kay watched them. She didn't check for a mark. She just rubbed her thumb against the handle of her mug, tracing the same spiral pattern Sam had on his chest, as if her hands remembered what her skin didn't need to carry.

"Can you teach us?" Celine asked. Her voice trembled, but it was not from fear. It was from standing on the edge of something and wanting to step over.

"Don't know how yet," Sam said. "Still trying to figure out how to survive it myself."

"Comforting," Hal said. His tone stayed gentle. "You sound like one of my old professors. 'We don't know how it works, but we're confident it does."

Kay watched Sam. There was something in her eyes now that had not been there in the kitchen. Not just worry. Recognition.

"Your uncle is going to see this in the morning," she said. "All of it. The mark. Maybe the ward if it is still up. You know how he is. He ran from this when Mama tried to show him. Slammed doors in her face." Her fingers tightened around her mug. "Wanted a normal life more than he wanted truth."

A shadow of Loyd, young and angry, crossed her face and was gone.

"Maybe I am done running," Sam said.

"Maybe he's scared you will do the same thing," Kay answered. "Maybe that's what has his voice shaking on the phone every time he calls me about you." Her gaze met his. "Silence takes people, Sammy. Takes whole families if you let it. He has lived in it a long time."

"How do you wall off something that does itself?" Sam asked. "I didn't build this. I am just the conduit that got volunteered."

Kay did not have an answer. She looked tired in a way that had nothing to do with the hour.

Audrey pushed herself to her feet. Her legs were unsteady. "This is real," she said. No more edge. Just stunned conviction. "Whatever else it is. It's real. We all saw it. Felt it."

"I think so," Sam said. "Unless I passed out in New Orleans and this is one long coma dream."

"Not funny," she said.

"Was not trying to be."

She looked at him for a long moment. "So what do we do?"

"Stand together," Celine said. The words came simple. Solid. "Whatever this is. We face it as a family. Like we should have been doing a long time ago."

Kay nodded. "She is right. Whatever is coming for him is coming for all of us one way or another. Might as well be ready to hit it as a pack instead of scattered."

Luke squeezed Sam's shoulder. "We'll figure it out. One thing at a time. You are not carrying this alone."

Hal sighed. "And we keep the coffee pot full. That part at least I can manage." He gave a small grin. "And maybe find a verse about glowing cousins somewhere in the back of the concordance."

The ward hummed under their feet. Not loud. Not intrusive. Just a steady low note that said: inside. Outside. Mine.

Something in Sam's chest finally let go. Not the seal. Deeper. A knot that had cinched down the day his mother died. Tightened with every funeral. Every loss. Every time he came back to Oklahoma and left again convinced he was fundamentally alone.

They stayed by the fire.

He told them what he could about the Vault. About the thing in stone. About the preacher. About the hospital hallway bending wrong. Left the parts his mind would not let him look at yet in the dark where they belonged, for now.

Audrey asked about Sovereign Hope. Who ran it. What they preached. Her questions sounded less like church and more like a woman considering a threat to her home.

Celine's questions came in bursts. What did the leyline feel like inside him. Could he hear anything when he ported. Did it feel like dying or like being born.

Luke's questions were surgical. Could the ward break. What would it take. Did Sam feel anything specific when the hunters bounced.

Hal mused aloud whether anyone else had ever written about things like this and who had buried those books.

Kay traced slow spirals on the side of her mug with her thumb. Old Velstra shapes. Howardson names. She did not seem aware she was doing it.

Stars wheeled overhead. Clear country sky. No city glow. The fire burned down to coals again.

Kay stood first. Chair scraping stone. "Let him rest," she said. The words carried more weight than just bedtime. "Morning is coming fast."

Audrey nodded. "I'm going to bed before my brain explodes." She looked at Sam. Her mouth opened. Closed. When she spoke it was simple. "Whatever you are now. You are still my cousin. We protect family. That has not changed."

Hal stood with her. "Come on, darlin'," he said to Audrey. "Before I start asking him to call down fire for the cookout."

He squeezed Sam's shoulder on his way past. "That was something, son. Still don't understand it. But it was something. Try not to do it in the kitchen."

Kay stepped close. Put her hand against his cheek. The touch grounded him more than the chair did.

"Sleeping in the guest room tonight," she said. "You three be careful walking back over to Luke's. Call if you feel anything go wrong. In your gut, not just out there."

Her eyes flicked up, like she could see the ward.

"We will talk more in the morning. When your uncle gets here."

Celine slung her bag over her shoulder. "I'm staying at Luke's. No way I'm missing whatever happens when Uncle Loyd sees that thing on your chest."

Luke huffed a laugh. "You say that like it is a movie premiere."

"Feels like one," she said.

They left the circle of light. Walked across the field. Dew soaked their shoes. The ward hummed under their steps, softer now, like a second heartbeat buried under the first.

"You really okay?" Luke asked.

"Don't know what I am," Sam said. The honesty tasted clean. "But I'm still here and that's something."

"Honest is better than pretending," Celine said. She bumped his arm with her elbow. "You glow a little. Did you know that?"

He snorted. "I am going back to bed."

Luke's house came into view. Squat against the treeline. Dark wood siding. Porch light off. The shape of it steadied something in him. Normal. Bills on the table. Work boots by the door. Life that had kept going without him.

"Couch or spare room?" Luke asked as he unlocked the door.

"Spare is fine," Sam said.

"Take the couch," Celine said. "I've slept on worse than a lumpy mattress."

Inside smelled of coffee grounds, old wood, machine oil. Luke flipped on a lamp. Soft yellow filled the living room.

"Bathroom down the hall," Luke said. "Clean towels under the sink."

Sam paused in the doorway of the spare room. Turned back.

"Luke," he said. "That thing I did tonight. The ward. The fire. I honestly don't know what I did."

Luke leaned against the frame across from him.

"That's what scares me," he said. "Not that you did it. That you didn't mean to."

He hesitated. The next words came low. "And I felt it. In my back. Right between the shoulders. When it went up. Like something woke up and stretched."

Celine nodded from the couch. "Same. In my wrist. For a second it was like remembering a song I never learned. I think it's in us too. Whatever this is. Just sleeping."

Sam's throat tightened. "Yeah."

Luke pushed off the frame. "All the more reason for us to stick together. Get some sleep. We'll handle tomorrow when it gets here."

Sam stepped into the spare room. Set the borrowed duffel down. Went to the window. The main house lights were going off one by one. Kitchen. Living room. Guest room where Kay moved behind the curtains.

The seal pulsed once. Not flaring. Just a single firm beat, like a knock answered.

Far off, thunder rolled.

He looked up. The sky stayed clear. No clouds. No storm. The sound came anyway. A low, deliberate rumble at the edge of hearing. It did not feel like weather. It felt like a signal.

It came again. His heartbeat climbed up to match it without asking.

He closed his eyes. Let the vibration wash through instead of pushing it away. The ward hummed under the property like a wire strung tight between anchors.

Across the field, four other heartbeats answered. Faint, then strong.

Kay. Audrey. Luke. Celine.

For one long breath they all beat in the same rhythm. Like chords on the same note.

Then the moment passed. Heartbeats fell back into their own patterns. The ward settled into its low patient hum.

Family safe inside its lines. For now.

Morning coming fast.

Whatever his body decided to do without consulting him, he would not face it alone anymore.

The circuit was open.

Alive.

# Chapter 22

# The Morning After

Audrey woke in her bedroom at Gooseneck Bend.

The numbers on the bedside clock glowed green. 4:44 a.m.

She stared at the glowing numbers, wondering if they meant anything or if her mind was clawing after patterns she had no business chasing.

Beside her, Hal breathed slow and steady. Dead asleep. Worn out from the weight of what he had witnessed last night.

But Audrey could not sleep.

Something hummed beneath the house.

She felt it through the mattress. Through the floorboards. Through the quiet between breaths. Not loud. Not threatening. Just present. Constant. As if the house had grown a heartbeat it never carried before yesterday.

She slipped out of bed. Pulled on her robe.

The hallway sat in soft dark. Pre-dawn light leaked through the kitchen window. Her bare feet found the cold boards. She moved toward the counter. Filled the reservoir. Measured grounds. Pressed the button. The machine sputtered awake. The smell of coffee began to bloom through the kitchen, warm and steady.

It did nothing for the rising knot in her chest.

The protection Sam raised still thrummed under her soles.

Audrey pressed both palms to the counter. Closed her eyes.

She no longer knew how to pray. Words would not come. Verses she had memorized when she was small felt too narrow to carry what last night had shown her. They cracked under the weight of it.

A sound came from the living room.

Kay sat in the recliner by the window, wrapped in the old afghan Grandma had crocheted years before Audrey was born. She stared forward. Awake. Still. She had not slept.

"Mom?"

Kay turned her head slowly. In the dim light she looked younger than seventy-three. Or older. Audrey could not tell.

"Couldn't sleep either?" Kay's voice came out thin. Soft. Like it hurt to use it.

Audrey crossed and sat on the couch. Pulled her knees up under her robe. "What Sam did last night. I can still sense it."

"I know," Kay said. She drew the afghan closer. "Like the ground remembering something it had no business forgetting."

They sat in the quiet. The coffee maker hissed behind them. The dark held the world still.

"You ever dream something so old it feels like it wasn't yours to begin with?" Audrey asked.

Kay's eyes found hers. "I used to. Then I learned not to remember."

"Why?"

"Because remembering made it real." Kay twisted the yarn at the blanket's edge. "And if it was real, then I had to do something about it. Had to choose."

"And you didn't want to choose."

"I wanted normal." Kay's voice broke. "I wanted my kids to be normal. I wanted to go to church and make casseroles and fret about ordinary things. That isn't terrible."

Audrey thought of her art classes, her small jobs, the neat life she had built to hold herself together after Aunt Janet died. The way she tried to make Sam normal too. Tried to sand him into a shape that would not draw attention.

"It isn't terrible," Audrey said softly. "Most people want normal. I did too. But after what I saw last night, I don't know if that's even possible anymore."

Kay looked down at the blanket. "Normal was never ours to keep. I just didn't want you to know that."

The coffee finished. Audrey poured two cups. Added cream to Kay's the way she had since childhood. Brought them back. Placed one in her mother's hands.

They drank in silence. Holding the same dawn for the first time in years. Two women who had spent a lifetime not looking at the truth. Now looking.

Sam woke in the spare room of Luke's house.

The seal burned beneath his sternum. Not pain. Not warning. Demand.

A heartbeat approaching the property line. Familiar without memory. Distant without being far.

He pressed a palm to his chest.

Across the field, morning shifted at the main house.

Luke stood in the doorway with two coffees. "You feel it too?"

"Yeah." Sam swung his legs to the floor. The pulse sharpened under his skin. "Someone's coming."

"Family?"

Celine appeared behind Luke. Dressed. Awake. Watchful.

"Uncle Loyd," Sam said.

He pulled on jeans and a shirt. Skipped the shoes.

The connection he raised last night stirred in answer to the approaching bloodline. Not acting on its own. Just echoing recognition. Fear that had been passed down. The long shadow of a man who ran from the same thing now waking in Sam.

"We should go," Luke said.

They crossed the field. Mist clung to their legs. The October air bit their throats. The ward parted cleanly for them. Kay and Audrey waited inside the house. Awake. Braced.

Loyd neared Gooseneck Bend when the radio cracked to static.

He had driven straight from Florida through the night, stopping only for gas and coffee. The highway gave him nothing but miles and thoughts he wished he could outrun.

The radio worked fine until he reached the ten-mile mark. Then the hissing began. Voices that weren't voices bleeding through the speakers. He shut it off and drove in silence.

Now, on the narrow road toward Audrey's place, pressure spread across his chest. Like a hand pressing down. Like the air thickened and carried weight it shouldn't.

His knuckles went white on the wheel.

He slowed the truck.

A white panel van sat parked on the shoulder, fifty yards from the driveway. No decals. No plates he could see. Tinted windows reflecting the pale morning like mirrors.

Loyd's stomach dropped.

He recognized that kind of van. Sovereign Hope didn't label their surveillance vehicles.

He drove past slow. Watched it through the rearview. It did not follow. Did not shift. Just watched.

When he turned into Audrey's driveway, the pressure doubled.

His skin prickled. Hair lifted on both arms. Something old and familiar pressed against him. Like a language he once knew but had forgotten how to speak.

He parked. Killed the engine. Sat while the weight in his chest refused to lift.

The house waited in the dark. Porch. Brick foundation. Windows he had never seen, yet something in them watched back.

But the ground beneath it thrummed.

He stepped out of the truck and staggered once. The sensation hit harder now. The field around the house felt alive in a way he did not want to name.

He steadied himself against the door. Looked down the road out of habit, scanning the tree line.

Nothing sat in Audrey's driveway. No van. No headlights. Just morning light and quiet.

But across the distant ridge near Luke's place, another white van idled where no vehicle should be, white against the treeline, half-hidden by brush. Watching from far enough that a normal man would miss it.

"Jesus Christ," he murmured.

The front door opened.

Kay stood wrapped in the afghan. When she looked at him, he saw their mother in her eyes. The same quiet certainty. The same way of seeing through people.

"Come inside," she said. "It's been too long."

Sam felt Loyd cross onto the property.

The seal flared. The connection he raised last night opened for the new heartbeat. Older. Carved by years of fear and denial.

They reached the porch. Audrey stood with a coffee mug held tight in both hands, shoulders tense despite the calm she tried to wear. She had been waiting for them the moment she saw the three of them crossing the field.

Sam scanned the treeline. The ridge beyond Luke's property pulled at him, a cold distortion in the air.

"Where's Uncle Loyd?" Sam asked.

"Inside," Audrey said. She watched him, confusion stirring behind her eyes. "What are you looking for? Uncle Loyd did the same thing when he got here."

Luke stepped up beside Sam, gaze following his line. Curious, alert.

Celine stopped a few feet back, studying the trees as if trying to see what Sam felt more than saw.

Sam didn't answer. The null pressure pressed again, faint but deliberate, sitting just past the boundary of the ward.

"Come on," he said. "Inside."

Luke and Celine followed him through the door.

The coffee smell couldn't cover what the room felt like.

Loyd sat at the table across from Kay. Both held their cups like anchors. Hal stood near the counter in work clothes. A man trying to be normal in a house that no longer was.

Loyd looked up. His gray eyes sharpened. He had Sam's grandfather's face. Same lines. Same weight.

"Well now," Loyd said. "You got the Howardson shoulders after all."

"Been a while," Sam answered.

Loyd nodded toward the window, jaw tight. "There's a van out on the county road. Just down from the driveway. Not sure for how long."

Kay lifted her head. "What van?"

"I have no idea how long that one's been sitting there," Loyd said. "But I had another one on me most of the trip. Kept its distance."

Kay frowned. "How do you know it was following you?"

Loyd let out a humorless breath. "Because, sis, the same damn vans have been tailing me for years. Never close enough to touch. Close enough to know."

Audrey froze at the stove. "You think it's them?"

"I don't think," Loyd said. "I know."

Luke planted himself behind Sam's chair. Celine took the window seat, watching the treeline with stillness that didn't belong to a teenager.

"That church," Loyd said. "Sovereign Hope. The one behind our house on Missouri Street."

Kay's breath hitched. "Yes."

"And the one near Hyde Park. Three blocks from where you moved."

The truth slid across their faces like dawn over still water. Slow, heavy, impossible to ignore.

"That isn't coincidence," Loyd said.

"No," Kay whispered. "No, I suppose not."

The air thickened.

Sam felt a pulse rise through his chest. Recognition. Blood answering blood. Loyd pressed a hand to his sternum as if something inside him had been struck. The lights flickered. The coffee maker sighed.

Heat climbed beneath Sam's shirt.

Loyd stared at him. "What's happening?"

"You're picking it up too," Sam said.

Audrey set platters down.

Biscuits. Gravy. Eggs. Sausage. A meal to hold the house together.

Hal moved beside her. Quiet. Steady.

Luke pulled up a chair next to Sam. Celine maintained watch at the window.

Kay pulled her chair close to her brother.

"Tell me what you remember," she said.

Loyd wrapped both hands around his cup. "Dad in the carport. Always carving symbols into wood. Said they were projects. They weren't."

Kay's eyes softened, unsure, searching old memories she had kept boxed up for decades. "Yes... I remember. But why, Loyd? Why would he do that?"

"And Mom," Loyd said. "The way she prayed. That language. Not Spanish. Not Latin. I tried researching it once. Nothing. Like it never existed."

Kay nodded slowly. "I looked too. Every trail I followed ended in nothing."

Everyone turned to Sam.

A word surfaced in his mind like something rising from deep water. It pressed against his tongue, heavy and familiar, asking to be spoken.

He swallowed it back. Not yet.

"Whatever they were doing," Sam said, "it's connected to what we carry now. I can feel that much."

The room stilled.

Audrey's voice cut through the silence. "How do you know that, Sam?"

Loyd exhaled. "Everywhere I moved, one of their churches showed up. Different names. Same symbol. Same rot underneath. I thought I was going crazy."

"You weren't," Kay said.

"They watched us," Loyd said. "Watched others like us. Families who didn't know what they carried."

Audrey slammed a spatula onto the counter. "Enough. They're a church. Not some shadow group."

Celine looked at Sam. "Show him."

Luke nodded. "Yeah. Show him."

Loyd frowned. "Show me what?"

A faint ringing pulsed in his damaged left ear. A frequency shaking something loose.

Sam stood. Lifted his shirt.

Light filled the kitchen. Gold circuitry moved under his skin like living metal. The seal pulsed once. Twice. The glow washed across every face.

Loyd froze. His hand tightened around the ceramic mug until his knuckles went white. Hot coffee sloshed over the rim, coating his fingers.

He didn't flinch.

He wiped the scalded skin against his jeans. A reflex. He didn't even look down.

"That pressure I felt," he whispered. "That was you."

Sam lowered his shirt. "It's the blood. Ours."

Loyd sat there, hand resting on his damp jeans, staring at the place where the light had been.

"No," Loyd said. "You can't."

"I didn't choose it," Sam said. "But it's here. And I need help."

Loyd shook his head. "I ran from this. Thirty years. Pretended it wasn't real."

"Running doesn't stop it," Sam said.

Luke turned. Lifted the back of his shirt.

Two faint crescents glowed between his shoulders.

Celine raised her wrist. A small spiral shimmered beneath her skin.

A pulse stirred in the room. Audrey's right ankle. Hidden. Denied. Awake.

She gripped the sink. Shoulders rigid. She didn't turn.

Five carriers. One resisting. One matriarch holding the center.

Silence deepened.

"All of you?" Loyd asked.

"Yes," Sam said.

Loyd looked toward Audrey. "Even you?"

A sharp throb hit her ankle. She ignored it. "I'm not part of this."

No one argued.

Loyd looked at Kay. "What did Mom say before I left?"

Kay swallowed. "She said the line would bend but never break. Said the circuit remembers even when we forget."

Loyd closed his eyes. "Thought she was losing her mind. She wasn't. She saw this coming."

Kay whispered, "No power but what's given." Tears rimmed her eyes. "She always knew."

The kitchen went still.

Outside, beyond fog and trees, the white van waited. Patient. Measuring what it could not understand.

Hal checked his watch. Stood. "Hate to break this up, but the plant doesn't care about bloodlines. Okies will riot without running water."

The tension loosened a fraction.

He shook Loyd's hand. "Stay as long as you need."

Audrey handed him his lunch sack. "Drive safe. Text me when you can."

Hal turned to Sam. Pulled him in. "Keep them safe."

"I will."

Hal nodded once. "Try not to blow anything up while I'm gone. Water pressure's bad enough."

A few brittle smiles moved through the room.

He stepped onto the porch. Straightened the crooked light fixture. Tested it once.

Kay watched him go. Hand pressed to her stomach. Grief rolled through the circuit hard enough to tighten Sam's chest.

Inside, the ward hummed.

Outside, the van waited.

# Chapter 23

# If the Mirrors Speak

The kitchen felt too quiet after Hal left.

Sam stood by the window, watching the empty driveway where Hal's truck had disappeared five minutes ago. The seal pulsed against his chest, counting the people left in the house and finding the number too small.

Kay sat at the table, turning her coffee cup between her palms. The ceramic was cold now, but her hands kept moving, waiting for something to make sense.

Loyd paced once from the table to the window, stopped, then sat heavily in the chair across from Kay. His legs wouldn't hold him anymore. Thirty years of running had weight, and it showed in the way his shoulders curved forward.

Audrey rinsed the same plate twice, water too hot, steam ghosting her face. She caught it before it slipped, breath snagging. Then she wiped the counter once, twice, again, until the rag squeaked.

"We should talk about what happens next," Luke said from the doorway.

Audrey turned and slammed the rag down.

"What happens next is we go back to our lives." She turned, hands dripping, eyes wide and frantic. "Sam figures out whatever this is on his own, and the rest of us stop pretending we're in some kind of supernatural drama."

Kay stood. "Audrey."

"No, Mom." Audrey grabbed her purse from the counter. "I love Sam. I do. But I can't do this. I can't sit here and pretend that what I saw last night makes any kind of sense. I have classes to teach. Bills to pay. I'm leaving."

She took a step toward the door.

A sharp heat spiked in her right ankle. Sudden. Warning. Like a wire pulled tight against the bone.

Audrey froze. Her hand hovered over the doorknob. She didn't turn it. Couldn't.

Kay reached for her bag on the counter, the gesture quiet and deliberate. Not magic, just a mother's instinct to do something, anything, when the air turned wrong.

She pulled out a small cream-colored envelope, yellowed at the edges. The paper looked old. Fragile. The words If The Mirrors Speak were written across the front in handwriting Sam didn't recognize but somehow knew.

"What's that?" Loyd asked.

"I don't know." Kay set the envelope on the table. "It was in the drawer with old bills and recipes. I've been through that drawer a hundred times, but I never saw it before. Not until this morning."

"When did you find it?" Sam moved closer to the table.

"Right after Celine was sleepwalked the other night." Kay looked at her daughter. "Something told me to look. And there it was, like it had been waiting."

Loyd let out a short laugh and rubbed his neck. "Can we ever just be normal?"

Audrey gave a dry smile, her hand dropping from the door. "Yes, let's do that. Pretend this never happened and move on."

"Please, Audrey." Kay's tone cut through the air. She turned to her brother. "What do you think it's about?"

Loyd sighed. "Only one way to find out."

Loyd opened the envelope carefully. A tarnished brass key slipped out first, heavy and old. Then he unfolded a sheet of paper and laid it flat on the table.

The page was blank.

"Well, that's not helpful," Kay said. "It's blank."

Sam leaned closer. The surface shimmered, light moving beneath still water. Shapes began to surface where no ink should exist. Curved lines, spirals, symbols his eyes knew before his mind could name them.

"No," Sam said quietly. "It's not."

Everyone turned toward him.

Kay frowned. "What do you see, Sam?"

"Letters," he said. "Not any alphabet I know. They're moving."

He reached for the paper. The moment his fingers touched it, the shapes flared to life.

Gold light spilled across the table, bright enough to pull everyone closer.

The symbols pulsed in rhythm with his heartbeat, the sound a low vibration that only Sam seemed to hear. Audrey hesitated by the door, then stepped back into the room as the light reached her.

A soft intake of breath came from Celine, still curled in the corner chair.

"It's glowing." Her voice barely carried.

Audrey stepped away from the doorway and looked at each of them.

Sam's vision tightened. The symbols folded into order, forming words that didn't belong to any alphabet he knew. Yet the meaning came through, clear and heavy, as the seal under his shirt began to hum.

"Aethrien," he said.

The word changed the air. The kitchen wavered. Not the room. The timeline.

Reality peeled back. He wasn't remembering. He was witnessing.

His grandmother sat at a table in a dim room. Paper before her, blank and waiting. She leaned close and whispered into it, each breath shaping the light around her. When she opened her eyes, they burned white, the glow spilling down her cheeks.

"Our cabin," she said, her voice carrying something ancient. "Protect what's here. You will know when you see it. Trust only the blood."

The light dimmed. Her eyes cleared. The paper carried words no one else could read.

Sam blinked, the kitchen snapping back into focus. His hand steadied on the table.

"Velstra," he said, the words slipping out before he realized he'd spoken.

"Velstra?" Loyd frowned. "That was Mom's maiden name."

Kay's gaze flicked toward Sam. "You've never heard that word, have you?"

"No," he said. "But I understand it."

He began to read. His voice dropped. The air tightened around him.

"When the mirror speaks what the mouth cannot, the carrier knows the threshold from the frame. Five lights, one dark, the circuit bends toward morning. What was buried breathes beneath the lake's second skin. Trust the eyes that read what isn't written. The line holds when memory fails the flesh."

The light climbed with each phrase. Shadows moved across the walls in rhythm.

Sam paused. The final line flared, hotter than the rest.

Signed in breath, not ink: "P. H."

The glow collapsed. The glyphs dissolved into blank paper, leaving only cream-colored stillness. The air cooled, darkened, as if a presence had withdrawn.

Sam swayed. He caught himself against the table edge. A sharp pain spiked behind his eyes. The physical cost of reading words meant for blood, not ink.

Kay covered her mouth, eyes shining. "My mother. She wrote that."

Loyd stared at the table. "What does it mean?"

Sam looked at them. Their faces were blank with confusion. They'd heard the words but not the meaning behind them.

He did. The pulse beneath his ribs answered each line like a heartbeat remembering its source.

"The mirrors," he murmured. "They're waiting."

No one moved. The paper lay pale and harmless between them, but the air itself felt awake, listening.

"They knew," Sam said quietly. "Grandma and Grandpa knew all of this was coming."

In the doorway between the kitchen and living room, Audrey's right ankle flared.

Heat climbed her leg, sharp and sudden. Her breath caught. Anxiety raced through her chest like current through wire. She pressed a hand to the doorframe to steady herself.

She closed her eyes. For a heartbeat the kitchen dimmed, and a memory pressed through.

Seven years old again, sitting cross-legged on the living-room carpet while her father read from the Bible. Whispering prayers she didn't understand to a God who felt too big for the room.

She opened her eyes. Sam was watching her.

Audrey quickly turned away, crossing into the living room.

Behind her, the mirror above the mantle seemed to darken. Not a trick of the light. A silent nod to the heat rising in her blood.

"The lake," Kay said, looking at Loyd. "She means Tenkiller."

Loyd nodded slowly. "The cabin. It has to be."

"What cabin?" Sam picked up the brass key. It was warm in his palm.

"Our parents' place," Kay said. "Out by Lake Tenkiller. Back in the woods. They built it when we were kids. Said it was for family vacations, but..." She glanced at her brother.

Loyd's jaw tightened. "We hardly ever went. Mostly they went alone. Said they were getting the place ready, but it was never ready. Always carving, measuring, sealing cracks that weren't there."

Kay's voice dropped, more to herself than anyone else. "They said it was so the house wouldn't sink. But that never made sense."

Sam turned the key in his hand. The brass caught the morning light and threw it back gold.

"The seal knows the road. It's already pulling us."

From the living room, Audrey's voice came flat. "Of course it is."

"Yes." Sam met Aunt Kay's eyes. "That's exactly what we need to do."

Silence settled over the kitchen. Outside, birds called through the thin morning air. The house went still. Waiting.

The walls gathered the quiet like breath held in stone.

Kay stood. "Then we pack."

## Chapter 24

# The Road to Tenkiller



GOOSENECK BEND

They dismantled the house with quiet purpose.

Sam crossed the field to grab his duffel from Luke's place. Luke loaded his truck with tools that might matter. Rope. Tarps. A toolbox that had seen decades of use.

Celine packed with the same precision she had shown since the ward rose. Her hands moved with a sharp intent, choosing only what the house would not mourn losing.

Kay moved through the house gathering what still felt solid. Her mother's notebook. A bundle of dried herbs wrapped in cloth. The envelope with the letter and key. At the hallway closet she reached for a cardboard box on the top shelf. Its weight surprised her. Dust covered the lid. She carried it to the truck and set it gently in the bed under the cover.

Inside were photographs. Birth certificates. Marriage licenses. A family threaded through decades. Beneath them, wrapped in old towels, lay things her parents had kept without explanation. A carved wooden disc marked with symbols. A small copper bowl warm even in shadow. A strip of fabric stitched in lines that looked almost like words.

She felt the weight of them like a past that had been waiting for her hands.

In Loyd's truck, the box hummed. Not loud. Not obvious. But a vibration that traveled through cardboard and towels.

Loyd stood by his truck, loading his go-bag into the back seat. His hand brushed the box in the bed. The vibration moved up his arm. Faint. Foreign. But stronger than it should have been. Stronger than it had been yesterday.

He was changing. Getting stronger. Proximity to Sam woke something that had slept for thirty years.

He didn't realize it. Sam didn't realize it. But the bloodline did.

Inside, Audrey packed slowly. Choosing. Rejecting. Choosing again. Everything carried impossible weight. She moved like someone preparing for exile.

Outside, engines idled. Ready. Kay waited by the porch, arms crossed against the chill.

Celine jogged back inside. "We're ready."

Audrey stood at the dresser, still holding a sweater she hadn't decided on.

"Take what matters," Celine said, crossing the room to help. She folded two shirts, zipped the bag, and pressed it into her mother's hands. "That's enough."

Audrey nodded. Silent. Her eyes glassy.

Minutes later they stepped outside. Two trucks waited in the drive. Engines low and patient.

Luke's truck sat first in line. Large and work-worn. Paint faded but engine solid. Loyd's white pickup idled behind it. Kay's box of family relics tucked safely beneath the bed cover.

Sam moved toward Luke's truck. Celine followed without a word. Luke climbed into the driver's seat. Turned the key.

Audrey stopped between the two vehicles. Her bag hung at her side. She looked at Luke's truck where Sam stood by the passenger door. Then turned and walked to Loyd's pickup. She opened the back door. Hesitated. Climbed in without speaking.

Sam watched her go. The seal under his shirt pulsed once. Sharp enough that he pressed his hand against it. He said nothing. Only slid into his seat and closed the door.

Across the yard, Kay settled into the front of Loyd's truck. The sound of her door closing echoed through the quiet morning.

Gravel shifted.

They pulled out of the driveway in a slow line. Luke's truck leading. The morning sun hung low, painting the world in gold and amber. Sam watched his mother's house shrink in the side mirror until trees swallowed it whole.

The protection he'd raised began to fade.

It didn't vanish all at once. The ward faded the way radio static fades. Softer mile by mile. Sam could feel it through the seal. A thread stretching thinner with every turn of the road.

They drove south toward the lake.

Inside Loyd's truck, silence held for the first twenty miles.

Kay watched trees blur past her window. Audrey sat in the back with her arms crossed. Eyes fixed on the forest. Loyd kept both hands on the wheel. Jaw set tight.

"You remember the cabin?" Kay asked.

Loyd nodded. "Haven't been there since I was seventeen. Fifty-five years."

"Dad took us every spring," Kay said. "Said he was checking the pipes. But he always brought that old tackle box full of tools."

"I caught him once," Loyd said. "Carving under the porch beam. He told me it was to keep the house from sinking. But it wasn't that kind of mark at all."

Kay turned to look at him. "What kind was it?"

"The kind that looked written in a language no one speaks anymore." His voice tightened. "Same kind Sam just read."

Audrey's hand found the door handle. Her knuckles whitened against the plastic. She stared out the window. As if the trees might give her an answer. They didn't.

"He used to hum while he worked," Kay said quietly. "At least I thought it was humming. Now I think it was some kind of chant. He said he learned it from the old Masons. The ones who met under the Shriner hall. Only the bloodline families were allowed to hear it."

"Maybe he was," Loyd said.

The words lingered between them. Audrey's grip on the door handle tightened.

In Luke's truck, the hum of the tires filled the silence. Sam could still feel the ward thinning. A faint pull behind his ribs.

"You okay?" Luke asked.

"The protection," Sam said, pressing a hand to his chest. "It's fading. Mile by mile."

Celine leaned forward. "You can still feel it?"

"Barely. It knows we're not coming back. Not for a while."

Luke's hands tightened on the wheel. "The house will stay safe?"

"It should," Sam said. "It's bound to my blood. Even if I stop feeling it, it should hold."

The words felt thin the moment he said them. The seal under his shirt flickered in reply. Caught between two heartbeats that refused to sync.

They drove in silence. The forest grew denser on both sides. Signal bars dropped away. Houses gave way to trees.

"How's Audrey doing?" Celine asked quietly.

Luke glanced in the rearview mirror at Loyd's truck behind them. "Not good. She's fighting this the whole way."

"She'll come around," Sam said.

Celine's tone stayed even. "You sure about that?"

"She's here," Sam said. "She could have stayed behind. That means something."

Luke's voice was low. "You think she feels like she had a choice?"

Sam looked out the window. Trees blurred into color. "We all have a choice. Do something or don't. I chose to do something. So will she."

Celine's question came softer. "What if she doesn't?"

"Then she doesn't." Sam rested a hand on his chest where the seal pulsed faintly. "I didn't understand before. I think I do now. At least a little."

Luke waited.

"When we're born, we're memory-wiped," Sam said. The words felt borrowed. As if read from somewhere deep inside him. "We have to live without remembering what came before. To rediscover who we are on our own."

Luke frowned. "Wiped from who?"

"I'm still working on that."

Sam reached into his pocket and felt the small pouch Sister Marie had given him. The objects inside pulsed softly against his palm. The seal answered each relic with a faint heat, as if it recognized something he had not learned to name.

He looked ahead. The road narrowing through shadow and light.

"Whatever is hunting us wants us to forget. To go blind again. To stay drunk on nothingness."

The forest swallowed the sound of the engine. The silence that followed felt older than the road itself.

Celine's voice sharpened. "Hunting?"

Sam turned in his seat to look at her. "Yeah. It's going to get worse. I can feel it. And Loyd's right. Sovereign Hope is part of it."

The air thickened as if something unseen tested the edge of his thoughts, probing for a door it no longer owned.

"Part of what?"

"Whatever's been watching bloodline families for generations. Tracking us. Waiting for the marks to wake up." Sam's grip tightened around the pouch in his hand. "I've seen things. Heard things. Maybe felt things that still don't make sense. But I'm trusting the unknown now. Following what the seal shows me."

Celine leaned forward. "I wonder how Audrey's doing."

Luke checked the mirror. "Not good. She'll fight this. She's deep in the church and has been for a long time. She's probably still mad at me for stopping attendance years ago."

"Well, we all did," Celine said. "It wasn't bad. Just... something felt off. Hard to explain."

Sam glanced at them both. "She will break before she opens. Some awaken through wounds."

Luke kept his eyes on the road. The weight of Sam's words settled in the cab like dust that refused to fall.

"You scared?" he asked.

Sam pressed a hand to his chest. The seal pulsed beneath it. Steady. Alive.

"Terrified. They're following us. Sovereign Hope knows where I am. They just can't get into my head anymore. That makes them more dangerous. I don't know when it hits."

"You will," Celine said softly.

Sam hoped she was right.

## THE GROCERY STOP

Kay stepped out of the station holding a folded map. "We should get food. There's a grocery store about ten miles up. Might be the last one before we lose civilization completely."

Luke nodded. "Good idea. We don't know what we'll find at the cabin."

They drove the ten miles in convoy and pulled into a small grocery store lot. The building hadn't changed since the seventies.

Inside, fluorescent lights buzzed overhead. The air smelled of linoleum and cold meat.

Without speaking, they split up. Luke grabbed a cart and went toward camping supplies. Kay turned down the aisle for canned goods. Celine drifted toward snacks.

Audrey moved in the opposite direction from Sam. Deliberate. She passed through produce. Picking apples. Lettuce. Tomatoes. Careful efficiency. As if planning for an ordinary week.

Sam found Luke near the back. "What are we getting?"

"Enough for a week, maybe more." Luke set lighter fluid in the cart. Then a bundle of firewood and cleaning supplies. "We don't know what shape the cabin's in. Better to have too much than not enough."

"Firewood's smart," Sam said. "If the power's out, we'll need it."

He looked at the cart. Thinking of the lake and the silence waiting there.

"Grab extra water too. If the pipes froze or the well's bad, we'll be glad we did."

Luke nodded and reached for a case. "Good call."

They worked quickly. Each had a cart. Celine filled hers with snacks and treats. Loyd stacked bread, lunch meat, cheese, and Dr Peppers in his. Kay gathered soup, chili ingredients, and spices. Moving with quiet purpose. Luke and Sam shared a cart, loading the heavy essentials.

Audrey moved down the opposite aisle. Filling her cart with ingredients for crockpot meals that could last the week. She set a new crockpot in the cart.

"If there isn't one at the cabin, we'll leave it for next time," she said quietly. "Crockpots are family."

Kay joined Luke and Sam near the back. "I got toilet paper," she said, setting four packs in the cart. "And more cleaning supplies. If we're gonna be there a while, we'll need them."

Celine rolled up beside them, her cart rattling. "I found marshmallows, chocolate bars, and graham crackers. For s'mores. By the fire."

Loyd grinned, pushing his cart closer. "Burgers, hotdogs, and enough Dr Pepper to keep us alive."

Celine smiled. "I like your style, Uncle Loyd."

They met at the register a few minutes later. Audrey appeared from the far aisle, her cart stacked high with bottled water. Eight cases in all.

"We'll need water," she said. Her tone was flat and practical. She wouldn't meet Sam's eyes.

Sam stepped forward before anyone could reach for their wallets. "I've got it," he said. "You've all looked out for me long enough. Let me cover this one."

No one argued.

The cashier rang them up without comment. Small town. Families stocked up for lake trips all the time. Nothing about this looked unusual.

Outside, as they loaded the trucks, Audrey's phone buzzed. She looked down. A brief relief crossed her face, thin and unsteady, as if the message steadied her and unsettled her in the same breath.

"Hal made it to work," she said, typing a reply. A single heart emoji. Simple. Normal.

Aunt Kay touched her daughter's arm. "He'll be alright."

Audrey nodded but did not answer.

They finished loading and climbed into their trucks.

The ward thinned until he could feel the air pressing against his ribs without its shield. The tether pulled thin, not breaking, waiting for him to choose which world claimed him.

# Chapter 25

# **The Arrival**

The forest swallowed the road.

Pavement ended. Gravel began. Houses disappeared. Canopy closed overhead. Dimming afternoon to twilight. Copper and gray.

Behind Loyd's truck, Luke maintained distance. Sam riding shotgun, Celine in back. Tactical spacing.

Radio crackled. "Fifteen miles. No signal. Dark."

In Loyd's truck, Kay stared ahead, Audrey quiet behind her.

Forest thickened. Trunks wide. Moss-choked. Air cooled. Scent of water. Soil. Deep earth remembering itself.

The seal pulsed. Hard. Recognition.

Then the snap.

Ward let go.

Not a fade. A break. Tether cut. Tension cable snapping miles away.

Sam gasped. Air punched from lungs. Heat flashed across chest. Bright. Sudden. Then gone.

House answered once. A heartbeat caught between worlds. Then gone.

Truck ahead swerved. Brake lights flared. Tires kicked up gravel as Loyd fought to keep it on the road. The radio cracked.

In back, Celine jerked forward. "You feel that?"

"Like a hammer," Luke said.

Sam said, "Yeah. It's going to get worse.

Luke's eyes flicked to mirrors. Scanning threats. "Loyd's slow-ing."

Sam exhaled. Long. Slow. "It's done."

Luke glanced over. "Ward?"

"Released."

No explanation. No metaphysics. Just the weight of the sev-ering. Hollow ache where protection used to hum.

"We keep moving," Luke said.

Trucks rolled forward. Road narrowed. Darkness pressed in.

Last mile. Silence heavier than before.

Gravel turned to dirt. Trees pressed closer. Ancient. Watchful. Sunlight broke through in ribbons. Slid across the hood like solid things. Undergrowth wild. Uncut.

Cabin appeared.

Stood in clearing. Small. Still. Wood gray with time. Solid. Porch leaned slightly. Windows dark. Waiting.

Beneath stillness, vibration.

Not the ward. Older. Deeper. Ground itself humming. Low frequency finding pulse. Matching it.

Loyd stopped. Engine cut.

Luke pulled alongside. Silence filled the clearing.

Sam stepped out.

Air shifted. Heavy. Alive. Seal responded. Steady rhythm. Skin prickled.

Loyd climbed out. Froze. "Ground's shifting under us."

Celine crouched. Palm to dirt. "Real."

Sam stayed quiet. Pulse grew stronger. Syncing.

Audrey stepped down. Boot touched earth.

She gasped and grabbed the door frame, knuckles white, weight jerking off her right leg as if she had stepped on a live wire. She did not look down.

She held still until the flare thinned.

Kay watched them.

Sam. Loyd. Celine. Audrey.

All reacting. All feeling the hum.

She stayed where she was, watching their faces change. Sam caught it on hers. The confusion. The silence.

While the rest of them shifted against the vibration, Kay stood perfectly still. No flinch. No bracing. As if the frequency stopped at her skin.

"It's the house," Loyd said, voice rough.

They turned.

The building stood perfect. Untouched by rot.

Audrey crossed her arms. Shivering. Stared at the wood. Afraid to look away.

Sam stepped forward. Brass key warm in pocket. Pouch humming against palm. Didn't know what waited beyond the door.

Sam reached the porch.

Light above the door quivered.

Everyone stopped.

Bulb glowed faint. Then bright. Steady. Gold light spilled across boards. Painting long shadows.

No switch touched. No power line connected.

House woke up.

Sam looked back. Kay pale. Loyd trembling. Celine entranced. Luke tight. Muscle coiled.

Audrey staring at the light. Hand pressed to chest.

Sam turned. Climbed steps. Key slid into lock. Belonged there.

Click.

Door opened.

Air rushed out. Dust. Rain. Metal. Charged air. Scent of a storm held in stasis for fifty years.

Sam crossed threshold.

Others followed.

Audrey's house was a home. This was a battery.

# Chapter 26

# The First Resonance

The main room spread before them. Furniture draped in sheets. Table centered under beams carved with symbols that shifted when you looked away. Walls marked in language and geometry both.

Air closed in, heavy as breath held too long.

Luke froze inside the threshold. Nostrils flared. Head turning. Tracking.

"You smell that?"

Sam nodded. "The orchard."

"Stronger in here." Luke moved deeper. Following scent like physical weight. "Rot and fruit." Jaw clenched. "But there's no orchard out here."

Hands fisted. Skin crawling.

Rotten. The smell underneath the sweet. Like meat left too long. Poison dressed as food.

His body knew before his mind caught up.

Celine touched his arm. "Luke..."

He jerked free. Pulse hammering. "It's everywhere." Stomach lurching. "How are you not smelling this?"

Audrey stood frozen. Eyes distant.

Flashes.

Fifth-wheel. Metal walls.

Arkansas.

Compound.

The first Sovereign Hope mission site.

She was twelve. Luke eight. Celine five.

Dad building. Always building. Churches for the mission. Teacher and builder. That's what the deacon said. Sell everything. Give it to the church.

The slogan painted on barn walls. The phrase still buried in her bones: *planted to obey*.

Apples for breakfast. Lunch. Dinner. Rows of trees. Fundraising, they said.

Sweet at first. Then wrong. Stomach cramping. Everyone eats. Everyone works.

Luke stopped drawing. Just worked. Eight years old lifting boxes.

Audrey stopped reading. Forgot what she loved. Twelve years old scrubbing floors.

But there was a moment. Before the forgetting. Dad lifting her onto his shoulders to see the land. "We're building something beautiful here, Audrey. Something that matters." His voice warm. Believing. She'd believed too.

Then Celine screaming. Five years old. Puking. Body rejecting the apples. Sick for days. Mom switched to boiling apples, hiding tomatoes in pots. Watching Celine turn gray.

Something wrong she couldn't name then. Can't name now.

Just apples and working and forgetting, Celine sick and metal walls, shame.

The smell filled the cabin. Overripe. Fermented.

Her ankle throbbed. Pulse matching rhythm buried in bone.

"Audrey?" Luke's voice pulled her back.

Audrey blinked. Room snapping into focus. "I'm fine."

Hands shaking. She pressed them against the wall.

Kay moved into routine. Bags to counter. Food sorted. Cabinets opened, dusty dishes wiped. Space made. Order built.

Loyd crossed to the refrigerator. Avocado green. Pulled the handle.

Door sucked open.

Interior light flickered. Empty shelves except the door.

Six-pack of glass bottles. Dr Pepper. Five remaining. Blue labels unmistakable.

Loyd stared. Smiled. Decades in that smile.

"Well look at what we have here." Pulled one out. Glass cold. "Dad's DP."

Drawer beneath. Bottle opener right in front. Worn smooth. Popped the cap. Metal clinked.

Tilted it back. Half gone. Eyes closed when he lowered it.

"Loyd, what are you doing?" Kay turned. "No telling how old those are."

Eyes opened. "Ahhhh. Now that's the way a DP should taste." Held bottle to light. "Check it out, sis. Blue label. Says 10-2-4."

Old formula. Before lawsuits. Before corn syrup.

Kay shook her head. "If you get sick, brother, you're on your own."

Sam laughed. First ease since arrival. "I'll have one too, Uncle."

Loyd grinned. "Atta boy." Handed Sam bottle and opener. Hands touched. Warm. Real.

Sam positioned opener. Loyd showed him when he was twelve. Cap hissed off.

Drank. Carbonation bit. Sweet but not too sweet. The way soda used to taste. Glass thick. Heavy. Made to last.

Celine stepped forward. "Me too."

Loyd handed her one. "There you go, kiddo."

She popped the cap. Drank. Eyes widened. "It tastes different."

"Better," Loyd said. "Real sugar."

Kay turned back to unpacking. But warmth underneath the complaint. "Great. Now everyone's going to get sick and we only have one bathroom here."

They stood drinking vintage Dr Pepper their grandfather left waiting. Like he'd known. Like he'd prepared for this exact moment.

Bottles sweated in their hands. Cold. Real. Proof someone had loved them before they knew they needed it.

Kay filled a pot. Tap sputtered brown, then clear. Can opener from drawer. Tomato soup.

Audrey crossed to the rotary phone. Yellow plastic. Dust thick.

Picked it up.

Dial tone. Thin.

Fingers shook dialing. Rotary clicked back. Patient. Mechanical.

One ring. Two. Three.

"Hey, sweetheart, you made it?" Hal's voice faint but clear.

Relief flooded her. "Yeah. We're here." Walls breathing around her. "It's different than I remember."

Hum rose in the walls. Low. Building.

Hal's voice distorted. Words stretching. "Everything okay? You sound...."

Line fractured.

Voices layered. Not words. Frequencies through copper wire. Musical and wrong. Teeth aching. Ankle throbbing.

Audrey yanked the receiver back. "Hal? Hal!"

Silence.

Dial tone. Steady. Empty.

She hung up. Plastic clicked.

Hum stopped.

Hand wouldn't release the phone. Breathing fast. Seeing Hal at the plant. Alone. Air turning toxic.

Luke crossed to her. "What happened?"

"The line." Throat closing. She looked at him. "I need him here. All of us together."

Luke nodded. "I'll drive back to Gooseneck. Grab a bag. Meet Hal halfway or get him and call him on the way."

"No." Kay turned from the stove. "We stay together."

"Hal needs to be here." Voice breaking. "I can't. Not without him." Couldn't finish.

Kay looked at her daughter. Fear naked on her face. Luke standing ready.

Exhaled slowly. "How long?"

"Three hours. Maybe four." Luke grabbed keys. "Back in a jiffy."

Kay nodded once. Agreement without peace.

Audrey grabbed her jacket. "I'm going."

Celine started to follow. Kay caught her arm. "You stay."

Celine looked between them. Torn.

"Go," Kay said. "Be careful. Come back."

They left. Engines. Gravel. Taillights into trees.

Cabin felt bigger. Emptier.

Sam stood by the hearth. Stone fireplace Charles built. Mortar perfect. Each stone fitted.

He knelt at the threshold. Iron nails driven at precise angles through the doorframe. Not random. Deliberate. Old method. Templar protection against passage of hostile intent.

His fingers traced one. Cold. Slightly magnetic.

Rug in front. Corner curled. Small imperfection.

Sam stopped. Looked.

The cabin showed him intention. Pointing.

Touched the corner. Felt the pull.

Not yet.

Stood. Turned.

Loyd moved to the window. "You see that?"

Sam joined him. At the treeline, moonlight caught shimmer. Heat rising but wrong. Moving in circles.

Loyd looked as far as he could see and then out through the dusty window. "What is it?"

Sam said quietly. "Boundary." The seal pulsed confirmation. "Field locked when we entered."

Loyd pressed palm to glass. Watched shimmer pulse. His fingers found the window frame. Copper wire woven through the joint. Thin. Almost invisible. But there.

Hair rose on his arms. The hairs on the back of his neck lifting. Static electricity gathering there. The air itself charged with something older than voltage.

He looked at Sam. Said nothing.

Sam nodded.

Loyd pulled his hand back. Rubbed his arms. "Dad built this for a reason."

"Built it for this," Sam said.

Silence. Two men recognizing protection that shouldn't exist.

Kay set bowls down. Chipped ceramic. Ladled soup. Steam rising.

"You need to eat."

Sam sat. Looked at the bowl. Throat closed. Body rejecting.

Celine touched hers, then pushed the bowl away. "I can't swallow."

Kay's shoulders dropped. She looked defeated.

"It's good, Aunt Kay," Sam said.

"I know." She smiled warmly at Sam.

Wind circled outside. Cabin hummed inside.

Seal pulsed beneath Sam's shirt. Matching walls. Matching ground.

They sat around the table. Bowls pushed aside. Empty bottles. Glass cold against wood.

Loyd looked at Sam. Really looked. The look that sees. Measures. Recognizes.

"You turned out good."

Throat tightening. "Yeah?"

"Yeah." Loyd leaned back. Wood creaked. "Better than good. Strong. You didn't break."

Sam didn't know how to name all the ways it had broken him. All the wrong ways he'd put himself back together before learning right.

"I never said thanks." Voice rough. "You taught me to drive when nobody would."

Eyes softening. "Course I remember."

"Passenger seat. I'd hold the wheel. You worked pedals." Hands moving like gripping leather. "I was twelve?"

"Eight, maybe nine?" Loyd paused. "Your mom had just. Well. You needed something."

After the funeral. Hospital smell wouldn't wash off. House too quiet. Silence meant thinking. Thinking meant drowning.

Loyd showed up with the truck. Going for a drive. Two hours to Tulsa. Sam in passenger seat. Teaching coordination without saying the word.

"You said you were taking a nap once. Said I was in control. Don't crash. Then closed your eyes."

Loyd laughed. Deep. Genuine. Filled the cabin. "I did."

"You didn't really sleep?"

"My eyes were closed?"

"Yes."

Smile carrying mischief. "Well, I was keeping lookout with the other eye."

Sam shook his head. Smiling despite everything. "You know there's no way anyone would do that now? Eleven-year-old on a highway?"

"Probably right." Warmth. Memory. Pride. "But it made you a great driver."

"It did." Voice catching. "Made me feel like I could control something."

Didn't finish. Didn't need to.

Loyd reached across. Gripped Sam's shoulder. Heavy. Steady. "You were never the problem, Sam."

Nodded. Couldn't speak.

"Your daddy. He loved you. But didn't know how without making it hurt. That's on him." Grip tightened. "Your mama did her best. But some people aren't built for this world. Too tender."

Eyes burning.

"But you got the best of both. Daddy's strength without his anger. Mama's gentleness without her fear. Took the good. Left the poison." Picked up empty bottle. "That's why the mark chose you. Strong enough to carry it."

Sam wiped eyes. Quick. Rough. "I don't feel strong."

Loyd shook his head. "Nobody does. That's the secret, and you keep moving anyways."

They sat in that. Understanding needing no more words.

Kay stood. Cleared bowls. Ceramic on ceramic. Celine helped unasked. Routine holding families together.

Seal pulsed. Three times. Deliberate. Knocking from inside. Recognition calling recognition.

Heat spread across sternum. Not burning. Calibrating. Heart rate slowing to match. Steady. Ancient. Patient.

Loyd pressed a hand to his chest, his breathing shifting. Deep. Resonant. As if something old was waking.

Celine rubbed her wrists, staring at her skin as if expecting fire to break through.

She looked at her palms. Unmarked. But the way she held them changed. Potential.

Kay folded the dish towel. Precise creases. She moved like she felt nothing. No flinch. No hesitation. Just routine while the family transformed.

She glanced at the rug by the hearth, the corner still curled, pointing down, then turned away, ignoring what lay beneath.

The cabin breathed. In. Out. Walls expanding. Contracting. Alive beyond waking. Aware.

Time passed. Clock stopped at 3:17. Minutes felt like hours.

Shimmer at the treeline pulsed. Gold through empty air.

Kay moved to window. Forehead against glass. "Where are they?"

Sam checked his watch. "Two hours."

Seal pulsed disagreement. Something building. Old strength waking on its own schedule.

Celine sat. Hands flat on wood, fingers tracing the grain. She looked around, eyes wide, as if the room was getting brighter.

Sam looked at the rug. Corner curled. Pointing.

At the box Kay had brought inside. The cardboard lid sat slightly askew. His grandmother's things. Vibrating faintly against the floorboards.

At his family here because something older than choice called them home.

All these years running. Loyd in Florida. Kay in Muskogee. Audrey in Gooseneck. Luke trying to forget. Sam in Texas, then New Orleans. Scattered. Afraid.

Charles and Pauline knew this day would come. Built this place. Carved these walls. Stocked Dr Pepper and waited. Sovereign Hope took them before they could see it. But they'd trusted bloodline would find its way home anyway.

Faith carved into wood and stone. Fifty-five years waiting.

Sam's throat tightened. Grief and rage mixing.

"It's like it's waiting for us," Celine said.

Sam looked at the walls. Symbols shifting. Carvings Charles spent years perfecting. Rug pointing beneath. Geometry holding them safe while teaching them dangerous.

"It's been waiting a long time."

Voice carrying weight. Recognition. Grief. Gratitude.

Nobody answered.

Lamplight pulsing. Golden. Alive.

Kay's hands stilled.

Loyd's breathing matched the cabin.

Celine's fire settled. Patient.

Seal pulsed once more. Gentle. Affirming.

You're home.

Outside, cabin glowed faint gold. Windows pulsing. One steady heartbeat from walls Charles raised. From ground Pauline blessed.

Clearing held breath.

Wind stilled. Insects quiet. Lake smooth as glass.

Everything waiting.

Deep beneath the floorboards, something ancient opened one eye, recognizing its own blood.

# Chapter 27

# **The Night Before**

The Night Before

The silence had weight now. The hum under the floor had faded but not vanished, buried itself beneath the house like a thing conserving breath. They moved through it, pretending normal, until the night grew soft enough for conversation.

Luke and Audrey were gone. Headlights disappearing down the drive hours ago, taillights swallowed by trees. Gone to bring Hal and supplies back. The cabin felt bigger without them. Emptier.

Kay had retreated to the bedroom. Celine slept in the chair, head tilted, breath slow and even.

Kay woke Celine just enough to get her moving, then walked her back to the bed.

The lamp burned low. Coffee hissed in the pot, sharp in the quiet. No one moved to pour it.

Loyd leaned back in his chair, smiling at nothing. Sam traced the rim of his mug, watching steam curl and fall.

"You remember those grocery runs?" Sam's voice half-whisper, half-laugh. "When you were running the game route?"

Loyd's grin widened. "You mean when I used child labor?"

Sam chuckled. "I don't see it that way."

"Well, most would." Loyd laughed with him, soft enough not to wake Kay or Celine. The sound settled between them like old light.

Sam stared into his coffee. "Ziploc bags full of quarters."

"Skateland," Loyd said. "Grocery stores. Arcades. You'd master a game faster than I could fix the next one."

"Mom stopped buying them. Said I'd finish too fast."

"You did." Loyd's smile faded into something gentler. "I'd give you three quarters, you'd help some kid get past the hard part, hand the game back. They'd keep playing. Kept the machines full." He shook his head. "Thought I was teaching you work ethic. Turns out you were teaching me how to see patterns."

Sam looked up. Held his uncle's gaze across thirty years and three feet of scarred wood table.

"You were the only one who let me try."

The words hung. No rush to fill them.

Outside, wind pressed against the cabin walls. The porch light flickered once, then held.

Under the table, beneath the floorboards, and the stone foundation Charles laid by hand, something hummed. Faint as a heartbeat under sleep.

Loyd felt it first. His smile went still.

Sam's mug trembled against the table though his hand was steady.

Headlights swept across the window glass sometime after midnight.

Sam rose. Loyd stayed seated, hand pressed flat to the table as if anchoring himself.

The truck doors opened. Closed. Boots on gravel, then wood.

Luke came through first, rifle across his shoulder, duffel in his other hand. Hal followed with his own rifle and a box of shells, overnight bag slung low. Audrey last, coat pulled tight, sleeping bags bundled under one arm, small suitcase in her grip.

No one spoke. Luke and Hal set the rifles beside the door, chambers checked in silence. The metal caught lamplight, clean and functional.

Kay stirred on the bed. Rose. Emerged from the bedroom wrapped in her cardigan, hair loose around her shoulders. She looked at the rifles. At Luke. At Audrey carrying more than she should.

"You came prepared," Kay said.

Luke set his duffel down. "Wasn't sure what you had out here. Figured better to bring it."

Hal unpacked the box of shells. Set them on the counter in neat rows. "Checkpoints north of Tulsa. Two of them. National Guard."

Sam watched him arrange the ammunition. Precise. Methodical. "What happened?"

"Blackout hit the city around ten," Hal said. "Whole grid down. We saw it from the highway. No lights for miles." He glanced at Luke. "Took the back roads after that."

Audrey dropped the sleeping bags by the couch. Smoothed her hair back. "Roads were empty. No one out. Felt wrong."

Celine shifted in the bed but didn't wake. Kay moved to the stove. Filled the kettle. "You're here now. That's what matters."

Luke pulled sleeping bags from their compression sacks. Laid one across the floor near the hearth. Another by the couch. Hal spread a third in the corner, testing the floor for level ground.

Audrey sat at the table, her shoulders finally dropping. Seeing Luke and Hal move like themselves again seemed to steady her.

"You okay?" Sam asked.

She nodded. "Better now."

Hal sat across from Loyd. Nodded once. Loyd nodded back.

The hum beneath the floor deepened. Everyone felt it but no one named it.

Kay poured water into mugs. Set them on the table. Steam rose between them, carrying the scent of something herbal and old.

Luke drank standing. Hal warmed his hands around the ceramic. Audrey just held hers, staring at nothing.

"Get some sleep," Kay said. "Morning will come whether we're ready or not."

They moved like people who'd been moving all day. Audrey to the bedroom to change. Luke settling into the chair by the window, feet propped on the coffee table. Hal stretching out on one of the sleeping bags near the hearth.

Kay returned to the bed. Celine curled beside her, still asleep, breath deepening.

Within minutes, the house settled into quiet.

Only Sam and Loyd stayed awake.

Loyd leaned back in his chair, stretched, watched the steam rise off his coffee. The rifles leaned by the door, metal cooling. House breathing quiet around them.

"You still scared of roller coasters?"

Sam laughed. "Umm, yeah. Still not my thing. I like speed, but only when I'm in control. Roller coasters, I'm strapped in. Don't like that."

Loyd chuckled, low and warm. "You're funny, Sam. You talked about Six Flags for a month till Grandma got tired of hearing it. Handed me money and said, 'Take that boy so he'll shut up about it.'"

Sam grinned, half-dazed by memory. "Oh yeah.  Those grape drinks with the twisty straws. The cups looked like plastic fruit. Man, those were good."

"They'd better be. Ten bucks a pop. Highway robbery back then." Loyd shook his head. "You burned through Grandma's money on sugar water and video games. Couldn't get you out of the arcade."

"Best day ever." Sam's voice softened. "I forgot all about those drinks. I'd love one right now." He stared into his mug. "Brings back good memories. Lot better than this hornet's nest we're sitting in, trying to find a pattern that doesn't make sense."

Loyd's smile faded into something quieter. "You'll figure it out. You always do."

The chair creaked. Coffee cooled between them. Outside, wind moved through pines.

Loyd's eyes closed. Head tilted back. His breathing deepened.

"Move to the couch," Sam said. "Or you'll regret that neck pain for days."

Loyd opened one eye. Smiled. "Yeah. You're right."

He pushed himself up from the chair. Crossed the room. Stretched out on the couch, one arm over his eyes. Within minutes, his breath settled into sleep.

Sam stayed at the table. Watched the last curl of steam rise and disappear.

The lamp burned lower. Shadows lengthened across walls where symbols carved fifty years ago caught the light and held it.

The hum beneath the floor grew louder. Not in the room. In his head. A frequency carrying information he couldn't parse yet. Words that weren't words. Patterns folding over patterns.

He tried to close his eyes. Couldn't.

His pulse matched the rhythm. The sound wouldn't stop.

Morning would come, and he'd still be sitting here.

Hours passed. Or minutes. Time moved wrong inside the hum.

Sam rose. Moved to the window. Pressed his palm against the glass.

Outside, the lake stretched dark and still. Steam rose from the surface in slow curls, catching moonlight. The treeline stood black against deeper black. No movement. No sound.

But something waited across the water.

He felt it the way you feel eyes on you in a crowded room. Present. Watching. Patient.

The symbols on the walls pulsed once. Faint enough he might have imagined it.

The floor beneath him thrummed. Steady. Insistent.

Behind him, Loyd's breathing stayed even. Luke shifted in the chair, feet sliding off the coffee table, head dropping to his chest. Hal turned in his sleeping bag but didn't wake.

The house held them. Protected them. Kept them sleeping while something deeper stirred.

Sam's chest flared heat. The glyph pulsed in time with the floor.

He looked down at the rug by the hearth. Saw it breathe. Rise and fall like lungs.

Not yet.

But soon.

He returned to the table. Sat. Wrapped his hands around the cold mug.

The hum continued. Language without translation. Meaning without words.

He would sit here until light broke the horizon. Until Kay woke and started coffee. Until the house decided it was time.

Whatever called from beneath the floor would wait until morning.

It had waited fifty-five years.

# Chapter 28

# The Cellar

The house settled around them, humming under the boards like a pulse that was not his. Everyone slept except Sam. He lay awake listening to it breathe until he couldn't stay inside anymore.

The back porch took him before dawn. Cold coffee from yesterday still sat in the pot. He poured it into a mug and went outside.

The lake steamed under stars that hadn't faded yet. The hum followed him through the walls, softer out here but still present, threading through his ribs like something alive. He sat on the narrow planks with his back against the cabin wall and let the frequency move through him.

His chest burned where the glyph sat beneath the seal, a low simmer that never stopped. The wrongness across the water felt closer now. Not moving, just there. Aware. Counting.

Morning had already taken the room, but the floor still carried last night's note.

Kay woke at five. Sam heard her through the screen door, moving quietly in the kitchen, starting the coffee maker. Water running. The soft clink of mugs. She found him on the porch a few minutes later, still holding the same cold cup.

"You sleep at all?"

Sam shook his head.

She studied him for a moment, then went back inside without another word. The fresh pot started brewing. The scent reached him through the screen, warm and ordinary, but it didn't cover the hum underneath.

Luke woke next. Sam heard him moving around inside, the quiet efficiency of someone who'd learned to wake sharp. Fifteen minutes later Luke emerged with a thermos he'd found in the cabinet and two clean mugs. He poured for himself, then topped off Sam's cold coffee without asking.

"You look rough."

"Couldn't sleep?"

Luke settled against the porch rail, eyes scanning the tree line.

"Feel it?"

Sam nodded once.

The lake breathed. The sun climbed. The presence across the water stayed fixed, patient and measuring.

Loyd stepped out next, mug in hand. He took the other chair, watching the lake. Watching Sam.

"You catch that shift?" Loyd said.

"Feels like it's counting the house," Sam said.

Loyd nodded once, slow.

They went back to watching.

Inside, the house filled with small sounds. Kay cooking. Audrey helping. Celine shuffling in near seven with her hair wild, going straight for the coffee without speaking.

Hal sat up from his sleeping bag on the bedroom floor, rubbed his face, checked his phone.

No signal.

He wandered into the main room and stopped when he saw the books.

They were everywhere. Stacked in the living room, lined along the floor edges, shoved into corners like someone had been collecting them for decades.

Hal moved toward them the way a kid moves toward something he'd been told he couldn't have. His hands shook slightly as he pulled the first book from a pile.

A blue cloth-bound Freemason proceedings book, year stamped 1954 on the spine. Next to it, a worn Oklahoma atlas with penciled marks near Tenkiller and Tulsa. Then a small church history booklet. Then leather journals, handwritten, spines cracked from use.

He opened a journal first. Pauline's handwriting, tight and precise. Names he didn't recognize. Dates that meant nothing yet. In the margin, one phrase: Draco Ruber Edict, 1213.

He turned the page.

Another note waited beneath it: Lyon archive beneath Saint-Jean, folio secured 1347.

"Lyon archive," Hal murmured aloud, the way historians do when something catches.

Sam's head turned from the porch.

"What?"

"What's it say, Hal?"

Hal read it again. "Lyon archive beneath Saint-Jean. Folio secured 1347."

The name hit Sam before thought could catch it.

"Lyon."

The glyph under his sternum pulsed once beneath the seal. Sharp.

Luke felt it ripple through the air. Celine's hand went to her wrist. Audrey shifted in her chair, wincing as she rubbed her ankle.

Hal noticed none of it.

"What does that mean, Sam?"

Sam struggled with the memory. It was there but distant, like something he'd heard through water.

"A woman in New Orleans said that name to me. Before the seal. I didn't understand it then. I still don't."

Everyone looked at him. Puzzled. Silent.

Hal just said, "Fascinating," and went back to reading the journal.

Inside, breakfast was ready. Scrambled eggs, bacon, toast, orange juice, fresh coffee. Everything looked fine.

But it wasn't.

The eggs had a faint metallic tang at the back of the tongue. The bacon smelled clean at first, then carried a sour note underneath.

Sam sat at the table and tried not to notice. Kay set a plate in front of him.

"Sam, eat a little. Just enough to stay upright."

He tried. Gave up after two bites. The glyph was too hot beneath the seal. The food felt wrong in his mouth.

Audrey scrunched her nose once but didn't say anything. Celine frowned at her bacon but kept eating. Luke and Hal didn't seem to notice. Kay refused to acknowledge it.

"Food's fine," she said when Audrey glanced at her. "It's the storm front."

No one argued.

Kay turned to Hal. "Hal, what exactly was going on in town? I didn't catch it last night."

Hal looked up from the Freemason book, blinking like he'd been somewhere else.

"412 past Broken Arrow is blacked out. National Guard's got a checkpoint they're not reporting anywhere."

He paused.

"I-44's doing rolling brownouts into downtown. And three towers blink off my map every few minutes. Tulsa's drawing a circle around itself."

The table went quiet. The hum under the floor tightened.

Sam felt it shift. Loyd did too. Their eyes met across the table. Loyd's jaw worked.

Something was pulling at him, instinctive and old, like the house was asking a question only he could answer.

Finally, Loyd looked toward the hearth.

The rug over the floor looked ordinary in the morning light, just a faded pattern covering old wood. But the hum underneath was louder now.

"It's calling," Loyd said quietly.

He stood.

"Instead of standing around staring at it, let's just see what's down there."

Hal grinned. "Hot dog. I hope there's stuff to explore."

Sam nodded. "Then we go together."

Kay's hand tightened on the countertop, knuckles going white. She didn't turn around at first. When she did, her shoulders were locked.

"I'm not going underground. I hated tornado cellars as a kid and I'm not starting again now. You all go. I'll stay up here where things can't crawl out at me."

No one pushed.

They moved to the hearth. Luke and Sam pulled the rug back.

Underneath, an old oak trapdoor with a cast-iron ring set into the center.

Luke crouched, examining the edges. "There's a keyhole."

Everyone looked at Sam.

He pulled the key from his back pocket. "Guess Grandma and Grandpa left us this."

The key slid in clean. One turn. A solid click.

Luke and Sam lifted together. The hatch came up heavy, revealing narrow stairs descending into darkness. Wooden steps, cinderblock walls reinforced with stone. Dark air rushed up, carrying the smell of dust and copper and something older.

The copper wire they'd seen in the walls ran downward along the stairwell, disappearing into the black.

Sam went first. Luke came right behind him, flashlight casting pale blue over the steps and Sam's shoulders.

The hum rose as they descended. At the top, it pressed into their knees and ribs. Halfway down, it split into layers, harmonic and deep. The copper wire along the wall pulsed faintly, responding to something.

Audrey hesitated at the top, gripping the rough wood. Hal moved just below her, guiding her down one painful step at a time, taking her weight where the ankle wouldn't hold.

At the bottom, the pressure peaked.

Celine stepped off the last stair and the nearest lantern ignited.

Everyone stopped.

Cold flame, visible but giving almost no heat. Old witch-fire, burning without fuel.

Celine pivoted toward the far wall and a second lantern bloomed. She raised her hand and two wall candles flared.

Celine flinched, rubbing her left wrist as if it burned. She touched the back of her neck, her skin flushing. As she did, the last lantern caught.

They were all staring at her now.

The space opened around them.

Octagonal, sixteen feet wall to wall, eight-foot ceiling. The air was cool and dry and thick, like it hadn't moved in decades. Dust lay heavy on everything. The smell of stone and copper and faint ozone pressed in from all sides.

Along the upper band of the walls ran a continuous thread of markings. Enochian script cut deep into the stone, overlaid with smaller runic patterns that looked like they'd been added later.

As the last person crossed the threshold, the markings gave a single soft glow, ember-light waking and then settling.

Sam's chest glyph tightened beneath the seal, then released.

He recognized the grammar. Not the meaning, but the shape. The same curves and intersections.

The chamber held them.

Four weather-sealed crates stenciled in faded military lettering sat against one wall: Project Sol-Ark 1943.

A copper astrolabe lay half-covered on a small side table, intricate radial arms etched with Enochian.

Church keys hung from iron hooks.

A half-melted ration tin sat on one of the crates, the Seal of Solomon engraved beneath the lid, rotated toward something only it understood.

Hal moved toward the astrolabe, hesitant but drawn in. He brushed the dust aside, tracing the lines.

"Some kind of navigation tool."

Luke found the ration tin and tried to pry it open. It didn't move.

Sam put a hand on his shoulder. "Leave it for now."

Celine crossed to the far wall. "There's a photo here."

Everyone moved toward her. Celine lifted the frame into lamplight. Luke raised his flashlight. The details sharpened under the beam.

Sepia. Soft edges. A group gathered outside a New Orleans house. Charles and Pauline stood at center, younger by decades. Beside them, two women. A boy in front, maybe eleven, eyes too old for his face. One woman rested her hand on her belly, pregnant.

Celine turned the frame. Ink on the back in Pauline's handwriting.

New Orleans, 1962.

Howardson and Dauvee families.

Yvette. Celestine. Leontine. Krishtan, age eleven.

Sam stilled.

"My friend from New Orleans."

They looked at him, waiting.

"I'll explain more later."

Celine studied him. "Is he the one who kept you safe at his place?"

"Yes. He called it his ward."

The air shifted. Not a sound, just a presence threading through the copper seams.

Celine stiffened, her hand going to her wrist again. Sam felt it too, steadying him when his knees wanted to buckle.

The others went still.

Then it passed.

On the opposite wall, another niche. This one held three things arranged with intention: a second photograph, a rosary, and a small leather-bound book wrapped in wax cloth.

The second photo was older. Cracked under glass.

Charles again, this time in his twenties, standing beside a man Sam had only seen once.

Brownlow.

Younger but not young. The same face. The same eyes.

Behind them, a construction site that looked like Tenkiller. The date on the corner: 1952.

Freemason men stood around them in formation. Under each name, symbols. Vatican sigils. Occult marks Sam had seen in history books but never understood.

A black sun. Keys interlocked.

Luke leaned closer. "That's Brownlow."

"He looks exactly the same," Audrey said.

No one answered.

The weight of it settled over them like stone.

The rosary lay coiled on top of the book. Black wood beads, the chain turned green with age. Each bead carved with tiny symbols.

Celine stepped closer, squinting in the lamplight. Her hand went to her wrist again.

"Sam," she said quietly. "That symbol is the one under your skin."

Sam didn't answer.

He was listening to something else.

A shift in the hum. A note that had been there a moment ago and now wasn't.

Loyd moved past them to a smaller box on a shelf against the octagonal wall. Wooden, locked.

He looked back at Sam. "Try the key."

Sam handed it over.

The key turned.

Inside, resting on old velvet, a necklace. Small cross, burned-looking, neither metal nor wood.

Loyd lifted it. Heavy. Impossibly heavy for its size.

The moment his fingers closed around it, Sam's chest ignited gold-blue beneath the seal.

The copper wiring along the walls lit like veins. Dust fell from the beams. The lanterns shook. The stone seams brightened, then snapped dark.

The astrolabe's etched lines flared once and cut out.

Then the room detonated.

Sound hit them in three layers. A high needle-tone. A deep sub-bass hum. A harmonic chord like a choir singing underwater.

It didn't come through their ears first. It came through their bones.

Pressure slammed into their chests. Ears popped. Air compressed. Heat flashed and vanished.

Audrey gasped, clutching her chest. Celine arched her back as if struck. Luke's knees buckled. Hal grimaced and tried to pop his ears.

One second. A single violent pulse.

Then absolute stillness.

From above, Kay's voice:

"Hey! What's going on down there?"

Loyd stood panting, the relic hanging from his hand. His face had gone white. His breath came in short, broken pulls.

He stared at the photo of Brownlow, then at the symbols beneath the names, then back at the relic.

"I need some air," he whispered.

Sam moved toward the stairs.

Loyd held up a hand. "You stay. Find the pattern, Sammy."

He didn't smile. Just turned and climbed the stairs with the relic still in his grip.

The others started moving again. Hal crouched by one of the crates, fingers brushing the stenciled letters. Celine and Audrey went back to the photos. Luke stayed near Sam, hand resting on the pistol at his back.

Sam stood in the center of the octagon and listened.

The hum was still there.

But something had changed.

Loyd's footsteps echoed on the stairs. Halfway up. Three-quarters.

Then he reached the top floor and crossed the threshold.

The note severed clean.

One frequency fell out of the chord.

The harmony tilted.

Pressure pulled sideways under Sam's ribs. Cold filled the space where heat had been.

His glyph dimmed beneath the seal by a half-step, and the absence hit him like a snapped string in his chest.

The family chord was broken.

The room kept humming, but the chord was broken now.

One note had gone with Loyd, and the house knew it before he did.

# Chapter 29

# The Severing

The family stood in the wake of Loyd's departure.

Sam stood in the center of the octagonal chamber.

The hum beneath the floor had changed.

One frequency missing. The chord lopsided.

A song with a broken string still trying to hold its shape.

Luke checked the Sol-Ark crates.

Fingers traced the stenciled letters.

Celine and Audrey studied the photographs under lamplight. Whispering about the faces staring back at them.

Hal crouched near the astrolabe. Turning it slowly. Watched Enochian etchings catch fire and not burn.

The relic was gone. Loyd had carried it upstairs.

Sam's chest tightened. The seal over his glyph flickered once. Then steadied. Something had shifted when Loyd crossed the threshold. The house knew before any of them did.

"We should go up," Audrey said quietly.

Luke nodded. "Mom's been up there alone too long."

They moved toward the stairs. Sam went last. Glancing back at the chamber one more time. The lanterns burned without fuel. The copper wiring pulsed faintly along the walls. The octagon held its secrets in stone and silence.

Upstairs, Kay stood at the kitchen sink. Hands braced against the counter. She looked through the window above the sink toward the lake.

The light was dying.

Not clouds. Not weather. The sky itself dimming. Like someone dragging a dimmer switch down.

It should be mid-morning. Bright. Clear. November sun cutting through bare branches.

Instead, darkness crept across the water.

It started at the far shore. A bruising. Purple-gray spreading like ink through wet cloth. The color was wrong. Sickly. Unnatural. It moved across the lake toward the cabin. Swallowing the water's reflection as it came.

The sky above shifted with it. Blue draining to slate. Then to something darker. Copper tones bled through at the edges like old blood.

She blinked hard. The light dropped another shade. Color drained from the trees. Green to gray to black. Shadows flattened against the ground. Losing dimension. Spreading like oil.

Her skin crawled. It wasn't just visual. The air itself felt thinner. Colder. Pressure dropping. Her arms prickled with goosebumps that had nothing to do with temperature.

Her lungs worked harder for each breath.

The hum beneath the floor stuttered.

Kay turned from the sink.

Loyd stood in the living room. Halfway to the front door.

His back was to her. One hand hung slack at his side. The other gripped the relic. Fingers white around it.

His head tilted toward the door like he was listening to someone she couldn't hear.

"Loyd?"

He didn't respond.

Kay stepped out of the kitchen. "Loyd, honey, you okay?"

He took another step toward the door.

That's when she saw his arm.

Black veins spread up from his hand. Thin lines branching beneath his skin. Ink bleeding through wet paper. They crawled toward his elbow in slow, deliberate patterns.

"Loyd." Her voice cracked. "What the hell is that in your hand?"

He flinched. Not at her voice. At something else.

His lips moved. Barely a whisper.

"Yeah... I hear you..."

Kay stopped breathing. "Hear who?"

A cold jolt ran down her spine.

The light outside dropped again. Deeper. Near-dusk in the middle of morning. Through the windows, the lake was invisible now. Just darkness where water should be.

Loyd's breath stuttered. His knees bent slightly. Like something was pulling him forward.

"...Butch..."

Kay's stomach dropped.

Butch. Only their father called him that. Only their Dad.

"Loyd, who are you talking to?"

He turned his head slowly. Looked at her. Eyes glazed. Unfocused.

"Hey, sis. Tell Dad I heard him."

The relic in his hand flared.

Dark light pulsed from its core. Violent. Rhythmic. The black veins up his arm lit from beneath his skin.

Pressure hit.

Kay stumbled. Her ears popped. Air compressed like a fist closing.

The front door exploded inward.

The sound was a cannon blast. Wood detonated. Splinters sprayed across the living room. The kitchen window shattered half a second later. Glass flew inward. Singing through the air.

The floor vibrated beneath Kay's feet. The smell of ozone and char filled the room.

Kay threw an arm up. Glass sliced her right side. Her forearm. Hot blood on cold skin. Pain bit deep.

Her breath broke.

They were already on him.

A swarm covering Loyd's body. Too many. Claws hooking into shoulders. Arms. Legs. Back. Teeth finding flesh.

Blood sprayed across the room. On the chair to her left. On her clothes. Her arm. Droplets hit the ceiling. Red mist in the air.

Loyd's body jerked backward. Violent. Bone cracked audibly. His head snapped. More blood. His boots left the floor. The thing stayed clenched in his fist.

Kay lunged.

Her fingers grazed his shirt. Fabric slipped through her grip.

They ripped him backward through the doorway. His free hand clawed at the floor. Found nothing.

She caught one glimpse. Just one. Something pale. Limbs bent wrong. Teeth.

Then blood. And her brother flying backward into darkness. Gone.

Loyd's voice cut the air once. Faint. Distant.

"Kay!"

Then nothing.

Silence.

Kay stood near the threshold. Blood dripping from her arm. Glass crunching beneath her boots. Breath came in short, jagged pulls.

She looked down.

Blood on the floor. Red where Loyd had stood. Dark puddles near the door. Smoking. The wood beneath hissed. Charred. Black rings spreading where the dark blood touched.

The smell was copper and burning meat. Wrong. Chemical.

Kay's knees buckled. She sank to the floor. Staring at her hands. Red and black. Mixed.

The light outside held its unnatural dim.

In the cellar, Sam heard it first.

A dull boom shook dust from the ceiling beams.

Then pressure slammed into his chest. The lanterns flickered. Copper wiring along the walls flared bright. Died.

The hum beneath the floor stopped.

Complete silence.

Luke's head snapped up. "What the hell was that?"

Celine grabbed Audrey's arm. "Gone. The hum's gone."

Sam's glyph burned cold beneath the seal. His throat closed. Air wouldn't come.

Weight. Crushing. Suffocating.

Chest pressure.

Wayne's shadow pressing down on his ribs.

Wordless. Heavy.

The belt. The hand on the back of his neck.

The shame that never washed off.

"Move!" Luke bolted for the stairs. Pistol already in his hand.

Hal followed, pulling Audrey up the steep steps as she scrambled against the pain. Celine came last.

Sam stood frozen.

One second. Two.

His legs remembered how to run.

He hit the stairs. Taking them two at a time. The air above was wrong. Thin. Charged. Tasted like metal and smoke.

Luke burst through the trapdoor.

He stopped.

Sam reached the top step and saw it.

Shattered door hanging from one hinge. Glass scattered across the floor like broken stars. Blood streaked across the threshold and up the wall.

Kay on her knees near the kitchen. Arms wrapped around herself. Staring at nothing.

Blood and glass everywhere.

Hal moved first. He froze for one heartbeat. Swallowed hard. Then crossed the room in three strides. He crouched beside Kay. Hands on her shoulders.

"Kay. Kay, look at me."

She didn't respond.

Luke scanned the room. Pistol raised. Breathing hard. "Where's Loyd?"

Kay's lips moved. No sound came out.

Celine stepped through the broken doorway. Hand over her mouth. "Oh my God."

The water was still. The sky held its dim. Shadows moved along the far shore. Retreating into the treeline.

Sam stepped into the room.

His boots crunched on glass. He moved past Luke. Past Hal and Kay. Past the blood and the shattered wood.

He stopped in the doorway.

The lake stretched before him. Dark. Silent. The sky flickered once, then settled into unnatural gloom.

His chest was hollow. Empty.

The chord was gone. The frequency that had been there since he stepped into this house had severed clean.

He looked down at the blood streaked across the threshold. Red and black. Mixed into patterns that were deliberate.

The relic and Uncle Loyd were gone. They'd taken everything.

Sam's eyes tracked back to Kay. Blood soaked her shirt. Spattered across her right arm. Dark streaks down her jeans. Glass cuts on her forearm wept red. But shallow. Survivable.

The blood wasn't hers. Most of it wasn't hers.

It was Loyd's.

She was covered in her brother's blood.

Her eyes were open but empty. Staring at nothing. Breathing but not here. Not physically destroyed. Worse.

She'd seen it happen. Watched them take him.

Sam knew that look. He'd worn it himself. The day his mother stopped breathing. The years Wayne made him small.

It wasn't shock. It was being hollowed out from the inside.

His windpipe slammed shut. Chest crushing inward. Couldn't breathe.

Vision graying. Childhood suffocation fear. Wayne's hand on his throat. The closet. The belt. The voice that said he was nothing and would always be nothing.

And now Loyd. Gone because Sam brought the frequency here. Because the glyph called them. Because he existed.

His voice came out small. Cracked. Barely there.

"This followed me. This is my fault."

The house didn't answer. The lake didn't move.

Nothing moved.

# Chapter 30

# **The Bait**

The observation room smelled of recycled air and age. Concrete walls pressed close under low ceilings. Brownlow stood alone at the glass, watching the prepared containment room beyond. Steel gurney. Biometric locks. LED strips casting blue light across spotless floor. A hum lived in the walls, steady and low, ancient breath rising through stone.

His desk sat behind him. Vatican insignia tucked in an open drawer beneath Paladin Trust memos. It pleased him. Two kingdoms, one throne.

He waited.

The door hissed. Three analysts entered carrying tablets, faces locked down to neutral. Military cut in the first man's posture. Lab coat on the woman. Corporate suit on the third, silk tie and dead eyes. They formed a loose line behind Brownlow, not quite at attention.

"Sir." The military analyst spoke first. "The pulse event data."

Brownlow didn't turn. "Show me."

Tablets angled forward. The monitors blew out when it hit. Readings spiked past anything calibrated. Dimensional sensors recording signatures that shouldn't exist. Seismic equipment registering tremors from Tenkiller Lake with no geological source. The waveform broke every pattern in their system. Four elements braided together in patterns their system couldn't categorize.

"We've never seen this configuration." The analyst's voice stayed level, but his thumb moved against the tablet edge. Nervous energy seeking exit.

The scientist leaned closer to her tablet. "One signature flaring. Fire first."

The suit scrolled through his data. "One signature suppressed."

The military analyst noted both, his face betraying nothing.

Brownlow smiled at the glass. "I felt it when it happened."

The corporate suit shifted weight. "Your vision."

"Yes." Brownlow's voice carried quiet certainty, the kind that didn't need volume. "Simultaneous with your instruments."

The scientist and the suit exchanged a glance. Brief. Calculated. Then back to neutral.

"The timing was exact," the suit confirmed. "Down to the millisecond."

Brownlow turned. The mural behind his desk showed a figure radiating false light, angels kneeling beneath in eternal submission. He moved past them to the desk itself, fingers trailing across a scripture page clipped to military logistics marked PT-47.13-B. The woman adjusted the cross at her throat. Reflexive. Ironic.

"The prophecy unfolds," Brownlow said.

The military analyst's hand twitched. A note passed behind Brownlow's back, suit to scientist, folded small. Professional silence held the room.

Brownlow's pupils dilated mid-breath.

Pressure folded in on itself, lights stuttering once, twice.

His voice deepened, the register shifting down into something that didn't quite fit his throat.

"One has awakened. Maybe more. We verify before the next one."

The analysts froze. The suit's knuckles whitened on his tablet. The scientist looked at her shoes. The military man's jaw set hard, a muscle jumping beneath skin.

The pressure lifted as suddenly as it came.

Brownlow blinked. Normal pupils. Normal voice. "How long until the subject arrives?"

"Inbound now," the military analyst said. His hand shook slightly. He pressed it flat against his thigh.

Brownlow turned back to the glass. "The rest will ignite soon."

The analysts exchanged another glance. The suit's jaw tightened.

The doors opened with a mechanical hiss.

Hyland wheeled the gurney through, breath already quickened.

The analysts kept a step back from him. No one ever stood close to the Handler.

"Ezekiel delivered the carrier," Brownlow said, and Hyland's mouth twitched at the old designation.

Loyd was strapped down across military-grade restraints. Semi-conscious. No bandages. Blood oozing freely from deep claw marks carved across shoulders and arms. Head trauma crusted dark in his hair. His chest rose and fell in shallow rhythms, ribs remembering violence.

Brownlow and the analysts moved to the observation window.

Glass between them and the containment room, view unobstructed.

Hyland leaned over Loyd, checking pulse at the wrist. His fingers lingered on torn flesh.

"Hyland," Brownlow said quietly. Warning in the name alone.

Hyland's breath hitched. "Yes, Sire." The words came out tight, a bridle forced between teeth.

He traced claw marks with a reverence that didn't belong in a lab. He lowered his head. His tongue dragged across the open wound on Loyd's forearm. Slow. Wet. Tasting the adrenaline in the red.

His breath hitched. Pupils flared wide. The hunger slipped through his mask like it had been waiting its turn.

Loyd flinched weakly. The restraints held.

Behind the glass, the scientist looked away. The suit's mouth pressed into a thin line. The military analyst watched without expression, taking mental notes.

Brownlow watched Hyland the way a sculptor watches clay.

A technician entered the containment room carrying a case. Glass and steel, biometric seal. The relic inside hummed faintly, audible even through the container. He set it on the examination table three feet from Loyd's gurney.

The response came instantly.

Violent hum. Air warped around the case, ripples lifting like something breathing under it. Monitors spiked. Loyd's body convulsed once, hard, restraints biting into already torn skin. The relic vibrated against containment, glass singing a single high note.

Brownlow leaned forward. "There."

Pressure surged through the room, heavy and hungry.

Hyland's excitement peaked. He grabbed Loyd's wrist, fingers digging into claw wounds. Loyd gasped, tried to pull away. Hyland produced a surgical tool from his coat, small and sharp, and pressed it into Loyd's shoulder wound.

Blood welled fresh.

Loyd's scream cut short as his body shut down, consciousness fleeing into shock.

Monitors flatlined for three seconds, then stabilized.

Brownlow's voice came through the intercom, calm and absolute. "Enough. He must live."

Hyland froze. Tool still pressed against flesh. Eyes wild. Then he withdrew slowly, obedient but barely, restraint a thin veneer over appetite.

The technician removed the relic. Hum stopped. Air pressure normalized. Monitors returned to baseline readings.

Proof. The relic needed the carrier.

Behind the glass, the corporate suit whispered to the scientist. he nodded once and made a note on her tablet, screen turned slightly out of Brownlow's line of sight.

"Bring in the father," Brownlow said.

Hyland wheeled Loyd's gurney out through the far door. Blood trail marked the floor. A sour, metallic odor drifted through the vents, the kind that rose from deep tunnels where air never moved clean. Another door opened. Guards shuffled Stellan Grimhold into the containment room.

Decades of drain showed in every line of his body. Hollow eyes. Skin gray like old paper. Hands trembling as guards strapped him into the examination chair. He didn't fight. No energy left for resistance.

The relic returned in its case. Placed on the table two feet from Stellan.

Nothing.

No hum. No air distortion. Monitors flat. The relic sat inert as stone.

Brownlow nodded once. "Hylic," he said. "Spent matter. Empty spark."

The military analyst made a notation. "Complete depletion."

Stellan's eyes tracked to the glass, seeing nothing, understanding less. They removed him without ceremony.

The third door opened. A woman entered between guards. Mid-forties. Creole features. Candlewax stains on her wrists, the kind altar-keepers carry. Beaten, exhausted, but her eyes held a thin defiance.

One guard wore a filter strip over his mouth. Not regulation. No one commented.

They strapped her into the chair.

The relic placed near her.

Faint hum began.

Not violent like Loyd's response. But present. Air shifted around the case. Monitors showed weak spike, readings climbing slow and steady.

Hyland's entire body went rigid. Rage flashed across his face, jaw clenched so hard teeth should crack.

"She wasn't supposed to have nothing left. The records showed nothing."

But the relic responded.

Brownlow leaned closer to the glass. "Generational echo."

Hyland moved toward the woman, hands forming fists.

"Leave her." Brownlow's voice stopped him mid-step.

Hyland froze. Breathing hard through his nose. Fists still clenched. He exited the containment room without looking back, door slamming behind him with more force than necessary.

The corporate suit made another note. The scientist glanced at the military analyst. Unspoken agreement passed between them. Hyland's instability noted. Filed. Useful later.

The analysts left at Brownlow's gesture. Door closed. He stood alone at the observation window. Loyd's unconscious form had been returned to the containment room, gurney replaced by a medical cot. Restraints still in place. Blood still oozing.

Brownlow spoke quietly. To himself. To something else.

"The boy will come for him."

His hand touched the glass. Fingers spread against cold surface.

"This confirms my calling."

Silence answered. The hum in the walls continued its ancient rhythm.

"Three signatures. Three threads. Something else moves beneath them."

His certainty filled the room like pressure. Absolute. Terrifying. Wrong.

A status light above the door flickered in perfect rhythm. Three. Six. Nine

Adjacent corridor. Door closed behind the analysts. Conversation resumed in low voices.

"He thinks this is his plan." The military analyst kept his voice below intercom range.

The corporate suit checked his tablet. "Let him. We need the structural reading first."

The scientist frowned at her data. "The pulse signature doesn't match Watcher frequencies. It's something unclassified."

"Whatever they are," the suit said, "we'll own it before he does."

Brief silence. Too long.

The military analyst glanced at the wall. "He's listening."

They returned to professional silence. Tablets held at neutral angles. Faces smooth.

Brownlow's eyes unfocused. Pupils blown wide.

Air pressure dropped heavily. Lights flickered, held, flickered again.

His voice shifted mid-sentence, register dropping into ancient spaces. "Bring the bloodline. Break the lock. Free the chains."

Pressure lifted.

Brownlow gasped. Blinked. Pupils normal. He wiped sweat from his temple with one hand. Then smiled.

Screens behind him showed data streams the analysts couldn't parse. Frequencies beyond their models. Signatures that shouldn't exist in their system.

Containment room. Loyd's eyes flickered beneath closed lids.

Monitors registered consciousness returning. Slow climb from shock into awareness.

Brownlow stood at the observation window. The analysts filed back in, silent as monks. The relic sat on a table near Loyd's cot. Separated but close. Biometric case unlocked now, glass open.

Low hum began again.

Loyd's lips moved.

Audible through the intercom. One word. Just the name.

"Sam..."

The relic's hum intensified for a single beat. Then stopped.

Air pressure shifted.

Brownlow's smile spread slowly across his face.

The air crushed inward, hunger in the pressure.

The analysts exchanged glances. The corporate suit's hand shook. The one in military cut took one step backward, unconscious retreat. The woman whispered through barely moving lips.

"What is he?"

Brownlow's voice came quiet, certain. "Inevitable."

Loyd's breathing changed, rhythms adjusting. The relic vibrated once on its table. Monitors spiked, held, spiked again. Data streams showed impossible readings. Four bands burned across the monitors, braided beyond the system's reach.

Air pressure dropped. Lights flickered, held, flickered again.

The corporate suit's tablet slipped in his grip. He caught it. Knuckles white.

The man's hand moved to his sidearm. Stopped. Hung there.

The woman's breathing went shallow.

Brownlow stepped closer to the glass. Loyd's eyes still closed. Blood still oozing. Restraints cutting into torn flesh. The relic hummed low and patient.

The hum in the walls held steady.

Brownlow tilted his head, listening to a voice no one else could hear.

He breathed once, slow, as if receiving instruction.

"Prepare the next retrieval," he said. "Broader net. No mistakes this time."

His fingers drifted from the glass like a blessing turned to sentence.

# Chapter 31

# The Thinning

The kitchen held a silence that didn't move.

Blood pooled near the doorway, still wet. Smeared where Loyd had been dragged. Alongside it, blackened streaks marked where the feeder's mouth had been on him. Charred wood. Darker than normal blood. Permanent as burn scars.

The smell was heavy. Copper and sulfur. A slaughterhouse sterilized with ozone.

Celine knelt beside the bucket, scrubbing at the red with a towel that kept soaking through. The water had turned dark. Thick. Her knees ached against the hard floor. Her breathing stayed steady but shallow. Control holding back a surge she couldn't name.

Kay sat on the floor against the lower cabinets. Knees pulled to her chest. Arms wrapped around her abdomen. Her breathing matched the rhythm of drowning on dry land. Quick. Shallow. Automatic.

She stared at the empty doorway. Guarding the space where her brother had vanished.

Sam sat on the stairs leading into the kitchen, head down, hands clasped between his knees. His back pressed against the wall. Heat pulsed in time with his heartbeat.

His thoughts kept pulling the same circle. They came because of him. The relic called them. Loyd bled because Sam carried something he didn't understand.

Luke stood in the doorway to the porch, hands gripping the frame hard enough to whiten his knuckles. His eyes tracked the lake. Scanning the dark water. The treeline across the lake. The sky beginning to shift toward the first edge of dawn. Not light yet. Just the faintest suggestion that night wouldn't last forever.

Audrey stood near the table, back straight as rebar, hands trembling at her sides. She hadn't moved in ten minutes. Frozen. Waiting for a sign that wasn't coming.

Hal paced between the table and the hallway. Three steps forward. Turn. Three steps back. His feet traced the same path over and over. Wearing a path into the boards.

He kept pacing.

The motion was all he had left.

The cabin creaked once. Settled. The hum beneath the floor lay dormant but present. A frequency just beneath the edge of sound.

Celine slammed the towel into the bucket. Water sloshed over the rim, spreading red across the floor. She stood. Knees cracking loud enough to cut the silence like a gunshot. The sound broke the room open.

"We should have gone after him."

Her voice came low and sharp. Not loud. Cutting.

Luke didn't turn from the doorway. His voice came colder than Celine's. Flatter. Stripped of everything but certainty.

"We will."

Audrey recoiled. Her shoulders pulled inward, collapsing toward her center. Her mouth opened. Closed. Opened again. Words scattered before they formed.

"This is warfare." The syllables came fast. Clipped. Desperate. "We're under attack. We need covering. We can't just go after them like this."

Celine's jaw tightened. Heat gathered in her chest. Pressed outward against her ribs. She gripped the edge of the counter to keep standing.

"Prayer won't bring him back."

Kay flinched. Her arms tightened around her knees. A small sound escaped her throat. Swallowed immediately.

Sam's head stayed down. His hands trembled. The stones in his pocket pulsed against his thigh. Vibration low and internal. A second heartbeat he couldn't silence.

He didn't defend himself. Didn't speak. The guilt sat on his chest like stone. Crushing breath. Crushing thought.

They came because of him. Loyd screamed because Sam opened a door he couldn't close.

His vision blurred at the edges.

Luke's head turned sharply toward the lake. His nostrils flared. The scent hit him cold and metallic. Sharp enough to taste. Wrong in a way he recognized but couldn't name.

He cataloged it. Stored it. Said nothing.

Sam caught the movement. Luke's head tilting. The tension in his shoulders shifting. Heat crawled between his shoulders.

Celine's pulse spiked. Too strong. Too fast. The heat in her chest spread outward, crawling up her throat, pressing against her ribs, pressure trying to escape. Her hair lifted slightly at the ends.

Static charge rippled across her scalp.

She gripped the counter harder. Knuckles bone-white.

The air around her hands distorted. Heat shimmer. Red crawled under her skin. Visible through the translucent flesh of her knuckles.

Sam finally looked up.

Their eyes locked.

Celine's breath caught. Her irises vanished. Black ate the green. The flare built beneath her sternum, burning outward. She couldn't stop it. Couldn't slow it. Metallic taste flooded her mouth. Copper. Ozone. The pressure in the room shifted. Oxygen thinned.

Kay whispered her name. The sound barely carried.

Celine swayed. Her knees buckled slightly. She braced harder against the counter. Fighting for breath. Fighting the heat that wanted to explode through her skin. Sweat beaded on her forehead. Her vision sharpened. Then blurred. Then sharpened again.

Hal stepped forward, hands raised like she was having a panic attack. His voice came soft. Placating.

"Celine, breathe..."

Sam's voice cut across the room. One word. Flat. Final.

"Don't."

Hal froze mid-step. Confusion flickered across his face. Then anger. Then fear. He backed away slowly. Three steps. Stopped. His hands dropped to his sides.

The lights flickered. Once. Twice. A plate in the sink cracked with a sharp pop. The sound rang through the kitchen, high and clean. The cabin hummed. Low. Steady. The walls vibrated with it. A frequency that lived in the bones of the structure.

The triangle under the rug pulsed heat once. Brief and intense. Radiating up through the floorboards.

Celine caught herself on the counter. Breath ragged. Chest heaving. Sweat ran down her temples. Her hair still lifted at the ends. Static that wouldn't let go.

She looked at Sam. Then at her hands. Then back at Sam.

Her throat tightened.

No words came.

Then, quiet, almost breaking:

"I feel him."

Everyone froze.

The hum in the walls kept breathing.

Audrey's knees gave out. She dropped beside the table, hand flying to her mouth. Prayer started silently. Lips moving without sound. Then whispers. Then audible fragments that tumbled over each other in desperate rhythm.

"Father God we need you. Cover us with your blood. Rebuke deception. Hedge of protection. The blood of the Lamb..."

She clung to her phone but didn't open the Bible app. Just held it. White-knuckled grip on black glass. Her breath came in shallow gasps between phrases.

No tears. Too shocked to cry.

Her body shook but her eyes stayed dry. Wide and glassy.

Hal's pacing stopped. His jaw set. He stepped between Audrey and the darkened window, blocking the line of sight.

"We need to call Pastor Mike." His voice cracked. "He'll know what to do. We need counsel. We can't..."

"No."

Celine's voice came out ice.

She straightened slowly, arms crossing over her chest. Her breathing still ragged but steadier now. The heat in her skin faded to a dull flush.

"We don't bring anyone else into this."

Audrey's head snapped up. Prayer cutting off mid-phrase. Her eyes found Hal's. Pleading.

"He's right. We need help. We need..."

Luke stepped away from the doorframe. One step inside. His voice came quiet but absolute.

"We keep this in the family."

Celine's head turned toward him. Something shifted in her expression. Surprise. Then approval. She nodded once.

"Finally. Something smart, brother."

Her eyes cut to Audrey. The temperature in the room dropped.

"Either help or go home. But don't bring that church in here. They'll call us delusional or possessed. We've lived that story already."

Kay's head lifted for the first time. Her eyes focused. Her voice came out raw but clear. Cutting through the tension like a blade through silk.

"Stop. He's alive."

The room froze.

Kay pressed her palm flat against the floorboards, reading the tremor.

"Celine's right. We've got enough going on without bringing more people into this."

Audrey's face crumpled. Her hands shook harder. She looked to Hal for support but found only his own uncertainty staring back at her. The prayer cycle started again. Quieter now. Fractured.

"Cover us, Father. Rebuke the enemy. We need your protection..."

Celine crossed her arms tighter. Her gaze never left Audrey.

"Keep this a family matter. We don't need more problems. Especially from people who'll just tell us we're going to hell."

Luke inhaled sharply. Copper. Burnt metal. Alive. Stronger than before. His jaw clenched. He took one small step outside the doorframe. Pupils still blown wide.

The instinct in him sharpened. Focusing on a signal he couldn't name yet.

Sam sat on the floor throughout it all. Watching. Dissociated. His breathing shallow. The guilt spiral tightened around his chest.

Crushing deeper with every second. The voices around him distorted, became ambient sound.

He heard nothing.

Felt it all.

Then he felt her.

Celine's frequency radiating outward like heat from a furnace. Not sound. Not sight. Pure sensation. It vibrated through the air. Through the floor. Through his ribs.

The triangle beneath the rug pulsed in response. Matching her rhythm. The geometry of the cabin pulling him back into alignment.

Sam closed his eyes.

Let the frequency wash over him.

Let it drag him up from the spiral.

The dread loosened. The guilt shifted from crushing weight to steel resolve.

He opened his eyes. Stood. Slow. Heavy.

The floorboards groaned beneath him, adjusting to his weight as if he were heavier than bone.

Celine's frequency still radiated. He moved toward her. Three steps. Wrapped his arms around her. She was still shaking. Still hot. But solid. Real.

"You're right," he said quietly into her hair. "We need to stop fucking around."

She exhaled hard against his shoulder. Her hands gripped his back.

Luke stepped fully into the room. His voice came stripped of everything but trust.

"What do we do next?"

Sam pulled back from Celine. Looked at Luke. Then at Kay, still sitting on the floor but awake now in a way she hadn't been before. Then at Audrey, collapsed beside the table, prayer whispers dying on her lips. Then at Hal, frozen between his wife and the family he didn't fully understand.

Sam reached for his pocket, fingers brushing the cold stone, then stopped.

He didn't pull it out.

The pressure he felt came from inside his chest, not from anything he carried.

Heat flared behind his sternum. A pulse he couldn't control.

The floor hummed in response. Boards tightened. The cabin leaned in.

Celine stood straighter. Her breath steadied. Her eyes cleared.

Luke's pupils stayed wide. His breathing deepened. Heat crawled down his spine. Copper. Burnt metal. Alive. Stronger now.

His jaw clenched hard. His shoulders squared without thought.

Fear and loyalty twisted together inside him, the same ignition Sam had survived in New Orleans. Love for Loyd. Terror of losing anyone else. Frequency rising without permission.

Kay lifted her head fully, the clarity returning to her gaze.

Audrey froze mid-prayer.

Hal stepped back, instinctively shielding her.

The cabin breathed around them.

The hum beneath the floor deepened once.

Then held steady.

Sam pressed a palm flat to his chest.

The Seed answered.

# Chapter 32

# The Ignition

The air thickened.

Sam felt it solidify in his lungs. Each breath required effort. The cabin pressed inward. Walls narrowing by fractions no eye could measure but every body registered. The space around them gained weight.

Outside, brush crowded closer. Branches scraped the siding with no wind to move them. The floorboards hummed beneath their feet. A vibration too low for sound, felt in bone.

Kay stayed on the floor near the cabinets. One hand flat against the wood. Celine stood by the counter. Shoulders tight. Breathing shallow. Luke held the doorway. Pupils wide. Jaw set.

Audrey knelt beside the table, where she had collapsed moments before. Hands pressed together. Lips moving without sound.

The geometry of the room tightened. Angles sharpened. Corners leaned in. The overhead light flickered once, twice, then steadied. Not quite warm. Not quite cold. Wrong in a way the skin noticed first.

Heat clicked behind Sam's sternum.

The Seed pulsed once. Hard. The pressure rolled through his chest and into the room. The floorboards answered with a deeper hum.

"We do not have time," he said.

Audrey's head snapped up.

Her right ankle burned.

Not the dull ache from earlier. Not the phantom itch she had blamed on Gooseneck Bend. Not the strange pulse in the cellar she had written off as nerves.

This was fire moving through bone.

She gasped. Her hand shot down, fingers clamping around her ankle through denim. Heat climbed higher. A thread of pressure spiraled up her calf, threading itself into muscle. Not surface. Deep. Precise.

Sam saw it. The way her knuckles whitened. The shake that hit her shoulders. The stutter in her breath.

"Audrey."

Her face drained of color. Years of sermons crashed through her all at once. Sunday mornings. Wednesday nights. Youth camp warnings. Every story of marks and judgments and spirits that branded the disobedient.

This was not blessing awakening.

This was punishment finding her.

"Something is wrong with me," she whispered.

The words came broken. Jagged with terror. She looked at Sam, then at Celine, then toward the place on Sam's chest he kept touching without noticing. The burn in her ankle intensified. The spiral climbed.

"I am not staying for this."

She stood. The movement jerked. Unsteady. Heat ripped up her leg but she forced it to take her weight.

Hal rose from where he had been frozen halfway between hallway and table.

"Audrey?"

"Hal, take me home. Now."

Her voice cut through the room. A command forged from fear, landing in the part of him trained to respond to crisis.

She turned toward the door. Limped. Hand still clamped around her ankle.

Hal stepped beside her. He hesitated. His eyes flicked to the darkened window. He knew what was out there. But he looked at her shaking hands. The choice took half a second.

"Alright. I have you."

His voice came firm. Directed. No blame. No debate. Authority wrapped around protection.

He shot one look back at the room. At Sam on the steps, at Kay folded near the cabinets, at Celine standing silent and rigid by the counter, at Luke a shadow in the doorway. The look said all of it without a word.

Then he turned.

"Come on," he said gently. Steadying her arm as she moved.

She did not pull away. She let him lead.

The front door opened. The sound of their exit cut through the charged quiet. The door shut. Gravel sprayed. The truck engine fired. Tires bit dirt. The noise twisted down the drive and vanished into trees and distance.

Silence flowed back in, heavier than before.

Kay's hand rose to her mouth. Celine stared at the empty doorway. Luke did not move.

Sam felt the absence like a wound opening in the room. One less frequency. One less anchor. The core in his chest spun faster. Its pulse slipped out of rhythm with his heartbeat. Pressure knotted under his ribs.

The cabin leaned inward.

A high, thin hum bled up through the floorboards. It climbed in pitch until it sat against the nerves just below conscious hearing.

Every muscle in Sam's body tightened. His vision frayed at the edges. Colors sharpened, then blurred.

Heat pooled behind his sternum until it tipped toward pain.

"I do not know what I am doing," he said. The words tore out low. Raw.

The pressure disappeared.

Not slowly. All at once. The air around him thinned, then steadied.

Sam's head turned.

She stood behind him.

Not close enough to touch. Close enough that the air remembered how to move around her. No footsteps. No shift from one point to another. She simply occupied a space she had not occupied a second before.

Sharp. Ancient. Unmoving.

He exhaled. "Please do not leave."

Inanna looked at him. No comfort lived in her face. No pity. No softening. Only recognition. As if she were watching a flame remember that it was fire.

She spoke once. Words quiet, weight enormous.

"Memory wakes when you stop pretending you are blind."

The cabin walls stopped pressing. Angles loosened by a fraction. His chest opened. Breath dropped into a rhythm that felt borrowed from a body that knew what to do.

The heat steadied.

Pulse after pulse aligned with something deeper than his own heart. A second metronome clicked into place beneath his sternum. Not foreign. Older than his first cry.

He saw.

Not with eyes. With recognition.

The Abzu. Depth before oceans. Black water that remembered light.

The nebggu. Matter caught mid-thought. Form waiting for command.

Light and density and soil threaded into human form. A pattern built to house charge. To carry flame. To stand in front of the breach instead of worshipping from a distance.

Inanna began to fade. Not dissolving. Withdrawing. The sense of her stepped backward without moving at all.

Sam spoke without sound.

Do not go.

Her eyes held his. That same mirror that had tracked him since the church in New Orleans. The answer sat in the silence.

You are the one who leaves.

She vanished.

The Seed pulsed once. Hard.

The cabin heard it.

The hum under the floor dropped into a lower register. Boards vibrated. Plates rattled in cabinets. The light overhead flickered again, then steadied to a harsher white.

Heat surged up Sam's chest and out into the room.

Celine doubled over. A cry ripped out of her raw, not fear but pain so sharp her ribs seized.

Pressure slammed behind her eyes. Her inner left wrist burned like iron pressed to bone. The faint glyph hidden since the cellar tore open beneath her skin. Light burst through flesh, blinding white, carving itself into shape as if it had always been there waiting to break free.

The pain doubled. She curled forward, palms to the floor. Fire punched up her arms, burning from the inside out, not surface flame but marrow-deep ignition.

She screamed, breath ragged. But she did not fall. She locked her knees. Forced her spine straight against the agony.

Then the light steadied.

Flames rose from her hands, white edged in blue. No comfort in them. Trial. Initiation.

Her body shook under it. Breath stuttered. A second heartbeat hammered behind her ribs like something remembering its name.

The flames bent toward her face, toward her ribs, as if greeting someone they had not seen in a very long time.

They knew her.

She knew them.

Next to her, the bloody water in the mop bucket began to steam. A low hiss cut the silence as the liquid started to boil just from the proximity of her skin.

She stared at the fire. Wide-eyed. Breath fast but not panicked. A quiet laid itself over her expression that had nothing to do with calm and everything to do with remembrance.

The fire didn't stop. It crawled through her lungs, spine, skull. She choked on heat and memory, gasping like someone drowning in light.

Then, slowly, the agony thinned enough for thought to form.

"I remember the fire," she whispered.

Her voice carried an undertone that did not belong to any present day. A strata of voices under her own. Women who had stood in temples and on gallows. Women who had burned cities and refused to apologize.

Luke's back flared hot.

The space between his shoulder blades lit up under his skin. Not visible, but precise. A brand any knife could not reach. He staggered a half step forward and caught the counter with one hand.

His pupils shrank to pinpoints, then expanded until green nearly vanished. For a heartbeat his eyes flashed a shade that belonged to wolves and old forests.

His sense of smell blew open.

Every scent in the cabin snapped into brutal clarity. Sweat in Kay's shirt. Copper ghosting off old blood and burned feeder flesh. Soap on Celine's skin beneath the reek of sulfur and ionized air. Lake water seeping through foundation. Cold. Deep. Corrupted.

He smelled them.

Out in the brush across the lake. Not bodies. Presence. A chemical wrongness pressed against branches and mud.

"They are back," he said. The words came quiet. Every syllable measured. His shoulders straightened without conscious thought. Instinct stood up inside him.

The Seed responded.

It did not leave his chest. It did not glow in his hand. It turned.

The pulse in his sternum shifted angle, as if an unseen compass had jerked toward a fixed point beyond the cabin walls. North. The awareness snapped into place with painful clarity. A straight line pinned him from ribs through distance through someone else's skin.

His vision jerked.

The room stayed where it was. The bodies stayed where they were.

Then, layered over the cabin, flooded an image that did not belong to this space at all.

Loyd.

Flat on a metal table. Arms strapped wide beneath a cold bar. Tubes in the crooks of his elbows. Blood crawling out of him in measured pulses into bags hanging above his head. Skin pale. Lips cracked. Breath shallow.

One eye open.

It turned. Not toward a camera. Straight toward Sam. Across distance that should have made that impossible.

Sam's body flinched.

Kay's hand flew to her mouth. She did not see what he saw, but she felt the impact in his chest as if someone had hit him.

Celine's flames wavered, then surged higher.

Loyd's lips moved. No sound reached the cabin, but the shape of the words carved itself straight into the Seed behind Sam's sternum.

Do not come here.

The vision cut.

A hit landed inside Sam's chest. Not emotional. Physical. A blow from the center itself. Heat flared behind his sternum so hard his knees buckled. The counter caught him before the floor did. Something had answered Loyd's pain and struck back through him.

The cabin snapped back into singular view. Counter. Stove. Table. Blood smear on planks. Kay on the floor. Celine kneeling with fire blooming from her hands. Luke braced in the doorway. Frost lacing the windows in patterns geometry could not parse.

Sam staggered. One hand slammed against the counter. The other pressed over his chest.

Loyd's absence roared louder than his warning.

Heat climbed through the glyph above Sam's heart. The lines engraved in his skin burned bright for three steady pulses, then cooled to a steady throb.

Kay's throat moved.

A word ripped out of her before she had time to be afraid of it.

"Narrow Point."

The sound shoved through the room. It landed in the air with weight, not volume. Every board under them seemed to twitch.

Kay blinked hard, stunned. Her fingers curled against the floor as if to hold herself in place.

"I do not know why I said that," she whispered.

Luke's head tilted slightly. He squinted at the space in front of Sam as if tracking a scent most noses did not register.

"Closer," he murmured. "Too close."

His focus stretched outward. His new sense mapped the perimeter. The feeders clustered just beyond the treeline. Not pressing in. Not backing off.

Waiting.

Celine's fire shifted color. A faint gold threaded through the blue-white. She turned her head toward the lake, eyes unfocused in normal sight, locked onto a plane only the Seed and the cabin could read.

"They are not alone," she said.

Sam straightened. His breathing found rhythm again. The pain in his chest thinned into direction. The pull north sharpened. Not a suggestion. A line.

"Someone is there," he said. "Beyond them."

His voice felt different in his own ears. Aligned with the pulse under his sternum. Carried by it.

The cabin acknowledged.

Beneath their feet, light bled through the cracks between floorboards. Faint, gold-white. It traced the hidden triangle embedded below the cabin. Each angle lit, then began a slow rotation.

The hum shifted key. Dropped half an octave. The sound settled into jaw and teeth and skull. Every cup, plate, and picture frame vibrated without moving.

The Eye beneath the cabin opened another fraction.

Not enough to reveal. Enough to register.

Sam swayed. The line of heat in his chest moved. Not outward. Inward. A new segment carved itself through the glyph over his heart. He felt it shift, threading through old lines, connecting points that had waited decades to close.

The pain lasted three seconds.

Then he inhaled.

The cabin settled around him in a new configuration. The weight of the walls felt similar, but the attention inside the geometry had changed. It watched with more focus. Less sleep. More interest.

Kay scrubbed at her eyes with the heel of her palm. Luke's jaw flexed. Celine's flames dropped in height but did not go out. They curled tight around her fingers, then rested there, not consuming, not cooling.

Sam looked at his own hands.

They looked unchanged. Skin. Lines. Scars.

He knew they were not the same.

The Seed beat slow behind his sternum. Not faster. Heavier. Deeper. Each pulse carried an answering pressure from the north. Something vast. A will he could not see. A presence that had turned, fully, toward him.

He met Luke's eyes. Then Celine's. Then Kay's.

"Loyd is alive," he said. The words came out with no room for argument. "For now."

A shiver moved through the floor. The unseen triangle stopped rotating. The gold light faded back into wood grain. The hum held its new key.

Outside, branches at the edge of the lake bowed toward the water, then stilled.

"They know where we are," Luke said quietly.

Celine's flames tightened around her palms. Her jaw set. Fear and fury braided clean in her eyes.

Sam touched the center of his chest once more. The Seed pushed back against his hand. Not comfort. A reminder.

He understood one thing with brutal clarity.

This was not awakening.

This was contact.

The breach had seen them.

And now it would not look away.

# Chapter 33

# The Rupture

The world stopped breathing.

Not wind. Not water. Not the scratch of leaves against wood. Silence pressed against Sam's eardrums like deep water. The cabin air turned heavy. Every breath felt like dragging stone through his lungs.

Celine stood near the window, hands shaking. The fire wasn't gone. It lived under her skin now, prowling her veins, looking for a way out. The flames that had danced there in the last heartbeat now hovered just beneath the surface.

Held by a thread.

Waiting.

Luke filled the doorway. Spine straight. Shoulders squared. Pupils wide enough to eat the color from his eyes. Every muscle in his body locked into predator stillness.

Kay stayed near the cabinets. One hand groped for the counter edge and clung tight. Her breath came shallow. Something old in her bones woke before her mind caught up. Ancestral fear, tasting of smoke and iron.

Sam stood at the center of the room. The Merkaba Seed pulsed, quiet behind his sternum. The cabin geometry tightened around him. Not crushing. Aligning. The floorboards under his feet recognized his specific weight, his exact placement in the triangle's hidden pattern.

The shadows moved first.

His shadow reached the wall a half second before his hand lifted. Kay's stretched toward the door while she stayed rooted near the cabinets. Luke's shadow slid across the floorboards ahead of his boots. Light sources did not change. The shadows shifted anyway, slightly out of sync with the bodies that cast them.

Celine's throat worked. "Tell me you see that."

Not a question.

Frost bloomed on the window glass. Not from the center outward, but backward. The ice grew tip-first, creeping toward points that didn't exist. The pattern held for three seconds, then broke and reformed the way it was supposed to.

One floorboard near Sam's left foot lifted a fraction. Not enough for the eye to track. Just enough for the body to register wrongness. Wood grain bent with it, warping around an angle that had not existed a heartbeat earlier.

The reflection in the glass delayed.

Sam turned his head. His reflection followed a breath late. Luke blinked. The mirrored Luke blinked second. Kay's hand lifted to her mouth. The hand in the glass rose after.

The cabin walls contracted.

Boards drew inward, shoulders hunched around a secret. Windows narrowed by some fraction without measurement. The ceiling dipped just enough to press on the top of Sam's awareness. Then the shift stopped. The new configuration held. Tighter. Protective. Awake.

Luke's nostrils flared. His head tilted toward the back window that faced the lake. The scent hit him like live wire. Burnt copper. Static. Wrong chemistry. Not smoke. Not rot. Something between states. Metal that had learned to breathe.

"They moved," Luke said.

His voice came low. Leveled. The glyph between his shoulder blades burned beneath his shirt. The heat stayed buried in muscle this time. His range expanded outward, mapping the property in invisible scent layers.

Pressure redistributed across the lake.

Not wind. Not ordinary weather. Air stepped aside for something that did not fit cleanly in space. The molecules re-arranged with a shiver. Luke's jaw clenched. He smelled them at the treeline. Multiple presences. They did not advance. They occupied.

Sam felt the pull north sharpen.

The Seed behind his sternum knocked once. The impact locked his breath mid-inhale. A directional pressure aligned his spine and tilted his head toward the back window. The new line carved into his chest glyph rotated a fraction. Not pain. Orien-tation. His entire body leaned toward a point he could not see.

Something across the lake stepped into visibility.

It did not walk forward. It resolved.

The shape coalesced at the thickest knot of brush on the far bank. Gray flesh bent the air around its edges. Light tried to cling and failed. Its head turned ninety degrees with no transition. One instant facing the trees. Next instant angled toward the cabin. No arc. No movement. Just new position.

The limbs were too long. Jointed in the wrong places. Pro-portions refused to settle into anything human or animal. Look-ing at it felt like staring at a bad edit in reality, a frame misaligned with the rest of the film.

It glitched.

One blink and it stood at the treeline. Another blink and it existed three feet to the left, same posture, no motion between. The world did not register travel. Only changed outcome.

It watched Sam.

Not the cabin. Not the lake. Not Luke in the doorway or Celine at the window or Kay gripping the counter to keep from falling.

Only Sam.

Empty eyes held no rage. No joy. No cruelty. Just attention. Focus so intense it felt like the barrel of a scope pressed against his soul. The sensation of being studied, measured, filed.

Behind it, silhouettes crowded the dark.

Not full bodies. Suggestions. Mass pressed into shadow. Rows of almost-there forms layered into the tree line. A wall of intent. They did not advance. Their weight sat in the background like a storm parked on the horizon.

Celine's palms heated.

Whatever lived inside her answered without permission. Light rose through her skin. Not full flame. A halo of white-blue shimmer. One thin strand of that light tugged toward the glass, a filament reaching in the direction of the thing on the far shore.

Her chest rose and fell in rhythm with the Seed's pulse.

She felt it. Breath syncing to the beat behind Sam's sternum. Her ribs adjusted around that pattern. Something inside her wrist glyph hummed in the same key. Her voice, when it arrived, sounded like it had come from a place halfway between memory and trance.

"It knows you."

Kay's jaw unlocked.

Her tongue moved before thought could get in the way. Syllables ripped from some place that existed before English, before Oklahoma, before cabins and lakes and Sunday school.

"Voras tal n'reth."

The words hit Sam like a thrown brick.

Pressure slammed his chest. Not impact on the outside. Recognition on the inside. The Seed lurched in place. His glyph flared hot under his shirt. Kay's phrase echoed against bone and light, resonating in a language his mouth did not speak but his blood did.

Kay slapped a hand over her lips. Eyes wide. Horrified.

"I did not mean to say that."

Light bled between the floorboards.

Thin, gold-white, seeping through hairline gaps in the planks. It traced the triangle buried beneath the cabin, angle by angle. Each point lit, then all three began a slow rotation around their center.

The hum in the bones of the house dropped half a note.

Lower. Heavier. The vibration tunneled through plaster and nail and tooth. The cabin inhaled on some invisible count. Windows stayed narrowed. Walls stayed compressed. Every molecule of air agreed to this new arrangement.

The Eye opened further.

Sam felt it under his feet. Not as an object. As awareness. Geometry that remembered what it had been built to do. A watcher built to face watchers. It recognized the thing across the lake. It recognized the Seed in his chest. It recognized the family standing inside its pattern.

The Seed answered.

A single clean pulse behind his sternum. Then another. Then a third.

A return signal.

His glyph line rotated again. The burn did not spread. It condensed. Clarified. His breath locked. The pull north intensified. The urge to step toward the lake rose up his legs like command.

Reality stuttered.

The shadows tore.

For a heartbeat, the room split into two frames.

Frame One held the cabin as it stood. Window glass whole. Luke in the doorway, alive and braced. Celine at the window, light sheathing her hands. Kay upright by the counter, mouth covered, shaking.

Frame Two overlaid the first with surgical cruelty.

Shattered glass across the floor. Curtains aflame. The far wall painted in impact. Luke slumped against the cabinets, red blooming across his ribs, his head lolling to one side. Celine on her knees, screaming, hands throwing fire in every direction without aim. Kay on the ground. The gray thing at the threshold. Not outside now. One elongated arm inside the room. Its hand clamped around Sam's throat. His feet off the floor. His body jerking once, then hanging slack.

Sam felt both.

The cool stillness of glass intact and the sting of shards in his forearms. The air in his lungs and the vacuum of strangled breath. The cabin's hum and the high whine of ruptured nerves. Two sets of sensory data crashed into the same skull.

He stood at the fulcrum.

The choice did not arrive as thought. It came as frequency.

One reality vibrated at a pitch of surrender. The other at a pitch of resistance. The Seed burned with the second.

Sam reached.

He grabbed the frame where they lived.

Not with hands. With alignment. With the glyph. With the law etched into his marrow when the Seed fused. He seized the stable version of the room and dragged it hard over the one where he died, forcing the images to overlap. Forcing the possible to overwrite the probable.

He slammed the lethal timeline shut.

The overlay held one second.

Sam felt the gray fingers on his throat and the air in his lungs at the same time. Felt flames eating curtains and flames sleeping in Celine's hands. Felt Luke's weight slumping against the cabinets and Luke standing unbroken in the doorway.

Then reality locked.

Shadows snapped back into correct obedience. Reflections in the window caught up to their sources. Frost patterns on the glass held only one geometry. The gray thing stood at the treeline again, where it had always stood.

Then it was not there at all.

Not retreating. Not stepping back.

Gone.

The silhouettes behind it vanished with it. The pressure at the far bank lifted. Air rushed into the space the watcher had occupied without making a sound.

One branch at the edge of the lake stayed bent at an angle that did not match the wind. One footprint pressed into mud near the waterline, too deep for the weight of any visible body. One patch of frost on the back window glowed faint green, a ghost stain of contact where nothing now stood.

Evidence. No explanation.

Luke sucked air into his lungs. His expanded senses shrank to human range. The scent of burnt copper thinned. The heat on his back cooled to ordinary warmth. His hand tightened on the edge of the doorframe.

"What just happened."

Sam did not answer.

The Seed did.

A knock inside his chest. Then another. The pull north yanked hard enough that his shoulders wanted to turn without his consent. Something on the other end of that line had noticed his refusal. Had noticed him slam shut a path it intended to use.

He saw Loyd.

Metal bar. Tubes. One eye open. That eye now flickered, searching for something beyond physical help.

The Seed pulsed one more time. Not warning.

Confirmation.

The signal he had sent when he reached for Loyd had not vanished with the watcher. It hung in the air. A thread. Someone, something, was holding the other end.

His glyph burned steady. Not higher. Not lower. Locked.

"It heard us," Sam said.

The words scraped past his teeth. Barely above a whisper.

The cabin held still.

Celine's light withdrew fully into her palms. Her fingers curled, closing over warmth that had no intention of going away. Kay gripped the counter with both hands. Color slowly returned to her cheeks.

Luke stayed at the door. His hand gripped the frame until the wood groaned. His eyes darted. Too much data. Too much scent. He looked like a man trying to hold back a flood with a plywood door.

The triangle beneath the floor slowed its rotation.

It stopped with one point aligned dead north, directly through Sam's chest. The gold-white light faded back into the grain of the wood. The hum held its lower key. No climb back to old resonance.

New normal. Not truce.

Outside, branches at the edge of the property shuddered and then pointed toward the lake as if bowing. The surface of the water lay unnaturally flat. No ripple. No wind scratch. A mirror waiting for something to appear.

Sam did not move.

He could feel it.

On the far side of that invisible line, beyond the feeders, beyond the trees and water and fence, something ancient recalibrated.

Not a creature. Not exactly.

An attention.

It had seen a human with a Seed reject one possible outcome and choose another. That should not have been available at his scale. At his level.

He had done it anyway.

Kay swallowed.

Her voice came small, hoarse. "Is it over?"

Luke answered before Sam could.

"No."

The certainty in his tone did not come from insight. It came from scent. From the way the air still tasted wrong. From the phantom presence on the far bank that had withdrawn its body but left its intent.

Celine pushed herself up from the window frame.

Fire traced along the inside of her veins, too bright to see, too loud to hear. She flexed her fingers. The urge to let it go, to call it fully, sat just under her skin.

"They will try again," she said.

Sam nodded once.

His hand lifted to his chest. Fingers pressed the fabric where his glyph burned, where the Seed sat lodged behind bone.

Heat answered his touch. One measured pulse.

The pull north throbbed in time with it, a second heart outside his body. Somewhere out there, in the direction his whole frame pointed toward now, Loyd hung between breaths. Blood feeding a system that did not deserve it. Somewhere further behind that, deeper into the grid, the intelligence that owned the watcher recalculated its strategy.

"They know we can see them," Sam said.

He thought of the place that called itself hopeful. Of the smiling man whose presence pressed like a lie. Of another who did not smile at all, who watched without motion. Of gatherings he had never seen yet could feel the residue of, cities away. Of a narrow place, unnamed, humming like a wound in the map.

Celine's jaw set. Fear and fury braided clean behind her eyes.

"Good," she said.

Kay flinched at the word.

Sam looked at her.

"We're staying together," Sam said. "All of us."

It was not a comfort. It was a tactical fact. The cabin, the Eye beneath it, the Seed, the fire in Celine, the scent opening in Luke, Kay's involuntary law-speech. All pieces in a pattern that would not allow anyone to stand alone in open ground again.

The Seed pulsed one more time.

Not warning. Confirmation.

A knot tied.

Across the water, a structure that had once been built for reverence came fully awake. Floodlights flared. Cameras aligned. Systems long left idle began to hum.

Somewhere much further behind those machines, watching through them, something smiled without a face.

Sam let his hand fall from his chest.

He felt no bigger. No stronger. Just a terrifying clarity that threatened to crack him open if he looked at it too long.

Only one thing had changed.

He now knew exactly what direction to walk if he wanted to tear open the world.

He also knew that the moment he started toward it, everything that had just looked back at him would move.

Celine's gaze dropped to the burn along Sam's arm. Her jaw tightened, not in fear but recognition.

"They think they marked you," she said quietly.

Sam kept his eyes on the back window. On the bent branch. On the faint green smear of frost that would not melt.

"They did," he said.

He let the truth sit in the air.

Then he added the part the watching presence did not know yet.

"I marked them back." The words felt heavy, like a sentence he had just passed on himself.

The cabin took that in.

Boards settled. Nails creaked. The Eye beneath the floor closed to a slit, enough to watch, not yet enough to act. The hum held a war drum's patience.

The world outside resumed breathing.

Wind picked up. Water lapped shore. Somewhere across the lake, an owl called as if night had not just almost split in half.

The pull north did not ease.

Sam stood in the center of the cabin, every line of his glyph hot with a change written too deep to undo, the Merkaba Seed beating in rhythm with something distant and vast and terrifyingly aware.

This was not deliverance.

This was not power.

This was contact.

The breach had seen them, answered him, and turned its full attention toward his line.

When he moved, the world would move with him.

# About the Author

Orion R. Veil was born in Oklahoma and now lives in Texas. He was married in New Orleans and remains connected to the city's culture and rhythm, returning often.

His fiction blends ancestry, trauma, and spiritual awakening into modern myth. The Bloodline Watchers began as an exploration of family, memory, and the hidden forces that shape ordinary lives.

He writes about lineage, awakening, and what rises when people remember who they are.

The story continues in  Book Two: The Covenant

Early access & updates at CosmicQuill.pub

# Acknowledgements

This book exists because a few people pushed when I needed it, questioned what deserved questioning, and told me the truth without soft edges.

Court, who read early drafts with sharp eyes and sharper honesty. Your notes forced this story to grow, and the book is stronger because you refused to let it stay small.

Sean, for structural insight and for pushing me to give the Howardson line the depth and weight it deserved. Your clarity cut through noise.

Keona, who heard the idea before it was a manuscript, and reminded me to keep going when the work felt heavier than the page.

My family, who shaped this story more than they know. The echoes are intentional.

And to the readers who made it here:

Stories only live when someone carries them forward.

Thank you for carrying this one.

— Orion R. Veil